LOW LIFE . . . HIGH TECH

"We're dead," says Doggy.

"Give them time to cool," says I.

"They'll never cool," says he. "There's no chance they'll forgive this even if they know the whole truth, because look at the names they give the cards to, it's like they got them for the biggest boys on the borderline, the habibs who bribe presidents of little countries and rank off cash from octopods like Shell and ITT and every now and then kill somebody and walk away clean. Now they're sitting there in jail with the whole life story of the organization in their brains, so they don't care if we meant to do it or not. They're hurting, and the only way they know to make the hurt go away is to pass it on to somebody else. And that's us. They want to make us hurt, and hurt real bad, and for a long time."

I never saw Dog so scared. . . .

—from "Dogwalker"

Plus many more
science fiction stories
by Orson Scott Card.

Tor Books by Orson Scott Card

*forthcoming

FLUX

TALES OF HUMAN FUTURES

by

Orson Scott Card

A TOM DOHERTY ASSOCIATES BOOK
NEW YORK

This is a work of fiction. All the characters and events portrayed in this book are fictitious, and any resemblance to real people or events is purely coincidental.

FLUX

Copyright © 1992 by Orson Scott Card

Previously published as book two of *Maps in a Mirror* by Orson Scott Card (Tor, 1990)

Cover art by Peter Scanlan

A Tor Book
Published by Tom Doherty Associates, Inc.
175 Fifth Avenue
New York, N.Y. 10010

Tor ® is a registered trademark of Tom Doherty Associates, Inc.

ISBN: 0-812-51685-0

First edition: September 1992

Printed in the United States of America

0 9 8 7 6 5 4 3 2 1

To Charlie Ben,
who can fly

CONTENTS

FLUX

INTRODUCTION

NEVER MIND THE question of why anybody would ever become a writer at all. The sheer arrogance of thinking that other people ought to pay to read my words should be enough to mark all us writers as unfit for decent society. But then, few indeed are the communities that reward proper modesty and disdain those who thrust themselves into the limelight. All human societies hunger for storytellers, and those whose tales we like, we reward well. In the meantime, the storytellers are constantly reinventing and redefining their society. We are paid to bite the hand that feeds us. We are birds that keep tearing down and rebuilding every nest in the tree.

So never mind the question of why I became a writer. Instead let's ask an easy one. Why did I choose to write science fiction?

The glib answer is to say that I didn't. Some are

born to science fiction, some choose science fiction, and some have science fiction thrust upon them. Surely I belong to the last category. I was a playwright by choice. Oh, I entered college as an archaeology major, but I soon discovered that being an archaeologist didn't mean being Thor Heyerdahl or Yigael Yadin. It meant sorting through eight billion potsherds. It meant moving a mountain with a teaspoon. In short, it meant work. Therefore it was not for me.

During the two semesters it took for me to make this personal discovery, I had already taken four theatre classes for every archaeology class I signed up for, and it was in theatre that I spent all my time. Because I attended Brigham Young High School, I was already involved with the BYU theatre program before I officially started college. In fact, I had already been in a student production, and continued acting almost continuously through all my years at the university. I was no great shakes as an actor—too cerebral, not able to use my body well enough to look comfortable or right on stage. But I gave great cold readings at auditions, so I kept getting cast. And when I gave up on archaeology, it was theatre that was there waiting for me. It was the first time I consciously made a decision based on autobiography. Instead of examining my feelings (which change hourly anyway) or making those ridiculous pro-and-con lists that always look so rational, I simply looked back at the last few years of my life and saw that the only thing I did that I really followed through on, the only thing I did over and over again regardless of whether it profited me in any way, was theatre. So I changed majors, thereby determining much of my future.

One obvious result was that I lost my scholarship. I was at BYU on a full-ride presidential scholarship—

tuition, books, housing. But I had to maintain a high grade point average, and while that was easy enough in academic subjects, it was devilishly hard in the subjective world of the arts. The matter hadn't come up before—presidential scholars hadn't ever gone into the arts before me. So there was no mechanism for dealing with the subjective grades that came out of theatre. If I worked my tail off in an academic subject, I got an *A*. Period. No question. But I could work myself half to death on a play, do my very best, and still get a *C* because the teacher didn't agree with my interpretation or didn't like my blocking or just plain didn't like *me*, and who could argue? There was nothing quantifiable. So choosing the arts cost me money. It also taught me that you can never please a critic determined to detest your work. I had to choose my professors carefully, or reconcile myself to low grades. I did both.

But if I wasn't working for grades and I wasn't trying to change myself to fit professors' preconceived notions of what my work ought to be, what *was* I working for? The answer came to me gradually, but once I understood it I never wavered. I rejected the notion, put forth by one English professor, that one should write for oneself. Indeed, his own life was a clear refutation of his lofty sentiment that "I write for myself and God." In fact he spent half his life pressing his writings on anyone who would hold still long enough to read or listen. He showed me what I was already becoming aware of: Art is a dialogue with the audience. There is no reason to create art except to present it to other people; and you present it to other people in order to change them. The world must be changed by what I create, I decided, or it isn't worth doing.

Within a year of becoming a theatre major, I was writing plays. I didn't plan it. Writing wasn't something I thought of as a career. In my family, writing was simply something that you *did*. My dad often bought *Writer's Digest;* I entered their contest a couple of times in my teens. But mostly I thought of writing as coming up with skits or assemblies at school or roadshows at church (Mormons have a longstanding commitment to theatre); it also meant that I could usually ace an essay exam if I knew even a little bit about the subject. It wasn't a *career*.

But as a fledgling director, I had run into the frustration of directing inadequate scripts. When I was assistant director of a college production of *Flowers for Algernon*, I finally got a professor—the director— to agree with me. The second act was terrible. I had read and loved the story, and so I was particularly frustrated by some bad choices made by the adapter. With the director's permission, I went home and rewrote the second act. We used my script.

About the same time (I think), I was taking a course in advanced interpretation, which included reader's theatre. I loved the whole concept of stripping the stage and letting the actors, in plain clothes, with no sets and minimal movements, act out the story for the audience. As part of the course, I wrote an adaptation of Marjorie Kellogg's *Tell Me That You Love Me, Junie Moon*. I had loved the book, and my adaptation was (and still is) one of my best works, because it preserved both the story and the madcap flavor of the writing. I asked for permission to direct it. I was told that advanced interp wasn't a course for which students were allowed to direct. There was only *one* course undergraduates could take that allowed them to direct a play, and I had taken it and received a *C*, and that was that.

No it wasn't. My professor in that course, Preston Gledhill, was sympathetic, and so he arranged to bend the rules and I got my performance. Two nights in the Experimental Theatre, doing reader's theatre as it had never been done before. The audience laughed in all the right places. They sobbed at the end. The standing ovation was earned. The actors still remember, as I do, that it was something remarkable. I may have been using someone else's story, but that student production told me, for the first time, that I could produce a script and a performance that audiences would take into themselves. I had changed people.

Because of those two adaptations, I resolved to try playwriting in a more serious way. Charles Whitman, who was the favorite among us undergraduates in those days (the late 1960s), was also the playwriting teacher and a fervent advocate of Mormon theatre. He thought that young Mormon theatre people ought to be producing plays for their own people, and I agreed—and still agree, enough that I have never stopped producing Mormon art throughout my career, often allowing it to take precedence over my more visible (and lucrative) career in "the world." Taking Whitman's class opened the floodgates. I wrote dozens of plays. I tried my hand at realism, comedy, verse drama, vignettes, anything that would hold still long enough for me to write it. I adapted stories from Mormon history and the Book of Mormon; I took personal stories out of my life and my parents' lives; and through all this writing, I *still* thought of myself as primarily an actor and director.

I mean, just because I wrote a lot of plays didn't mean I *was* a playwright. I also designed costumes and did makeup and composed music and designed and built stage sets. The only reason I didn't do lighting was because of a healthy case of acrophobia. No, I wasn't a playwright, I was an all-around theatre person. I didn't make the decision that I was a writer until one day I was sitting in the Theatre Department office with a group—some meeting, I don't remember what—and a professor happened to say to me, "So you're going to be a playwright." I found something about his statement to be offensive. It flashed through my mind that I had already written a dozen plays that had been produced to sold-out houses. I was at least as much a writer as he was an actor or director or teacher—because I had done it to the satisfaction of an audience. So I answered, rather coldly, "I'm not *going* to be a playwright. I *am* a playwright."

A short while later, I happened to be sitting in on a class he was teaching, and he referred to that conversation in front of his class. "Some of you are going to be actors and some directors and some playwrights," he said. Then, pointing at me, he said, "Except for Scott Card, there, who already *is* a playwright." It was a great laugh line. The mockery I thought I heard in his words left me angry and frustrated. Later I would learn that he had intended his comments as a kind of respect; and we have worked together well on other projects. But I interpreted things then with the paranoia normal to "sensitive" adolescents, and took his words as a challenge. I brooded on them for days. Weeks. And at the end of that time, in my own mind I *was* a playwright, and all my other theatrical enterprises were secondary. I could succeed or fail at them without it making much difference—my future was tied to my writing.

Skip a few years now. Years in which I started a repertory theatre company, which by some measures was a resounding success; but at the end of that time I found myself $20,000 in debt on an annual income of about $5,000. My own scripts had been quite successful in the company, but some bad business decisions—*my* decisions, I must add—had made a good thing go sour. I folded the company, and probably should have declared personal and corporate bankruptcy, but instead decided to pay it all off.

How? My income as an editor at BYU Press would never be enough to make a dent in what I owed. I had to make money on the side. Doing what? The only thing I knew how to do was write, and because my plays were all aimed at the Mormon audience, there was no way that a script of mine would bring in that kind of money—not from royalties. There just weren't enough warm bodies with dollars in their pockets to bring me what I needed. I thought of writing plays for the New York audience, but that would be so chancy and require so much investment in time that I rejected it. Instead, I thought of writing fiction.

In a way, that was as scary as trying to write plays for the American audience at large. The difference was that with fiction, you find out much sooner whether you've failed. You can take years flogging a few scripts around in New York and regional theatre and end up with nothing—no audience, no money, no future. But you can find yourself in exactly that condition after only a few months of mailing out fiction manuscripts.

And when considering what kind of fiction to write, science fiction was an easy choice. I wanted to start with short stories, and when it comes to short fiction, science fiction was then and is now the most open market there is. First, because the money is fairly low, the established novelists generally stay out of the short fiction market, making it more open to new names. Second, because science fiction thrives on strangeness, new writers are more welcome in this field than any other. True strangeness is the product of genius, but a good substitute is the strangeness inherent in every writer's unique voice, so that when a science fiction writer is both competent and new, he gives off the luster of an ersatz kind of genius, and the field welcomes him with open arms. (Others might say that the field chews you up, swallows you, and pukes you back, but that would be crude and unkind, and it doesn't *always* happen that way.)

So for purely commercial reasons, deep in debt, I chose science fiction. I was lucky enough that the second story I sent out sold after only a couple of tries (told about elsewhere) and went on to come in second for a Hugo and win me the Campbell Award for best new writer. So as long as people were paying me to write science fiction why should I stop?

That's the colorful, devil-may-care answer. It's also a crock.

Because during that whole time that I "was" a playwright, I was also writing science fiction. I had not yet written a play when at sixteen I first came up with the story idea that eventually became "Ender's Game." I was taking fiction-writing courses at BYU right along with my playwriting courses, and, although I had brains enough not to turn in sci-fi for class credit, my heart went into the Worthing stories I was already writing before my first play was produced. Like my plays, my stories were all written on narrow-ruled paper in spiral notebooks, and at first my mother typed them for me. Then I mailed them out and treasured the very kind rejection notes I got. Not many—only a couple of submissions, only a couple of rejections. But between rejections—and between plays—I worked on my fiction as assiduously as I ever worked on anything else in my life.

So now, glib answers aside, why science fiction? Why is it that, left to myself, the stories I am drawn to write are all science fiction and fantasy? It wasn't because sci-fi was all I read. On the contrary, while I went through several science fiction binges, during high school and college I usually read only the sci-fi and fantasy that were making the rounds. I read *Dune* when everybody read *Dune*; the same with *Lord of the Rings* and *Foundation* and *I Sing the Body Electric* and *Dandelion Wine*. At the same time, I was reading Hersey's *The Wall* and *White Lotus*, Ayn Rand's *Fountainhead*, Rod McKuen's *Stanyan Street and Other Sorrows*. Hell, I even read Khalil Gibran. I may not have dropped acid, but I wasn't totally cut off from my generation. (Fortunately, by the time *Jonathan Livingston Seagull* came out I had matured enough to recognize it immediately as drivel.) I never, not once, not for a moment, thought of myself as a "science fiction reader." Some science fiction books came to me like revelations, yes, but so did many other books—and none had anything like the influence on me that came from Shakespeare and Joseph Smith, the two writers who, more than any others, formed the way I think and write.

If I wasn't a science fiction reader, per se, why did my impulse toward storytelling come out in science fictional forms? I think it was the same reason that my playwriting impulses always expressed themselves in stories aimed at and arising from the Mormon audience. The possibility of the transcendental is part of it. More important, though—for Mormonism is *not* a transcendental religion—is the fact that science fiction, like Mormonism, offered a vocabulary for rationalizing the transcendental. That is, within science fiction it is possible to find the meaning of life without resorting to Mystery. I detest Mystery (though I love mysteries); I think it is the name we put on our decision to stop trying to understand. From Joseph Smith I learned to reject any philosophy that requires you to swallow paradox as if it were profound; if it makes no sense, it's probably hogwash. Within the genre of science fiction, I could shuck off the shackles of realism and make up worlds in which the issues I cared about were clear and powerful. The tale could be told direct. It could be *about something*.

Since then I have learned ways to make more realistic fiction be *about something* as well—but not the ways my literature professors tried to teach me. The oblique methods used by contemporary American literateurs are bankrupt because they have forsaken the audience. But there are writers doing outside of science fiction the things that I thought, at the age of twenty-three, could only be done within it. I think of Olive Ann Burns's *Cold Sassy Tree* as the marker that informed me that all the so-called Mysteries could still be reached through stories that told of love and sex and death; the need to belong, the hungers of the body, and the search for individual worth; Community, Carnality, Identity. Ultimately, that triad is what all stories are about. The great stories are simply the ones that do it better for a particular audience at a particular place and time. So I'm gradually reaching out to write other stories, outside of both the Mormon and the science fiction communities. But the fact remains that it was in science fiction that I first found it possible to speak to non-Mormons about the things that mattered most to me. That's why I wrote science fiction, and write science fiction, and will write it for many years to come.

A THOUSAND DEATHS

"**Y**OU WILL MAKE no speeches," said the prosecutor.

"I didn't expect they'd let me," Jerry Crove answered, affecting a confidence he didn't feel. The prosecutor was not hostile; he seemed more like a high school drama coach than a man who was seeking Jerry's death.

"They not only won't let you," the prosecutor said, "but if you try anything, it will go much worse for you. We have you cold, you know. We don't need anywhere near as much proof as we have."

"You haven't proved anything."

"We've proved you knew about it," the prosecutor insisted mildly. "No point arguing now. Knowing about treason and not reporting it is exactly equal to committing treason."

Jerry shrugged and looked away.

The cell was bare concrete. The door was solid

steel. The bed was a hammock hung from hooks on the wall. The toilet was a can with a removable plastic seat. There was no conceivable way to escape. Indeed, there was nothing that could conceivably occupy an intelligent person's mind for more than five minutes. In the three weeks he had been here, he had memorized every crack in the concrete, every bolt in the door. He had nothing to look at, except the prosecutor. Jerry reluctantly met the man's gaze.

"What do you say when the judge asks you how you plead to the charges?"

"Nolo contendere."

"Very good. It would be much nicer if you'd consent to say 'guilty'," the prosecutor said.

"I don't like the word."

"Just remember. Three cameras will be pointing at you. The trial will be broadcast live. To America, you represent all Americans. You must comport yourself with dignity, quietly accepting the fact that your complicity in the assassination of Peter Anderson—"

"Andreyevitch—"

"*Anderson* has brought you to the point of death, where all depends on the mercy of the court. And now I'll go have lunch. Tonight we'll see each other again. And remember. No speeches. Nothing embarrassing."

Jerry nodded. This was not the time to argue. He spent the afternoon practicing conjugations of Portuguese irregular verbs, wishing that somehow he could go back and undo the moment when he agreed to speak to the old man who had unfolded all the plans to assassinate Andreyevitch. "Now I must trust you," said the old man. "*Temos que confiar no senhor americano.* You love liberty, *né?*"

Love liberty? Who knew anymore? What was liberty? Being free to make a buck? The Russians had been smart enough to know that if they let Americans make money, they really didn't give a damn which language the government was speaking. And, in fact, the government spoke English anyway.

The propaganda that they had been feeding him wasn't funny. It was too true. The United States had never been so peaceful. It was more prosperous than it had been since the Vietnam War boom thirty years before. And the lazy, complacent American people were going about business as usual, as if pictures of Lenin on buildings and billboards were just what they had always wanted.

I was no different, he reminded himself. I sent in my work application, complete with oath of allegiance. I accepted it meekly when they opted me out for a tutorial with a high Party official. I even taught his damnable little children for three years in Rio.

When I should have been writing plays.

But what do I write about? Why not a comedy— *The Yankee and the Commissar*, a load of laughs about a woman commissar who marries an American blue blood who manufactures typewriters. There are no women commissars, of course, but one must maintain the illusion of a free and equal society.

"Bruce, my dear," says the commissar in a thick but sexy Russian accent, "your typewriter company is suspiciously close to making a profit."

"And if it were running at a loss, you'd turn me in, yes, my little noodle?" (Riotous laughs from the Russians in the audience; the Americans are not amused, but then, they speak English fluently and don't need broad humor. Besides, the reviews are all approved by the Party, so we don't have to worry about the critics. Keep the Russians happy, and screw the American audience.) Dialogue continues:

"All for the sake of Mother Russia."

"Screw Mother Russia."

"Please do," says Natasha. "Regard me as her personal incarnation."

Oh, but the Russians do love onstage sex. Forbidden in Russia, of course, but Americans are *supposed* to be decadent.

I might as well have been a ride designer for Disneyland, Jerry thought. Might as well have written shtick for vaudeville. Might as well go stick my head in an oven. But with my luck, it would be electric.

He may have slept. He wasn't sure. But the door opened, and he opened his eyes with no memory of having heard footsteps approach. The calm before the storm: and now, the storm.

The soldiers were young, but unSlavic. Slavish, but definitely American. Slaves to the Slavs. Put that in a protest poem sometime, he decided, if only there were someone who wanted to read a protest poem.

The young American soldiers (But the uniforms were wrong. I'm not old enough to remember the old ones, but these are not made for American bodies.) escorted him down corridors, up stairs, through doors, until they were outside and they put him into a heavily armored van. What did they think, he was part of a conspiracy and his fellows would come to save him? Didn't they know that a man in his position would have no friends by now?

Jerry had seen it at Yale. Dr. Swick had been very popular. Best damn professor in the department. He could take the worst drivel and turn it into a *play*, take terrible actors and make them look good, take apathetic audiences and make them, of all things, enthusiastic and hopeful. And then one day the police had broken into his home and found Swick with four actors putting on a play for a group of maybe a score of friends. What was it—*Who's Afraid of Virginia Woolf?* Jerry remembered. A sad script. A despairing script. But a sharp one, nonetheless, one that

showed despair as being an ugly, destructive thing,
one that showed lies as suicide, one that, in short,
made the audience feel that, by God, something was
wrong with their lives, that the peace was illusion,
that the prosperity was a fraud, that America's ambi-
tions had been cut off and that so much that was
good and proud was still undone—

And Jerry realized that he was weeping. The soldiers sitting across from him in the armored van
were looking away. Jerry dried his eyes.

As soon as news got out that Swick was arrested,
he was suddenly unknown. Everyone who had letters
or memos or even class papers that bore his name
destroyed them. His name disappeared from address
books. His classes were empty as no one showed up.
No one even hoping for a substitute, for the university suddenly had no record that there had ever been
such a class, ever been such a professor. His house
had gone up for sale, his wife had moved, and no one
said good-bye. And then, more than a year later, the
CBS news (which always showed official trials then)
had shown ten minutes of Swick weeping and saying,
"Nothing has ever been better for America than
Communism. It was just a foolish, immature desire
to prove myself by thumbing my nose at authority.
It meant nothing. I was wrong. The government's
been kinder to me than I deserve." And so on. The
words were silly. But as Jerry had sat, watching, he
had been utterly convinced. However meaningless
the words were, Swick's face was meaningful: he
was utterly sincere.

The van stopped, and the doors in the back opened
just as Jerry remembered that he had burned his copy
of Swick's manual on playwriting. Burned it, but
not until he had copied down all the major ideas.
Whether Swick knew it or not, he had left something
behind. But what will I leave behind? Jerry wondered.

Two Russian children who now speak fluent English and whose father was blown up in their front yard right in front of them, his blood spattering their faces, because Jerry had neglected to warn him? What a legacy.

For a moment he was ashamed. A life is a life, no matter whose or how lived.

Then he remembered the night when Peter Andreyevitch (no—Anderson. Pretending to be American is fashionable nowadays, so long as everyone can tell at a glance that you're *really* Russian) had drunkenly sent for Jerry and demanded, as Jerry's employer (i.e., owner), that Jerry recite his poems to the guests at the party. Jerry had tried to laugh it off, but Peter was not that drunk: he insisted, and Jerry went upstairs and got his poems and came down and read them to a group of men who could not understand the poems, to a group of women who understood them and were merely amused. Little Andre said afterward, "The poems were good, Jerry," but Jerry felt like a virgin who had been raped and then given a two-dollar tip by the rapist.

In fact, Peter had given him a bonus. And Jerry had spent it.

Charlie Ridge, Jerry's defense attorney, met him just inside the doors of the courthouse. "Jerry, old boy, looks like you're taking all this pretty well. Haven't even lost any weight."

"On a diet of pure starch, I've had to run around my cell all day just to stay thin." Laughter. Ha ho, what a fun time we're having. What jovial people we are.

"Listen, Jerry, you've got to do this right, you know. They have audience response measurements. They can judge how sincere you seem. You've got to really *mean* it."

"Wasn't there once a time when defense attorneys tried to get their clients off?" Jerry asked.

"Jerry, that kind of attitude isn't going to get you anywhere. These aren't the good old days when you could get off on a technicality and a lawyer could delay trial for five years. You're guilty as hell, and so if you cooperate, they won't do anything to you. They'll just deport you."

"What a pal," Jerry said. "With you on my side, I haven't a worry in the world."

"Exactly right," said Charlie. "And don't you forget it."

The courtroom was crowded with cameras. (Jerry had heard that in the old days of freedom of the press, cameras had often been barred from courtrooms. But then, in those days the defendant didn't usually testify and in those days the lawyers didn't both work from the same script. Still, there was the press, looking for all the world as if they thought they were free.)

Jerry had nothing to do for nearly half an hour. The audience (Are they paid? Jerry wondered. In America, they must be.) filed in, and the show began at exactly eight o'clock. The judge came in looking impressive in his robes, and his voice was resonant and strong, like a father on television remonstrating his rebellious son. Everyone who spoke faced the camera with the red light on the top. And Jerry felt very tired.

He did not waver in his determination to try to turn this trial to his own advantage, but he seriously wondered what good it would do. And was it to his own advantage? They would certainly punish him more severely. Certainly they would be angry, would cut him off. But he had written his speech as if it were an impassioned climactic scene in a play (*Crove Against the Communists* or perhaps *Liberty's Last*

Cry), and he the hero who would willingly give his life for the chance to instill a little bit of patriotism (a little bit of intelligence, who gives a damn about patriotism!) in the hearts and minds of the millions of Americans who would be watching.

"Gerald Nathan Crove, you have heard the charges against you. Please step forward and state your plea."

Jerry stood up and walked with, he hoped, dignity to the taped X on the floor where the prosecutor had insisted that he stand. He looked for the camera with the red light on. He stared into it intently, sincerely, and wondered if, after all, it wouldn't be better just to say *nolo contendere* or even *guilty* and have an easier time of it.

"Mr. Crove," intoned the judge, "America is watching. How do you plead?"

America was watching indeed. And Jerry opened his mouth and said not the Latin but the English he had rehearsed so often in his mind:

"There is a time for courage and a time for cowardice, a time when a man can give in to those who offer him leniency and a time when he must, instead, resist them for the sake of a higher goal. America was once a free nation. But as long as they pay our salaries, we seem content to be slaves! I plead not guilty, because any act that serves to weaken Russian domination of any nation in the world is a blow for all the things that make life worth living and against those to whom power is the only god worth worshiping!"

Ah. Eloquence. But in his rehearsals he had never dreamed he would get even this far, and yet they still showed no sign of stopping him. He looked away from the camera. He looked at the prosecutor, who was taking notes on a yellow pad. He looked at Charlie, and Charlie was resignedly shaking his head and putting his papers back in his briefcase. No one seemed to be particularly worried that Jerry was saying these things over live television. And the broadcasts *were* live—they had stressed that, that he must be careful to do everything correctly the first time because it was all live—

They were lying, of course. And Jerry stopped his speech and jammed his hands into his pockets, only to discover that the suit they had provided for him had no pockets (Save money by avoiding nonessentials, said the slogan), and his hands slid uselessly down his hips.

The prosecutor looked up in surprise when the judge cleared his throat. "Oh, I beg your pardon," he said. "The speeches usually go on much longer. I congratulate you, Mr. Crove, on your brevity."

Jerry nodded in mock acknowledgment, but he felt no mockery.

"We always have a dry run," said the prosecutor, "just to catch you last-chancers."

"Everyone knew that?"

"Well, everyone but you, of course, Mr. Crove. All right, everybody, you can go home now."

The audience arose and quietly shuffled out.

The prosecutor and Charlie got up and walked to the bench. The judge was resting his chin on his hands, looking not at all fatherly now, just a little bored. "How much do you want?" the judge asked.

"Unlimited," said the prosecutor.

"Is he really that important?" Jerry might as well have not been there. "After all, they're doing the actual bombers in Brazil."

"Mr. Crove is an American," said the prosecutor, "who chose to let a Russian ambassador be assassinated."

"All right, all right," said the judge, and Jerry marveled that the man hadn't the slightest trace of a Russian accent.

"Gerald Nathan Crove, the court finds you guilty of murder and treason against the United States of America and its ally, the Union of Soviet Socialist Republics. Do you have anything to say before sentence is pronounced?"

"I just wondered," said Jerry, "why you all speak English."

"Because," said the prosecutor icily, "we are in America."

"Why do you even bother with trials?"

"To stop other imbeciles from trying what you did. He just wants to argue, Your Honor."

The judge slammed down his gavel. "The court sentences Gerald Nathan Crove to be put to death by every available method until such time as he convincingly apologizes for his action to the American people. Court stands adjourned. Lord in heaven, do I have a headache."

They wasted no time. At five o'clock in the morning, Jerry had barely fallen asleep. Perhaps they monitored this, because they promptly woke him up with a brutal electric shock across the metal floor where Jerry was lying. Two guards—this time Russians— came in and stripped him and then dragged him to the execution chamber even though, had they let him, he would have walked.

The prosecutor was waiting. "I have been assigned your case," he said, "because you promise to be a challenge. Your psychological profile is interesting, Mr. Crove. You long to be a hero."

"I wasn't aware of that."

"You displayed it in the courtroom, Mr. Crove. You are no doubt aware—your middle name implies it—of the last words of the American Revolutionary War espionage agent named Nathan Hale. 'I regret that I have but one life to give for my country,' he said. You shall discover that he was mistaken. He should be very glad he had but one life.

"Since you were arrested several weeks ago in Rio de Janeiro, we have been growing a series of clones for you. Development is quite accelerated, but they have been kept in zero-sensation environments until the present. Their minds are blank.

"You are surely aware of somec, yes, Mr. Crove?"

Jerry nodded. The starship sleep drug.

"We don't need it in this case, of course. But the mind-taping technique we use on interstellar flights—that is quite useful. When we execute you, Mr. Crove, we shall be continuously taping your brain. All your memories will be rather indecorously dumped into the head of the first clone, who will immediately become *you*. However, he will clearly remember all your life up to and including the moment of death.

"It was so easy to be a hero in the old days, Mr. Crove. Then you never knew for sure what death was like. It was compared to sleep, to great emotional pain, to quick departure of the soul from the body. None of these, of course, is particularly accurate."

Jerry was frightened. He had heard of multiple death before, of course—it was rumored to exist because of its deterrent value. "They resurrect you and kill you again and again," said the horror story, and now he knew that it was true. Or they wanted him to believe it was true.

What frightened Jerry was the way they planned to kill him. A noose hung from a hook in the ceiling. It could be raised and lowered, but there didn't seem to be the slightest provision for a quick, sharp drop to break his neck. Jerry had once almost choked to death on a salmon bone. The sensation of not being able to breathe terrified him.

"How can I get out of this?" Jerry asked, his palms sweating.

"The first one, not at all," said the prosecutor. "So you might as well be brave and use up your heroism this time around. Afterward we'll give you a screen test and see how convincing your repentance is. We're fair, you know. We try to avoid putting anyone through this unnecessarily. Please sit."

Jerry sat. A man in a lab coat put a metal helmet on his head. A few needles pricked into Jerry's scalp.

"Already," said the prosecutor, "your first clone is becoming aware. He already has all your memories. He is right now living through your panic—or shall we say your attempts at courage. Make sure you concentrate carefully on what is about to happen to you, Jerry. You want to make sure you remember every detail."

"Please," Jerry said.

"Buck up, my man," said the prosecutor with a grin. "You were wonderful in the courtroom. Let's have some of that noble resistance now."

Then the guards led him to the noose and put it around his neck, being careful not to dislodge the helmet. They pulled it tight and then tied his hands behind his back. The rope was rough on his neck. He waited, his neck tingling, for the sensation of being lifted in the air. He flexed his neck muscles, trying to keep them rigid, though he knew the effort would be useless. His knees grew weak, waiting for them to raise the rope.

The room was plain. There was nothing to see, and the prosecutor had left the room. There was, however, a mirror on a wall beside him. He could barely see into it without turning his entire body. He was sure it was an observation window. They would watch, of course.

Jerry needed to go to the bathroom.

Remember, he told himself, I won't really die. I'll be awake in the other room in just a moment.

But his body was not convinced. It didn't matter a bit that a new Jerry Crove would be ready to get up and walk away when this was over. *This* Jerry Crove would die.

"What are you waiting for?" he demanded, and as if that had been their cue the guards pulled the rope and lifted him into the air.

From the beginning it was worse than he had thought. The rope had an agonizingly tight grip on his neck; there was no question of resisting at all. The suffocation was nothing, at first. Like being under water holding your breath. But the rope itself was painful, and his neck hurt, and he wanted to cry out with the pain; but nothing could escape his throat.

Not at first.

There was some fumbling with the rope, and it jumped up and down as the guards tied it to the hook on the wall. Once Jerry's feet even touched the floor.

By the time the rope held still, however, the effects of the strangling were taking over and the pain was forgotten. The blood was pounding inside Jerry's head. His tongue felt thick. He could not shut his eyes. And now he wanted to breathe. He had to breathe. His body demanded a breath.

His body was not under control. Intellectually, he knew that he could not possibly reach the floor, knew that this death would be temporary, but right now his mind was not having much influence over his body. His legs kicked and struggled to reach the ground. His hands strained at the rope behind him. And all the exertion only made his eyes bulge more with the pressure of the blood that could not get past the rope; only made him need air more desperately.

There was no help for him, but now he tried to scream for help. The sound now escaped his throat—

but at the cost of air. He felt as if his tongue were being pushed up into his nose. His kicking grew more violent, though every kick was agony. He spun on the rope; he caught a glimpse of himself in the mirror. His face was turning purple.

How long will it be? Surely not much longer!

But it was much longer.

If he had been underwater, holding his breath, he would now have given up and drowned.

If he had a gun and a free hand, he would kill himself now to end this agony and the sheer physical terror of being unable to breathe. But he had no gun, and there was no question of inhaling, and the blood throbbed in his head and made his eyes see everything in shades of red, and finally he saw nothing at all.

Saw nothing, except what was going through his mind, and that was a jumble, as if his consciousness were madly trying to make some arrangement that would eliminate the strangulation. He kept seeing himself in the creek behind his house, where he had fallen in when he was a child, and someone was throwing him a rope, but he couldn't and he couldn't and he couldn't catch it, and then suddenly it was around his neck and dragging him under.

Spots of black stabbed at his eyes. His body felt bloated, and then it erupted, his bowel and bladder and stomach ejecting all that they contained, except that his vomit was stopped at his throat, where it burned.

The shaking of his body turned into convulsive jerks and spasms, and for a moment Jerry felt himself reaching the welcome state of unconsciousness. Then, suddenly, he discovered that death is not so kind.

There is no such thing as slipping off quietly in

your sleep. No such thing as being "killed immediately" or having death mercifully end the pain.

Death woke him from his unconsciousness, for perhaps a tenth of a second. But that tenth of a second was infinite, and in it he experienced the infinite agony of impending nonexistence. His life did not flash before his eyes. The lack of life instead exploded, and in his mind he experienced far greater pain and fear than anything he had felt from the mere hanging.

And then he died.

For an instant he hung in limbo, feeling and seeing nothing. Then a light stabbed at his eyes and soft foam peeled away from his skin and the prosecutor stood there, watching as he gasped and retched and clutched at his throat. It seemed incredible that he could now breathe, and if he had experienced only the strangling, he might now sigh with relief and say, "I've been through it once, and now I'm not afraid of death." But the strangling was nothing. The strangling was a prelude. And he was afraid of death.

They forced him to come into the room where he had died. He saw his body hanging, black-faced, from the ceiling, the helmet still on the head, the tongue protruding.

"Cut it down," the prosecutor said, and for a moment Jerry waited for the guards to obey. Instead, a guard handed Jerry a knife.

With death still heavy in his mind, Jerry swung around and lunged at the prosecutor. But a guard caught his hand in an irresistible grip, and the other guard held a pistol pointed at Jerry's head.

"Do you want to die again so soon?" asked the prosecutor, and Jerry whimpered and took the knife and reached up to cut himself down from the noose. In order to reach above the knot, he had to stand close enough to the corpse to touch it. The stench was incredible. And the fact of death was unavoidable. Jerry trembled so badly he could hardly control the knife, but eventually the rope parted and the corpse slumped to the ground, knocking Jerry down as it fell. An arm lay across Jerry's legs. The face looked at Jerry eye-to-eye.

Jerry screamed.

"You see the camera?"

Jerry nodded, numbly.

"You will look at the camera and you will apologize for having done anything against the government that has brought peace to the earth."

Jerry nodded again, and the prosecutor said, "Roll it."

"Fellow Americans," Jerry said, "I'm sorry. I made a terrible mistake. I was wrong. There's nothing wrong with the Russians. I let an innocent man be killed. Forgive me. The government has been kinder to me than I deserve." And so on. For an hour Jerry babbled, insisting that he was craven, that he was guilty, that he was worthless, that the government was vying with God for respectability.

And when he was through, the prosecutor came back in, shaking his head.

"Mr. Crove, you can do better than that.

"Nobody in the audience believed you for one minute. Nobody in the test sample, not one person, believed that you were the least bit sincere. You still think the government ought to be deposed. And so we have to try the treatment again."

"Let me try to confess again."

"A screen test is a screen test, Mr. Crove. We have to give you a little more experience with death before we can permit you to have any involvement with life."

This time Jerry screamed right from the beginning. He made no attempt at all to bear it well. They hung him by the armpits over a long cylinder filled with boiling oil. They slowly lowered him. Death came when the oil was up to his chest—by then his legs had been completely cooked and the meat was falling off the bones in large chunks.

They made him come in and, when the oil had cooled enough to touch, fish out the pieces of his own corpse.

He wept all through his confession this time, but the test audience was completely unconvinced. "The man's a phony," they said. "He doesn't believe a word of what he's saying."

"We have a problem," said the prosecutor. "You seem so willing to cooperate after your death. But you have reservations. You aren't speaking from the heart. We'll have to help you again."

Jerry screamed and struck out at the prosecutor. When the guards had pulled him away (and the prosecutor was nursing an injured nose), Jerry shouted, "Of course I'm lying! No matter how often you kill me it won't change the fact that this is a government of fools by vicious, lying bastards!"

"On the contrary," said the prosecutor, trying to maintain his good manners and cheerful demeanor despite the blood pouring out of his nose, "if we kill you enough, you'll completely change your mind."

"You can't change the truth!"

"We've changed it for everyone else who's gone through this. And you are far from being the first who had to go to a third clone. But this time, Mr. Crove, do try to forget about being a hero."

They skinned him alive, arms and legs first, and then, finally, they castrated him and ripped the skin off his belly and chest. He died silently when they cut his larynx out—no, not silently. Just voiceless. He found that without a voice he could still whisper a scream that rang in his ears when he awoke and was forced to go in and carry his bloody corpse to the disposal room. He confessed again, and the audience was not convinced.

They slowly crushed him to death, and he had to scrub the blood out of the crusher when he awoke, but the audience only commented. "Who does the jerk think he's fooling?"

They disemboweled him and burned his guts in front of him. They infected him with rabies and let his death linger for two weeks. They crucified him and let exposure and thirst kill him. They dropped him a dozen times from the roof of a one-story building until he died.

Yet the audience knew that Jerry Crove had not repented.

"My God, Crove, how long do you think I can keep doing this?" asked the prosecutor. He did not seem cheerful. In fact, Jerry thought he looked almost desperate.

"Getting a little tough on you?" Jerry asked, grateful for the conversation because it meant there would be a few minutes between deaths.

"What kind of man do you think I am? We'll bring him back to life in a minute anyway, I tell myself, but I didn't get into this business in order to find new, hideous ways of killing people."

"You don't like it? And yet you have such a natural talent for it."

The prosecutor looked sharply at Crove. "Irony? Now you can joke? Doesn't death mean anything to you?"

Jerry did not answer, only tried to blink back the

tears that these days came unbidden every few minutes.

"Crove, this is not cheap. Do you think it's cheap? We've spent literally billions of rubles on you. And even with inflation, that's a hell of a lot of money."

"In a classless society there's no need for money."

"What is this, dammit! *Now* you're getting rebellious? *Now* you're trying to be a hero?"

"No."

"No wonder we've had to kill you eight times! You keep thinking up clever arguments against us!"

"I'm sorry. Heaven knows I'm sorry."

"I've asked to be released from this assignment. I obviously can't crack you."

"Crack me! As if I didn't long to be cracked."

"You're costing too much. There's a definite benefit in having criminals convincingly recant on television. But you're getting too expensive. The cost-benefit ratio is ridiculous now. There's a limit to how much we can spend on you."

"I have a way for you to save money."

"So do I. Convince the damned audience!"

"Next time you kill me, don't put a helmet on my head."

The prosecutor looked absolutely shocked. "That would be final. That would be capital punishment. We're a humane government. We never kill anybody permanently."

They shot him in the gut and let him bleed to death. They threw him from a cliff into the sea. They let a shark eat him alive. They hung him upside down so that just his head was under water, and when he finally got too tired to hold his head out of the water he drowned.

But through all this, Jerry had become more inured to the pain. His mind had finally learned that none of these deaths was permanent after all. And now when the moment of death came, though it was still terrible, he endured it better. He screamed less. He approached death with greater calm. He even hastened the process, deliberately inhaling great draughts of water, deliberately wriggling to attract the shark. When they had the guards kick him to death he kept yelling, "Harder," until he couldn't yell anymore.

And finally when they set up a screen test, he fervently told the audience that the Russian government was the most terrifying empire the world had ever known, because this time they were efficient at keeping their power, because this time there was no outside for barbarians to come from, and because they had seduced the freest people in history into loving slavery. His speech was from the heart—he loathed the Russians and loved the memory that once there had been freedom and law and a measure of justice in America.

And the prosecutor came into the room ashen-faced.

"You bastard," he said.

"Oh. You mean the audience was live this time?"

"A hundred loyal citizens. And you corrupted all but three of them."

"Corrupted?"

"Convinced them."

Silence for a moment, and then the prosecutor sat down and buried his head in his hands.

"Going to lose your job?" Jerry asked.

"Of course."

"I'm sorry. You're good at it."

The prosecutor looked at him with loathing. "No one ever failed at this before. And I had never had to take anyone beyond a second death. You've died a dozen times, Crove, and you've got used to it."

"I didn't mean to."

"How did you do it?"

"I don't know."

"What kind of animal are you, Crove? Can't you make up a lie and *believe* it?"

Crove chuckled. (In the old days, at this level of amusement he would have laughed uproariously. But inured to death or not; he had scars. And he would never laugh loudly again.) "It was my business. As a playwright. The willing suspension of disbelief."

The door opened and a very important looking man in a military uniform covered with medals came in, followed by four Russian soldiers. The prosecutor sighed and stood up. "Good-bye, Crove."

"Good-bye," Jerry said.

"You're a very strong man."

"So," said Jerry, "are you." And the prosecutor left.

The soldiers took Jerry out of the prison to a different place entirely. A large complex of buildings in Florida. Cape Canaveral. They were exiling him, Jerry realized.

"What's it like?" he asked the technician who was preparing him for the flight.

"Who knows?" the technician asked. "No one's ever come back. Hell, no one's ever arrived yet."

"After I sleep on somec, will I have any trouble waking up?"

"In the labs, here on earth, no. Out there, who knows?"

"But you think we'll live?"

"We send you to planets that look like they might be habitable. If they aren't, so sorry. You take your chances. The worst that can happen is you die."

"Is that all?" Jerry murmured.

"Now lie down and let me tape your brain."

Jerry lay down and the helmet, once again, recorded his thoughts. It was irresistible, of course: when you are conscious that your thoughts are being taped, Jerry realized, it is impossible not to try to think something important. As if you were performing. Only the audience would consist of just one person. Yourself when you woke up.

But he thought this: That this starship and the others that would be and had been sent out to colonize in prison worlds were not really what the Russians thought they were. True, the prisoners sent in the Gulag ships would be away from earth for centuries before they landed, and many or most of them would not survive. But some would survive.

I will survive, Jerry thought as the helmet picked up his brain pattern and transferred it to tape.

Out there the Russians are creating their own barbarians. I will be Attila the Hun. My child will be Mohammed. My grandchild will be Genghis Khan.

One of us, someday, will sack Rome.

Then the somec was injected, and it swept through him, taking consciousness with it, and Jerry realized with a shock of recognition that this, too, was death: but a welcome death, and he didn't mind. Because this time when he woke up he would be free.

He hummed cheerfully until he couldn't remember how to hum, and then they put his body with hundreds of others on a starship and pushed them all out into space, where they fell upward endlessly into the stars. Going home.

CLAP HANDS AND SING

O N THE SCREEN the crippled man screamed at the lady, insisting that she must not run away. He waved a certificate. "I'm a registered rapist, damnit!" he cried. "Don't run so fast! You have to make allowances for the handicapped!" He ran after her with an odd, left-heavy lope. His enormous prosthetic phallus swung crazily, like a clumsy propeller that couldn't quite get started. The audience laughed madly. Must be a funny, funny scene!

Old Charlie sat slumped in his chair, feeling as casual and permanent as glacial debris. *I am here only by accident, but I'll never move.* He did not switch off the television set. The audience roared again with laughter. Canned or live? After more than eight decades of watching television, Charlie couldn't tell anymore. Not that the canned laughter had got any more real: It was the real laughter that had gone tinny, premeditated. As if the laughs were timed to come *now*, no matter what, and the poor actors could strain to get off their gags in time, but always they were just *this* much early, *that* much late.

"It's late," the television said, and Charlie started awake, vaguely surprised to see that the program had changed: Now it was a demonstration of a convenient electric breast pump to store up natural mother's milk for those times when you just can't be with baby. "It's late."

"Hello, Jock," Charlie said.

"Don't sleep in front of the television again, Charlie."

"Leave me alone, swine," Charlie said. And then: "Okay, turn it off."

He hadn't finished giving the order when the television flickered and went white, then settled down into its perpetual springtime scene that meant *off*. But in the flicker Charlie thought he saw—who? Name? From the distant past. A girl. Before the name came to him, there came another memory: a small hand resting lightly on his knee as they sat together, as light as a long-legged fly upon a stream. In his memory he did not turn to look at her; he was talking to others. But he knew just where she would be if he turned to look. Small, with mousy hair, and yet a face that was always the child Juliet. But that was not her name. Not Juliet, though she was Juliet's age in that memory. *I am Charlie*, he thought. *She is—Rachel.*

Rachel Carpenter. In the flicker on the screen hers was the face the random light had brought him, and so he remembered Rachel as he pulled his ancient body from the chair; thought of Rachel as he peeled the clothing from his frail skeleton, delicately, lest some rough motion strip away the wrinkled skin like cellophane.

And Jock, who of course did not switch himself off with the television, recited:

"An aged man is a paltry thing, a tattered coat upon a stick."

"Shut up," Charlie ordered.

"Unless Soul clap its hands."

"I said shut up!"

"And sing, and louder sing, for every tatter in its mortal dress."

"Are you finished?" Charlie asked. He knew Jock was finished. After all, Charlie had programmed him to recite—*it* to recite—just that fragment every night when his shorts hit the floor.

He stood naked in the middle of the room and thought of Rachel, whom he had not thought of in years. It was a trick of being old, that the room he was in now so easily vanished, and in its place a memory could take hold. *I've made my fortune from time machines*, he thought, *and now I discover that every aged person is his own time machine*. For now he stood naked. No, that was a trick of memory; memory had these damnable tricks. He was not naked. He only felt naked, as Rachel sat in the car beside him. Her voice—he had almost forgotten her voice—was soft. Even when she shouted, it got more whispery, so that if she shouted, it would have all the wind of the world in it and he wouldn't hear it at all, would only feel it cold on his naked skin. That was the voice she was using now, saying yes. I loved you when I was twelve, and when I was thirteen, and when I was fourteen, but when you got back from playing God in São Paulo, you didn't call me. All those letters, and then for three months you didn't call me and I knew that you thought I was just a child and I fell in love with—Name? Name gone. Fell in love with a *boy*, and ever since then you've been treating me like. Like. No, she'd never say *shit*, not in that voice. And take some of the anger out, that's right. Here are the words . . . here they come: You could have had me, Charlie, but now all you can do is try to make me miserable. It's too late, the time's gone by, the time's over, so stop criticizing me. Leave me *alone*.

First to last, all in a capsule. The words are nothing, Charlie realized. A dozen women, not least his dear departed wife, had said exactly the same words to him since, and it had sounded just as maudlin, just as unpleasantly uninteresting every time. The difference was that when the others said it, Charlie felt himself insulated with a thousand layers of unconcern. But when Rachel said it to his memory, he stood naked in the middle of his room, a cold wind drying the parchment of his ancient skin.

"What's wrong?" asked Jock.

Oh, yes, dear computer, a change in the routine of the habitbound old man, and you suspect what, a heart attack? Incipient death? Extreme disorientation?

"A name," Charlie said. "Rachel Carpenter."

"Living or dead?"

Charlie winced again, as he winced every time Jock asked that question; yet it was an important one, and far too often the answer these days was Dead. "I don't know."

"Living and dead, I have two thousand four hundred eighty in the company archives alone."

"She was twelve when I was—twenty. Yes, twenty. And she lived then in Provo, Utah. Her father was a pianist. Maybe she became an actress when she grew up. She wanted to."

"Rachel Carpenter. Born 1959. Provo, Utah. Attended—"

"Don't show off, Jock. Was she ever married?"

"Thrice."

"And don't imitate my mannerisms. Is she still alive?"

"Died ten years ago."

Of course. Dead, of course. He tried to imagine her—where? "Where did she die?"

"Not pleasant."

"Tell me anyway. I'm feeling suicidal tonight."

"In a home for the mentally incapable."

It was not shocking; people often outlived their minds these days. But sad. For she had always been bright. Strange perhaps, but her thoughts always led to something worth the sometimes-convoluted path. He smiled even before he remembered what he was smiling at. Yes. Seeing through your knees. She had been playing Helen Keller in *The Miracle Worker*, and she told him how she had finally come to understand blindness. "It isn't seeing the red insides of your eyelids, I knew that. I knew it isn't even seeing black. It's like trying to see where you never had eyes at all. Seeing through your knees. No matter how hard you try, there just isn't any *vision* there." And she had liked him because he hadn't laughed. "I told my brother, and he laughed," she said. But Charlie had not laughed.

Charlie's affection for her had begun then, with a twelve-year-old girl who could never stay on the normal, intelligible track, but rather had to stumble her own way through a confusing underbrush that was thick and bright with flowers. "I think God stopped paying attention long ago." she said. "Any more than Michelangelo would want to watch them whitewash the Sistine Chapel."

And he knew that he would do it even before he knew what it was that he would do. She had ended in an institution, and he, with the best medical care that money could buy, stood naked in his room and remembered when passion still lurked behind the lattices of chastity and was more likely to lead to poems than to coitus.

You overtold story, he said to the wizened man who despised him from the mirror. You are only tempted because you're bored. Making excuses because you're cruel. Lustful because your dim old dong is long past the exercise.

And he heard the old bastard answer silently, You *will* do it, because you can. Of all the people in the world, *you* can.

And he thought he saw Rachel look back at him, bright with finding herself beautiful at fourteen, laughing at the vast joke of knowing she was admired by the very man whom she, too, wanted. Laugh all you like, Charlie said to his vision of her. I was too kind to you then. I'm afraid I'll undo my youthful goodness now.

"I'm going back," he said aloud. "Find me a day."

"For what purpose?" Jock asked.

"My business."

"I have to know your purpose, or how can I find you a day?"

And so he had to name it. "I'm going to have her if I can."

Suddenly a small alarm sounded, and Jock's voice was replaced by another. "Warning. Illegal use of THIEF for possible present-altering manipulation of the past."

Charlie smiled. "Investigation has found that the alteration is acceptable. Clear." And the program release: "Byzantium."

"You're a son of a bitch," said Jock.

"Find me a day. A day when the damage will be least—when I can. . ."

"Twenty-eight October 1973."

That was after he got home from São Paulo, the contracts signed, already a capitalist before he was twenty-three. That was during the time when he had been afraid to call her, because she was only fourteen, for God's sake.

"What will it do to her, Jock?"

"How should I know?" Jock answered. "And what difference would it make to you?"

He looked in the mirror again. "A difference."

I won't do it, he told himself as he went to the THIEF that was his most ostentatious sign of wealth, a private THIEF in his own rooms. I won't do it, he decided again as he set the machine to wake him in twelve hours, whether he wished to return or not. Then he climbed into the couch and pulled the shroud over his head, despairing that even this, even doing it to *her*, was not beneath him. There was a time when he had automatically held back from doing a thing because he knew that it was wrong. *Oh, for that time!* he thought, but knew as he thought it that he was lying to himself. He had long since given up on right and wrong and settled for the much simpler standards of effective and ineffective, beneficial and detrimental.

He had gone in a THIEF before, had taken some of the standard trips into the past. Gone into the mind of an audience member at the first performance of Handel's *Messiah* and listened. The poor soul whose ears he used wouldn't remember a bit of it afterward. So the future would not be changed. That was safe, to sit in a hall and listen. He had been in the mind of a farmer resting under a tree on a country lane as Wordsworth walked by and had hailed the poet and asked his name, and Wordsworth had smiled and been distant and cold, delighting in the countryside more than in those whose tillage made it beautiful. But those were legal trips—Charlie had done nothing that could alter the course of history.

This time, though. This time he would change

Rachel's life. Not his own, of course. That would be impossible. But Rachel would not be blocked from remembering what happened. She would remember, and it would turn her from the path she was meant to take. Perhaps only a little. Perhaps not importantly. Perhaps just enough for her to dislike him a little sooner, or a little more. But too much to be legal, if he were caught.

He would not be caught. Not Charlie. Not the man who owned THIEF and therefore could have owned the world. It was all too bound up in secrecy. Too many agents had used his machines to attend the enemy's most private conferences. Too often the Attorney General had listened to the most perfect of wiretaps. Too often politicians who were willing to be in Charlie's debt had been given permission to lead their opponents into blunders that cost them votes. All far beyond what the law allowed; who would dare complain now if Charlie also bent the law to his own purpose?

No one but Charlie. *I can't do this to Rachel*, he thought. And then the THIEF carried him back and put him in his own mind, in his own body, on 28 October 1973, at ten o'clock, just as he was going to bed, weary because he had been wakened that morning by a six A.M. call from Brazil.

As always, there was the moment of resistance, and then peace as his self of that time slipped into unconsciousness. Old Charlie took over and saw, not the past, but the now.

A moment before, he was standing before a mirror, looking at his withered, hanging face; now he realizes that this gazing into a mirror before going to bed is a lifelong habit. *I am Narcissus*, he tells himself, *an unbeautiful idolator at my own shrine*. But now he is not unbeautiful. At twenty-two, his body still has the depth of young skin. His belly is soft, for he is not athletic, but still there is a litheness to him that he will never have again. And now the vaguely remembered needs that had impelled him to this find a physical basis; what had been a dim memory has him on fire.

He will not be sleeping tonight, not soon. He dresses again, finding with surprise the quaint print shirts that once had been in style. The wide-cuffed pants. The shoes with inch-and-a-half heels. *Good God, I wore that!* he thinks, and then wears it. No questions from his family; he goes quietly downstairs and out to his car. The garage reeks of gasoline. It is a smell as nostalgic as lilacs and candlewax.

He still knows the way to Rachel's house, though he is surprised at the buildings that have not yet been built, which roads have not yet been paved, which intersections still don't have the lights he knows they'll have soon, should surely have already. He looks at his wristwatch; it must be a habit of the body he is in, for he hasn't worn a wristwatch in decades. The arm is tanned from Brazilian beaches, and it has no age spots, no purple veins drawing roadmaps under the skin. The time is ten-thirty. *She'll doubtless be in bed.*

He almost stops himself. Few things are left in his private catalog of sin, but surely this is one. He looks into himself and tries to find the will to resist his own desire solely because its fulfillment will hurt another person. He is out of practice—so far out of practice that he keeps losing track of the reason for resisting.

The lights are on, and her mother—Mrs. Carpenter, dowdy and delightful, scatterbrained in the most attractive way—her mother opens the door suspiciously until she recognizes him. "Charlie," she cries out.

"Is Rachel still up?"

"Give me a minute and she will be!"

And he waits, his stomach trembling with anticipation. *I am not a virgin*, he reminds himself, *but this body does not know that.* This body is alert, for it has not yet formed the habits of meaningless passion that Charlie knows far too well. At last she comes down the stairs. He hears her running on the hollow wooden steps, then stopping, coming slowly, denying the hurry. She turns the corner, looks at him.

She is in her bathrobe, a faded thing that he does not remember ever having seen her wear. Her hair is tousled, and her eyes show that she had been asleep.

"I didn't mean to wake you."

"I wasn't really asleep. The first ten minutes don't count anyway."

He smiles. Tears come to his eyes. Yes, he says silently. This is Rachel, yes. The narrow face; the skin so translucent that he can see into it like jade; the slender arms that gesture shyly, with accidental grace.

"I couldn't wait to see you."

"You've been home three days. I thought you'd phone."

He smiles. In fact he will not phone her for months. But he says, "I hate the telephone. I want to talk to you. Can you come out for a drive?"

"I have to ask my mother."

"She'll say yes."

She does say yes. She jokes and says that she trusts Charlie. And the Charlie she knows was trustworthy. *But not me*, Charlie thinks. You are putting your diamonds into the hands of a thief.

"Is it cold?" Rachel asks.

"Not in the car." And so she doesn't take a coat. It's all right. The night breeze isn't bad.

As soon as the door closes behind them, Charlie begins. He puts his arm around her waist. She does not pull away or take it with indifference. He has never done this before, because she's only fourteen, just a child, but she leans against him as they walk, as if she had done this a hundred times before. As always, she takes him by surprise.

"I've missed you," he says.

She smiles, and there are tears in her eyes. "I've missed you, too," she says.

They talk of nothing. It's just as well. Charlie does not remember much about the trip to Brazil, does not remember anything of what he's done in the three days since getting back. No problem, for she seems to want to talk only of tonight. They drive to the Castle, and he tells her its history. He feels an irony about it as he explains. She, after all, is the reason he knows the history. A few years from now she will be part of a theater company that revives the Castle as a public amphitheater. But now it is falling into ruin, a monument to the old WPA, a great castle with turrets and benches made of native stone. It is on the property of the state mental hospital, and so hardly anyone knows it's there. They are alone as they leave the car and walk up the crumbling steps to the flagstone stage.

She is entranced. She stands in the middle of the stage, facing the benches. He watches as she raises her hand, speech waiting at the verge of her lips. He remembers something. Yes, that is the gesture she made when she bade her nurse farewell in *Romeo and Juliet*. No, not *made*. Will make, rather. The gesture must already be in her, waiting for this stage to draw it out.

She turns to him and smiles because the place is

strange and odd and does not belong in Provo, but it does belong to her. She should have been born in the Renaissance, Charlie says softly. She hears him. He must have spoken aloud. "You belong in an age when music was clean and soft and there was no makeup. No one would rival you then."

She only smiles at the conceit. "I missed you," she says.

He touches her cheek. She does not shy away. Her cheek presses into his hand, and he knows that she understands why he brought her here and what he means to do.

Her breasts are perfect but small, her buttocks are boyish and slender, and the only hair on her body is that which tumbles onto her shoulders, that which he must brush out of her face to kiss her again. "I love you," she whispers. "All my life I love you."

And it is exactly as he would have had it in a dream, except that the flesh is tangible, the ecstasy is real, and the breeze turns colder as she shyly dresses again. They say nothing more as he takes her home. Her mother has fallen asleep on the living room couch, a jumble of the *Daily Herald* piled around her feet. Only then does he remember that for her there will be a tomorrow, and on that tomorrow Charlie will not call. For three months Charlie will not call, and she'll hate him.

He tries to soften it. He tries by saying, "Some things can happen only once." It is the sort of thing he might then have said. But she only puts her finger on his lips and says, "I'll never forget." Then she turns and walks toward her mother, to waken her. She turns and motions for Charlie to leave, then smiles again and waves. He waves back and goes out of the door and drives home. He lies awake in this bed that feels like childhood to him, and he wishes it could have gone on forever like this. *It should have gone on like this*, he thinks. *She is no child. She* was *no child*, he should have thought, for THIEF was already transporting him home.

"What's wrong, Charlie?" Jock asked.

Charlie awoke. It had been hours since THIEF brought him back. It was the middle of the night, and Charlie realized that he had been crying in his sleep. "Nothing," he said.

"You're crying, Charlie. I've never seen you cry before."

"Go plug into a million volts, Jock. I had a dream."

"What dream?"

"I destroyed her."

"No, you didn't."

"It was a goddamned selfish thing to do."

"You'd do it again. But it didn't hurt her."

"She was only fourteen."

"No, she wasn't."

"I'm tired. I was asleep. Leave me alone."

"Charlie, remorse isn't your style."

Charlie pulled the blanket over his head, feeling petulant and wondering whether this childish act was another proof that he was retreating into senility after all.

"Charlie, let me tell you a bedtime story."

"I'll erase you."

"Once upon a time, ten years ago, an old woman named Rachel Carpenter petitioned for a day in her past. And it was a day *with* someone, and it was a day with *you*. So the routine circuits called me, as they always do when your name comes up, and I found her a day. She only wanted to visit, you see, only wanted to relive a good day. I was surprised, Charlie. I didn't know you ever had good days."

This program had been with Jock too long. It knew too well how to get under his skin.

"And in fact there were no days as good as she thought," Jock continued. "Only anticipation and disappointment. That's all you ever gave anybody, Charlie. Anticipation and disappointment."

"I can count on you."

"This woman was in a home for the mentally incapable. And so I gave her a day. Only instead of a day of disappointment, or promises she knew would never be fulfilled, I gave her a day of answers. I gave her a night of answers, Charlie."

"You couldn't know that I'd have you do this. You couldn't have known it ten years ago."

"That's all right, Charlie. Play along with me. You're dreaming anyway, aren't you?"

"And don't wake me up."

"So an old woman went back into a young girl's body on twenty-eight October 1973, and the young girl never knew what had happened; so it didn't change her life, don't you see?"

"It's a lie."

"No, it isn't. I can't lie, Charlie. You programmed me not to lie. Do you think I would have let you go back and *harm* her?"

"She was the same. She was as I remembered her."

"Her body was."

"She hadn't changed. She wasn't an old woman, Jock. She was a girl. She was a girl, Jock."

And Charlie thought of an old woman dying in an institution, surrounded by yellow walls and pale gray sheets and curtains. He imagined young Rachel inside that withered form, imprisoned in a body that would not move, trapped in a mind that could never again take her along her bright, mysterious trails.

"I flashed her picture on the television," Jock said.

And yet, Charlie thought, *how is it less bearable than that beautiful boy who wanted so badly to do the right thing that he did it all wrong, lost his chance, and now is caught in the sum of all his wrong turns? I got on the road they all wanted to take, and I reached the top, but it wasn't where I should have gone. I'm still that boy. I did not have to lie when I went home to her.*

"I know you pretty well, Charlie," Jock said. "I knew that you'd be enough of a bastard to go back. And enough of a human being to do it right when you got there. She came back happy, Charlie. She came back satisfied."

His night with a beloved child was a lie then; it wasn't young Rachel any more than it was young Charlie. He looked for anger inside himself but couldn't find it. For a dead woman had given him a gift, and taken the one he offered, and it still tasted sweet.

"Time for sleep, Charlie. Go to sleep again. I just wanted you to know that there's no reason to feel any remorse for it. No reason to feel anything bad at all."

Charlie pulled the covers tight around his neck, unaware that he had begun that habit years ago, when the strange shadowy shapes hid in his closet and only the blanket could keep him safe. Pulled the covers high and tight, and closed his eyes, and felt her hand stroke him, felt her breast and hip and thigh, and heard her voice as breath against his cheek.

"O chestnut tree," Jock said, as he had been taught to say, ". . . great rooted blossomer,

"Are you the leaf, the blossom, or the bole?

"O body swayed to music, O brightening glance,

"How can we know the dancer from the dance?"

The audience applauded in his mind while he

slipped into sleep, and he thought it remarkable that they sounded genuine. He pictured them smiling and nodding at the show. Smiling at the girl with her hand raised so; nodding at the man who paused forever, then came on stage.

DOGWALKER

I WAS AN INNOCENT pedestrian. Only reason I got in this in the first place was I got a vertical way of thinking and Dogwalker thought I might be useful, which was true, and also he said I might enjoy myself, which was a prefabrication, since people done a lot more enjoying on me than I done on them.

When I say I think vertical, I mean to say I'm metaphysical, that is, simular, which is to say, I'm dead but my brain don't know it yet and my feet still move. I got popped at age nine just lying in my own bed when the goat next door shot at his lady and it went through the wall and into my head. Everybody went to look at them cause they made all the noise, so I was a quart low before anybody noticed I been poked.

They packed my head with supergoo and light pipe, but they didn't know which neutron was supposed to butt into the next so my alchemical brain got turned from rust to diamond. Goo Boy. The Crystal Kid.

From that bright electrical day I never grew another inch, anywhere. Bullet went nowhere near my gonadicals. Just turned off the puberty switch in my head. Saint Paul said he was a eunuch for Jesus, but who am I a eunuch for?

Worst thing about it is here I am near thirty and I still have to take barkeepers to court before they'll sell me beer. And it ain't hardly worth it even though the judge prints out in my favor and the barkeep has to pay costs, because my corpse is so little I get toxed on six ounces and pass out pissing after twelve. I'm a lousy drinking buddy. Besides, anybody hangs out with me looks like a pederast.

No, I'm not trying to make you drippy-drop for me—I'm used to it, OK? Maybe the homecoming queen never showed me True Love in a four-point spread, but I got this knack that certain people find real handy and so I always made out. I dress good and I ride the worm and I don't pay much income tax. Because I am the Password Man. Give me five minutes with anybody's curriculum vitae, which is to say their autopsychoscopy, and nine times out of ten I'll spit out their password and get you into their most nasty sticky sweet secret files. Actually it's usually more like three times out of ten, but that's still a lot better odds than having a computer spend a year trying to push out fifteen characters to make just the right P-word, specially since after the third wrong try they string your phone number, freeze the target files, and call the dongs.

Oh, do I make you sick? A cute little boy like me, engaged in critical unspecified dispopulative behaviors? I may be half glass and four feet high, but I can simulate you better than your own mama, and the better I know you, the deeper my hooks. I not only know your password *now*, I can write a word on a paper, seal it up, and then you go home and *change* your password and then open up what I wrote and there it'll be, your *new* password, three times out of ten. I am *vertical*, and Dogwalker knowed it. Ten percent more supergoo and I wouldn't even be legally human, but I'm still under the line, which is more than I can say for a lot of people who are a hundred percent zoo inside their head.

Dogwalker comes to me one day at Carolina Circle, where I'm playing pinball standing on a stool. He didn't say nothing, just gave me a shove, so naturally he got my elbow in his balls. I get a lot of twelve-year-olds trying to shove me around at the arcades, so I'm used to teaching them lessons. Jack the Giant Killer. Hero of the fourth graders. I usually go for the stomach, only Dogwalker wasn't a twelve-year-old, so my elbow hit low.

I knew the second I hit him that this wasn't no kid. I didn't know Dogwalker from God, but he gots the look, you know, like he been hungry before, and he don't care what he eats these days.

Only he got no ice and he got no slice, just sits there on the floor with his back up against the Eat Shi'ite game, holding his boodle and looking at me like I was a baby he had to diaper. "I hope you're Goo Boy," he says, "cause if you ain't, I'm gonna give you back to your mama in three little tupperware bowls." He doesn't sound like he's making a threat, though. He sounds like he's chief weeper at his own funeral.

"You want to do business, use your mouth, not your hands," I says. Only I say it real apoplectic, which is the same as apologetic except you are also still pissed.

"Come with me," he says. "I got to go buy me a truss. You pay the tax out of your allowance."

So we went to Ivey's and stood around in children's wear while he made his pitch. "One P-word," he says, "only there can't be no mistake. If there's a mistake, a guy loses his job and maybe goes to jail."

So I told him no. Three chances in ten, that's the best I can do. No guarantees. My record speaks for itself, but nobody's perfect, and I ain't even close.

"Come on," he says, "you got to have ways to make sure, right? If you can do three times out of ten, what if you find out more about the guy? What if you meet him?"

"OK, maybe fifty-fifty."

"Look, we can't go back for seconds. So maybe you can't get it. But do you *know* when you ain't got it?"

"Maybe half the time when I'm wrong, I know I'm wrong."

"So we got three out of four that you'll know whether you got it?"

"No," says I. "Cause half the time when I'm right, I don't know I'm right."

"Shee-it," he says. "This is like doing business with my baby brother."

"You can't afford me anyway," I says. "I pull two dimes minimum, and you barely got breakfast on your gold card."

"I'm offering a cut."

"I don't want a cut. I want cash."

"Sure thing," he says. He looks around, real careful. As if they wired the sign that said Boys Briefs Sizes 10–12. "I got an inside man at Federal Coding," he says.

"That's nothing," I says. "I got a bug up the First Lady's ass, and forty hours on tape of her breaking wind."

I got a mouth. I know I got a mouth. I especially

know it when he jams my face into a pile of shorts
and says, "Suck on this, Goo Boy."

I hate it when people push me around. And I know
ways to make them stop. This time all I had to do
was cry. Real loud, like he was hurting me. Everybody looks when a kid starts crying. "I'll be good." I
kept saying it. "Don't hurt me no more! I'll be good."

"Shut up," he says. "Everybody's looking."

"Don't you ever shove me around again," I says.
"I'm at least ten years older than you, and a hell of
a lot more than ten years smarter. Now I'm leaving
this store, and if I see you coming after me, I'll start
screaming about how you zipped down and showed
me the pope, and you'll get yourself a child-molest-
ing tag so they pick you up every time some kid gets
jollied within a hundred miles of Greensboro." I've
done it before, and it works, and Dogwalker was no
dummy. Last thing he needed was extra reasons for
the dongs to bring him in for questioning. So I figured
he'd tell me to get poked and that'd be the last of it.

Instead he says, "Goo Boy, I'm sorry, I'm too quick
with my hands."

Even the goat who shot me never said he was sorry.
My first thought was, what kind of sister is he, ab-
jectifying right out like that. Then I reckoned I'd
stick around and see what kind of man it is who
emulsifies himself in front of a nine-year-old-looking
kid. Not that I figured him to be purely sorrowful.
He still just wanted me to get the P-word for him,
and he knew there wasn't nobody else to do it. But
most street pugs aren't smart enough to tell the right
lie under pressure. Right away I knew he wasn't your
ordinary street hook or low arm, pugging cause they
don't have the sense to stick with any kind of job.
He had a deep face, which is to say his head was
more than a hairball, by which I mean he had brains
enough to put his hands in his pockets without seek-

ing an audience with the pope. Right then was when I decided he was my kind of no-good lying son-of-a-bitch.

"What are you after at Federal Coding?" I asked him. "A record wipe?"

"Ten clean greens," he says. "Coded for unlimited international travel. The whole ID, just like a real person."

"The President has a green card," I says. "The Joint Chiefs have clean greens. But that's all. The U.S. Vice-President isn't even cleared for unlimited international travel."

"Yes he is," he says.

"Oh, yeah, you know everything."

"I need a P. My guy could do us reds and blues, but a clean green has to be done by a burr-oak rat two levels up. My guy knows how it's done."

"They won't just have it with a P-word," I says. "A guy who can make green cards, they're going to have his finger on it."

"I know how to get the finger," he says. "It takes the finger *and* the password."

"You take a guy's finger, he might report it. And even if you persuade him not to, somebody's gonna notice that it's gone."

"Latex," he says. "We'll get a mold. And don't start telling me how to do my part of the job. You get P-words, I get fingers. You in?"

"Cash," I says.

"Twenty percent," says he.

"Twenty percent of pus."

"The inside guy gets twenty, the girl who brings me the finger, she gets twenty, and I damn well get forty."

"You can't just sell these things on the street, you know."

"They're worth a meg apiece," says he, "to certain buyers." By which he meant Orkish Crime, of course. Sell ten, and my twenty percent grows up to be two megs. Not enough to be rich, but enough to retire from public life and maybe even pay for some high-level medicals to sprout hair on my face. I got to admit that sounded good to me.

So we went into business. For a few hours he tried to do it without telling me the baroque rat's name, just giving me data he got from his guy at Federal Coding. But that was real stupid, giving me second-hand face like that, considering he needed me to be a hundred percent sure, and pretty soon he realized that and brought me in all the way. He hated telling me anything, because he couldn't stand to let go. Once I knew stuff on my own, what was to stop me from trying to go into business for myself? But unless he had another way to get the P-word, he had to get it from me, and for me to do it right, I had to know everything I could. Dogwalker's got a brain in his head, even if it is all biodegradable, and so he knows there's times when you got no choice but to trust somebody. When you just got to figure they'll do their best even when they're out of your sight.

He took me to his cheap condo on the old Guilford College campus, near the worm, which was real congenital for getting to Charlotte or Winston or Raleigh with no fuss. He didn't have no soft floor, just a bed, but it was a big one, so I didn't reckon he suffered. Maybe he bought it back in his old pimping days, I figured, back when he got his name, running a string of bitches with names like Spike and Bowser and Prince, real hydrant leg-lifters for the tweeze trade. I could see that he used to have money, and he didn't anymore. Lots of great clothes, tailor-tight fit, but shabby, out of sync. The really old ones, he tore all the wiring out, but you could still see where the diodes used to light up. We're talking neanderthal.

"Vanity, vanity, all is profanity," says I, while I'm holding out the sleeve of a camisa that used to light up like an airplane coming in for a landing.

"They're too comfortable to get rid of," he says. But there's a twist in his voice so I know he don't plan to fool nobody.

"Let this be a lesson to you," says I. "This is what happens when a walker don't walk."

"Walkers do steady work," says he. "But me, when business was good, it felt bad, and when business was bad, it felt good. You walk cats, maybe you can take some pride in it. But you walk dogs, and you know they're getting hurt every time—"

"They got a built-in switch, they don't feel a thing. That's why the dongs don't touch you, walking dogs, cause nobody gets hurt."

"Yeah, so tell me, which is worse, somebody getting tweezed till they scream so some old honk can pop his pimple, or somebody getting half their brain replaced so when the old honk tweezes her she can't feel a thing? I had these women's bodies around me and I knew that they used to be people."

"You can be glass," says I, "and still be people."

He saw I was taking it personally. "Oh hey," says he, "you're under the line."

"So are dogs," says I.

"Yeah well," says he. "You watch a girl come back and tell about some of the things they done to her, and she's *laughing*, you draw your own line."

I look around his shabby place. "Your choice," says I.

"I wanted to feel clean," says he. "That don't mean I got to stay poor."

"So you're setting up this grope so you can return to the old days of peace and propensity."

"Propensity," says he. "What the hell kind of word is that? Why do you keep using words like that?"

"Cause I know them," says I.

"Well you *don't* know them," says he, "because half the time you get them wrong."

I showed him my best little-boy grin. "I know," says I. What I don't tell him is that the fun comes from the fact that almost nobody ever *knows* I'm using them wrong. Dogwalker's no ordinary pimp. But then the ordinary pimp doesn't bench himself halfway through the game because of a sprained moral qualm, by which I mean that Dogwalker had some stray diagonals in his head, and I began to think it might be fun to see where they all hooked up.

Anyway we got down to business. The target's name was Jesse H. Hunt, and I did a real job on him. The Crystal Kid really plugged in on this one. Dogwalker had about two pages of stuff—date of birth, place of birth, sex at birth (no changes since), education, employment history. It was like getting an armload of empty boxes. I just laughed at it. "You got a jack to the city library?" I asked him, and he shows me the wall outlet. I plugged right in, visual onto my pocket sony, with my own little crystal head for ee-i-ee-i-oh. Not every goo-head can think clear enough to do this, you know, put out clean type just by thinking the right stuff out my left ear interface port.

I showed Dogwalker a little bit about research. Took me ten minutes. I know my way right through the Greensboro Public Library. I have P-words for every single librarian and I'm so ept that they don't even guess I'm stepping upstream through their access channels. From the Public Library you can get all the way into North Carolina Records Division in Raleigh, and from there you can jumble into federal personnel records anywhere in the country. Which meant that by nightfall on that most portentous day we had hardcopy of every document in Jesse H. Hunt's whole life, from his birth certificate and first grade report card to his medical history and security clearance reports when he first worked for the feds.

Dogwalker knew enough to be impressed. "If you can do all that," he says, "you might as well pug his P-word straight out."

"No puedo, putz," says I as cheerful as can be. "Think of the fed as a castle. Personnel files are floating in the moat—there's a few alligators but I swim real good. Hot data is deep in the dungeon. You can get in there, but you can't get out clean. And P-words—P-words are kept up the queen's ass."

"No system is unbeatable," he says.

"Where'd you learn that, from graffiti in a toilet stall? If the P-word system was even a little bit break-able, Dogwalker, the gentlemen you plan to sell these cards to would already be inside looking out at us, and they wouldn't need to spend a meg to get clean greens from a street pug."

Trouble was that after impressing Dogwalker with all the stuff I could find out about Jesse H., I didn't know that much more than before. Oh, I could guess at some P-words, but that was all it was—guessing. I couldn't even pick a P most likely to succeed. Jesse was one ordinary dull rat. Regulation good grades in school, regulation good evaluations on the job, probably gave his wife regulation lube jobs on a weekly schedule.

"You don't really think your girl's going to get his finger," says I with sickening scorn.

"You don't know the girl," says he. "If we needed his flipper she'd get molds in five sizes."

"You don't know this guy," says I. "This is the straightest opie in Mayberry. I don't see him cheating on his wife."

"Trust me," says Dogwalker. "She'll get his finger so smooth he won't even know she took the mold."

I didn't believe him. I got a knack for knowing things about people, and Jesse H. wasn't faking. Unless he started faking when he was five, which is pretty unpopulated. He wasn't going to bounce the first pretty girl who made his zipper tight. Besides which he was smart. His career path showed that he was always in the right place. The right people always seemed to know his name. Which is to say he isn't the kind whose brain can't run if his jeans get hot. I said so.

"You're really a marching band," says Dogwalker. "You can't tell me his P-word, but you're obliquely sure that he's a limp or a wimp."

"Neither one," says I. "He's hard and straight. But a girl starts rubbing up to him, he isn't going to think it's because she heard that his crotch is cantilevered. He's going to figure she wants something, and he'll give her string till he finds out what."

He just grinned at me. "I got me the best Password Man in the Triass, didn't I? I got me a miracle worker named Goo-Boy, didn't I? The ice-brain they call Crystal Kid. I got him, didn't I?"

"Maybe," says I.

"I got him or I kill him," he says, showing more teeth than a primate's supposed to have.

"You got me," says I. "But don't go thinking you can kill me."

He just laughs. "I got you and you're so good, you can bet I got me a girl who's at least as good at what she does."

"No such," says I.

"Tell me his P-word and then I'll be impressed."

"You want quick results? Then go ask him to give you his password himself."

Dogwalker isn't one of those guys who can hide it

when he's mad. "I want quick results," he says. "And if I start thinking you can't deliver, I'll pull your tongue out of your head. Through your nose."

"Oh, that's good," says I. "I always do my best thinking when I'm being physically threatened by a client. You really know how to bring out the best in me."

"I don't want to bring out the best," he says. "I just want to bring out his password."

"I got to meet him first," says I.

He leans over me so I can smell his musk, which is to say I'm very olfactory and so I can tell you he reeked of testosterone, by which I mean ladies could fill up with babies just from sniffing his sweat. "Meet him?" he asks me. "Why don't we just ask him to fill out a job application?"

"I've read all his job applications," says I.

"How's a glass-head like you going to meet Mr. Fed?" says he. "I bet you're always getting invitations to the same parties as guys like him."

"I don't get invited to *grown-up* parties," says I. "But on the other hand, grown-ups don't pay much attention to sweet little kids like me."

He sighed. "You really have to meet him?"

"Unless fifty-fifty on a P-word is good enough odds for you."

All of a sudden he goes nova. Slaps a glass off the table and it breaks against the wall, and then he kicks the table over, and all the time I'm thinking about ways to get out of there unkilled. But it's me he's doing the show for, so there's no way I'm leaving, and he leans in close to me and screams in my face. "That's the last of your fifty-fifty and sixty-forty and three times in ten I want to hear about, Goo Boy, you hear me?"

And I'm talking real meek and sweet, cause this boy's twice my size and three times my weight and

I don't exactly have no leverage. So I says to him, "I can't help talking in odds and percentages, Dogwalker, I'm vertical, remember? I've got glass channels in here, they spit out percentages as easy as other people sweat."

He slapped his hand against his own head. "This ain't exactly a sausage biscuit, either, but you know and I know that when you give me all them *exact* numbers it's all guesswork anyhow. You don't know the odds on this beakrat anymore than I do."

"I don't know the odds on *him*, Walker, but I know the odds on *me*. I'm sorry you don't like the way I sound so precise, but my crystal memory has every P-word I ever plumbed, which is to say I can give you exact to the third decimal percentages on when I hit it right on the first try after meeting the subject, and how many times I hit it right on the first try just from his curriculum vitae, and right now if I don't meet him and I go on just what I've got here you have a 48.838 percent chance I'll be right on my P-word first time and a 66.667 chance I'll be right with one out of three."

Well that took him down, which was fine I must say because he loosened up my sphincters with that glass-smashing table-tossing hot-breath-in-my-face routine he did. He stepped back and put his hands in his pockets and leaned against the wall. "Well I chose the right P-man, then, didn't I," he says, but he doesn't smile, no, he *says* the back-down words but his eyes don't back down, his eyes say don't try to flash my face because I see through you, I got most excellent inward shades all polarized to keep out your glitz and see you straight and clear. I never saw eyes like that before. Like he knew me. Nobody ever knew me, and I didn't think he *really* knew me either, but I didn't like him looking at me as if he *thought* he knew me cause the fact is I didn't know

me all that well and it worried me to think he might
know me better than I did, if you catch my drift.

"All I have to do is be a little lost boy in a store,"
I says.

"What if he isn't the kind who helps little lost
boys?"

"Is he the kind who lets them cry?"

"I don't know. What if he is? What then? Think
you can get away with meeting him a second time?"

"So the lost boy in the store won't work. I can
crash my bicycle on his front lawn. I can try to sell
him cable magazines."

But he was ahead of me already. "For the cable
magazines he slams the door in your face, if he even
comes to the door at all. For the bicycle crash, you're
out of your little glass brain. I got my inside girl
working on him right now, very complicated, because he's not the playing around kind, so she has
to make this a real emotional come-on, like she's
breaking up with a boyfriend and he's the only shoulder she can cry on, and his wife is so lucky to have
a man like him. This much he can believe. But then
suddenly he has this little boy crashing in his yard,
and because he's paranoid, he begins to wonder if
some weird rain isn't falling, right? I know he's paranoid because you don't get to his level in the fed
without you know how to watch behind you and kill
the enemy even before *they* know they're out to get
you. So he even suspects, for one instant, that somebody's setting him up for something, and what does
he do?"

I knew what Dogwalker was getting at now, and
he was right, and so I let him have his victory and I
let the words he wanted march out all in a row. "He
changes all his passwords, all his habits, and watches
over his shoulder all the time."

"And my little project turns into compost. No clean greens."

So I saw for the first time why this street boy, this ex-pimp, why he was the one to do this job. He wasn't vertical like me, and he didn't have the inside hook like his fed boy, and he didn't have bumps in his sweater so he couldn't do the girl part, but he had eyes in his elbows, ears in his knees, by which I mean he noticed everything there was to notice and then he thought of new things that weren't even noticeable yet and noticed them. He earned his forty percent. And he earned part of my twenty, too.

Now while we waited around for the girl to fill Jesse's empty aching arms and get a finger off him, and while we were still working on how to get me to meet him slow and easy and sure, I spent a lot of time with Dogwalker. Not that he ever asked me, but I found myself looping his bus route every morning till he picked me up, or I'd be eating at Bojangle's when he came in to throw cajun chicken down into his ulcerated organs. I watched to make sure he didn't mind, cause I didn't want to piss this boy, having once beheld the majesty of his wrath, but if he wanted to shiver me he gave me no shiv.

Even after a few days, when the ghosts of the cold hard street started haunting us, he didn't shake me, and that includes when Bellbottom says to him, "Looks like you stopped walking dogs. Now you pimping little boys, right? Little catamites, we call you Catwalker now, that so? Or maybe you just keep him for private use, is that it? You be Boypoker now?" Well like I always said, someday somebody's going to kill Bellbottom just to flay him and use his skin for a convertible roof, but Dogwalker just waved and walked on by while I made little pissy bumps at Bell. Most people shake me right off when they start getting splashed on about liking little boys, but Doggy, he didn't say we were friends or nothing, but he didn't give me no Miami howdy, neither, which is to say I didn't find myself floating in the Bermuda Triangle with my ass pulled down around my ankles, by which I mean he wasn't ashamed to be seen with me on the street, which don't sound like a six-minute orgasm to you but to me it was like a breeze in August, I didn't ask for it and I don't trust it to last but as long as it's there I'm going to like it.

How I finally got to meet Jesse H. was dervish, the best I ever thought of. Which made me wonder why I never thought of it before, except that I never before had Dogwalker like a parrot saying "stupid idea" every time I thought of something. By the time I finally got a plan that he didn't say "stupid idea," I was almost drowned in the deepest lightholes of my lucidity. I mean I was going at a hundred watts by the time I satisfied him.

First we found out who did babysitting for them when Jesse H. and Mrs. Jesse went out on the town (which for Nice People in G-boro means walking around the mall wishing there was something to do and then taking a piss in the public john). They had two regular teenage girls who usually came over and ignored their children for a fee, but when these dar-lettes were otherwise engaged, which meant they had a contract to get squeezed and poked by some half-zipped boy in exchange for a humbuger and a vid, they called upon Mother Hubbard's Homecare Hotline. So I most carefully assinuated myself into Mother Hubbard's estimable organization by passing myself off as a lamentably prepubic fourteen-year-old, specializing in the northwest section of town and on into the county. All this took a week, but Walker was in no hurry. Take the time to do it right, he said, if we hurry somebody's going to notice the blur of motion and look our way and just by looking at us they'll undo us. A horizontal mind that boy had.

Came a most delicious night when the Hunts went out to play, and both their diddle-girls were busy being squeezed most delectably (and didn't we have a lovely time persuading two toddle-boys to do the squeezing that very night). This news came to Mr. and Mrs. Jesse at the very last minute, and they had no choice but to call Mother Hubbard's, and isn't it lovely that just a half hour before, sweet little Stevie Queen, being *moi*, called in and said that he was available for baby-stomping after all. Ein and ein made zwei, and there I was being dropped off by a Mother Hubbard driver at the door of the Jesse Hunt house, whereupon I not only got to look upon the beatific face of Mr. Fed himself, I also got to have my dear head patted by Mrs. Fed, and then had the privilege of preparing little snacks for fussy Fed Jr. and foul-mouthed Fedene, the five-year-old and the three-year-old, while Microfed, the one-year-old (not yet human and, if I am any judge of character, not likely to live long enough to become such) sprayed uric acid in my face while I was diapering him. A good time was had by all.

Because of my heroic efforts, the small creatures were in their truckle beds quite early, and being a most fastidious baby-tucker, I browsed the house looking for burglars and stumbling, quite by chance, upon the most useful information about the beak-rat whose secret self-chosen name I was trying to learn. For one thing, he had set a watchful hair upon each of his bureau drawers, so that if I had been inclined to steal, he would know that unlawful access of his drawers had been attempted. I learned that he and his wife had separate containers of everything in the bathroom, even when they used the same brand of toothpaste, and it was he, not she, who took care of all their prophylactic activities (and not a moment too soon, thought I, for I had come to know their children). He was not the sort to use lubrificants or little pleasure-giving ribs, either. Only the regulation government-issue hard-as-concrete rubber rafts for him, which suggested to my most pernicious mind that he had almost as much fun between the sheets as me.

I learned all kinds of joyful information, all of it trivial, all of it vital. I never know which of the threads I grasp are going to make connections deep within the lumens of my brightest caves. But I never before had the chance to wander unmolested through a person's own house when searching for his P-word. I saw the notes his children brought home from school, the magazines his family received, and more and more I began to see that Jesse H. Hunt barely touched his family at any point. He stood like a waterbug on the surface of life, without ever getting his feet wet. He could die, and if nobody tripped over the corpse it would be weeks before they noticed. And yet this was not because he did not care. It was because he was so very very careful. He examined everything, but through the wrong end of the microscope, so that it all became very small and far away. I was a sad little boy by the end of that night, and I whispered to Microfed that he should practice pissing in male faces, because that's the only way he would ever sink a hook into his daddy's face.

"What if he wants to take you home?" Dogwalker asked me, and I said, "No way he would, nobody does that," but Dogwalker made sure I had a place to go all the same, and sure enough, it was Doggy who got voltage and me who went limp. I ended up riding in a beak-rat buggy, a genuine made-in-America rattletrap station wagon, and he took me to the for-sale house where Mama Pimple was waiting crossly for me and made Mr. Hunt go away because he kept me out too late. Then when the door was closed Mama Pimple giggled her gig and chuckled her chuck, and Walker himself wandered out of the back room and said, "That's one less favor you owe me, Mama Pimple," and she said, "No, my dear boyoh, that's one more favor *you* owe *me*" and then they kissed a deep passionate kiss if you can believe it. Did you imagine anybody ever kissed Mama Pimple that way? Dogwalker is a boyful of shocks.

"Did you get all you needed?" he asks me.

"I have P-words dancing upward," says I, "and I'll have a name for you tomorrow in my sleep."

"Hold onto it and don't tell me," says Dogwalker. "I don't want to hear a name until after we have his finger."

That magical day was only hours away, because the girl—whose name I never knew and whose face I never saw—was to cast her spell over Mr. Fed the very next day. As Dogwalker said, this was no job for lingeree. The girl did not dress pretty and pretended to be lacking in the social graces, but she was a good little clerical who was going through a most distressing period in her private life, because she had undergone a premature hysterectomy, poor lass, or so she told Mr. Fed, and here she was losing her womanhood and she had never really felt like a woman at all. But he was so kind to her, for weeks he had been so kind, and Dogwalker told me afterward how he locked the door of his office for just a few minutes, and held her and kissed her to make her feel womanly, and once his fingers had all made their little impressions on the thin electrified plastic microcoating all over her lovely naked back and breasts, she began to cry and most gratefully informed him that she did not want him to be unfaithful to his wife for her sake, that he had already given her such a much of a lovely gift by being so kind and understanding, and she felt better thinking that a man like him could bear to touch her knowing she was defemmed inside, and now she thought she had the confidence to go on. A very convincing act, and one calculated to get his hot naked handprints without giving him a crisis of conscience that might change his face and give him a whole new set of possible Ps.

The microsheet got all his fingers from several angles, and so Walker was able to dummy out a finger mask for our inside man within a single night. Right index. I looked at it most skeptically, I fear, because I had my doubts already dancing in the little lightpoints of my inmost mind. "Just one finger?"

"All we get is one shot," said Dogwalker. "One single try."

"But if he makes a mistake, if my first password isn't right, then he could use the middle finger on the second try."

"Tell me, my vertical pricket, whether you think Jesse H. Hunt is the sort of burr oak rat who makes mistakes?"

To which I had to answer that he was not, and yet I had my misgivings and my misgivings all had to do with needing a second finger, and yet I am vertical, not horizontal, which means that I can see the present as deep as you please but the future's not mine to see, que sera, sera.

From what Doggy told me, I tried to imagine Mr. Fed's reaction to this nubile flesh that he had pressed. If he had poked as well as peeked, I think it would have changed his P-word, but when she told him that she would not want to compromise his uncompromising virtue, it reinforced him as a most regular or even regulation fellow and his name remained pronouncedly the same, and his P-word also did not change. "InvictusXYZrwr," quoth I to Dogwalker, for that was his veritable password, I knew it with more certainty than I had ever had before.

"Where in hell did you come up with that?" says he.

"If I knew how I did it, Walker, I'd never miss at all," says I. "I don't even know if it's in the goo or in the zoo. All the facts go down, and it all gets mixed around, and up come all these dancing P-words, little pieces of P."

"Yeah but you don't just make it up, what does it mean?"

"Invictus is an old poem in a frame stuck in his bureau drawer, which his mama gave him when he was still a little fed-to-be. XYZ is his idea of randomizing, and rwr is the first U.S. President that he admired. I don't know why he chose these words now. Six weeks ago he was using a different P-word with a lot of numbers in it, and six weeks from now he'll change again, but right now—"

"Sixty percent sure?" asked Doggy.

"I give no percents this time," says I. "I've never roamed through the bathroom of my subject before. But this or give me an assectomy, I've never been more sure."

Now that he had the P-word, the inside guy began to wear his magic finger every day, looking for a chance to be alone in Mr. Fed's office. He had already created the preliminary files, like any routine green card requests, and buried them within his work area. All he needed was to go in, sign on as Mr. Fed, and then if the system accepted his name and P-word and finger, he could call up the files, approve them, and be gone within a minute. But he had to have that minute.

And on that wonderful magical day he had it. Mr.

Fed had a meeting and his secretary sprung a leak a day early, and in went Inside Man with a perfectly legitimate note to leave for Hunt. He sat before the terminal, typed name and P-word and laid down his phony finger, and the machine spread wide its lovely legs and bid him enter. He had the files processed in forty seconds, laying down his finger for each green, then signed off and went on out. No sign, no sound that anything was wrong. As sweet as summertime, as smooth as ice, and all we had to do was sit and wait for green cards to come in the mail.

"Who you going to sell them to?" says I.

"I offer them to no one till I have clean greens in my hand," says he. Because Dogwalker is careful. What happened was not because he was not careful.

Every day we walked to the ten places where the envelopes were supposed to come. We knew they wouldn't be there for a week—the wheels of government grind exceeding slow, for good or ill. Every day we checked with Inside Man, whose name and face I have already given you, much good it will do, since both are no doubt different by now. He told us every time that all was the same, nothing was changed, and he was telling the truth, for the fed was most lugubrious and palatial and gave no leaks that anything was wrong. Even Mr. Hunt himself did not know that aught was amiss in his little kingdom.

Yet even with no sign that I could name, I was jumpy every morning and sleepless every night. "You walk like you got to use the toilet," says Walker to me, and it is verily so. Something is wrong, I say to myself, something is most deeply wrong, but I cannot find the name for it even though I know, and so I say nothing, or I lie to myself and try to invent a reason for my fear. "It's my big chance," says I. "To be twenty percent of rich."

"Rich," says he, "not just a fifth."

"Then you'll be double rich."

And he just grins at me, being the strong and silent type.

"But then why don't you sell nine," says I, "and keep the other green? Then you'll have the money to pay for it, and the green to go where you want in all the world."

But he just laughs at me and says, "Silly boy, my dear sweet pinheaded lightbrained little friend. If someone sees a pimp like me passing a green, he'll tell a fed, because he'll know there's been a mistake. Greens don't go to boys like me."

"But you won't be dressed like a pimp," says I, "and you won't stay in pimp hotels."

"I'm a low-class pimp," he says again, "and so however I dress that day, that's just the way pimps dress. And whatever hotel I go to, that's a low-class pimp hotel until I leave."

"Pimping isn't some disease," says I. "It isn't in your gonads and it isn't in your genes. If your daddy was a Kroc and your mama was an Iacocca, you wouldn't be a pimp."

"The hell I wouldn't," says he. "I'd just be a high-class pimp, like my mama and my daddy. Who do you think gets green cards? You can't sell no virgins on the street."

I thought that he was wrong and I still do. If anybody could go from low to high in a week, it's Dogwalker. He could be anything and do anything, and that's the truth. Or almost anything. If he could do *anything* then his story would have a different ending. But it was not his fault. Unless you blame pigs because they can't fly. *I* was the vertical one, wasn't I? I should have named my suspicions and we wouldn't have passed those greens.

I held them in my hands, there in his little room, all ten of them when he spilled them on the bed. To celebrate he jumped up so high he smacked his head on the ceiling again and again, which made them ceiling tiles dance and flip over and spill dust all over the room. "I flashed just one, a single one," says he, "and a cool million was what he said, and then I said what if ten? And he laughs and says fill in the check yourself."

"We should test them," says I.

"We can't test them," he says. "The only way to test it is to use it, and if you use it then your print and face are in its memory forever and so we could never sell it."

"Then sell one, and make sure it's clean."

"A package deal," he says. "If I sell one, and they think I got more by I'm holding out to raise the price, then I may not live to collect for the other nine, because I might have an accident and lose these little babies. I sell all ten tonight at once, and then I'm out of the green card business for life."

But more than ever that night I am afraid, he's out selling those greens to those sweet gentlebodies who are commonly referred to as Organic Crime, and there I am on his bed, shivering and dreaming because I know that something will go most deeply wrong but I still don't know what and I still don't know why. I keep telling myself, You're only afraid because nothing could ever go so right for you, you can't believe that anything could ever make you rich and safe. I say this stuff so much that I believe that I believe it, but I don't really, not down deep, and so I shiver again and finally I cry, because after all my body still believes I'm nine, and nine-year-olds have tear ducts very easy of access, no password required. Well he comes in late that night, and I'm asleep he thinks, and so he walks quiet instead of dancing, but I can hear the dancing in his little sounds, I know he has the money all safely in the bank, and so when he leans over to make sure if I'm asleep, I say, "Could I borrow a hundred thou?"

So he slaps me and he laughs and dances and sings, and I try to go along, you bet I do, I know I should be happy, but then at the end he says, "You just can't take it, can you? You just can't handle it," and then I cry all over again, and he just puts his arm around me like a movie dad and gives me play-punches on the head and says, "I'm gonna marry me a wife, I am, maybe even Mama Pimple herself, and we'll adopt you and have a little spielberg family in Summerfield, with a riding mower on a real grass lawn."

"I'm older than you *or* Mama Pimple," says I, but he just laughs. Laughs and hugs me until he thinks that I'm all right. Don't go home, he says to me that night, but home I got to go, because I know I'll cry again, from fear or something, anyway, and I don't want him to think his cure wasn't permanent. "No thanks," says I, but he just laughs at me. "Stay here and cry all you want to, Goo Boy, but don't go home tonight. I don't want to be alone tonight, and sure as hell you don't either." And so I slept between his sheets, like with a brother, him punching and tickling and pinching and telling dirty jokes about his whores, the most good and natural night I spent in all my life, with a true friend, which I know you don't believe, snickering and nickering and ickering your filthy little thoughts, there was no holes plugged that night because nobody was out to take pleasure from nobody else, just Dogwalker being happy and wanting me not to be so sad.

And after he was asleep, I wanted so bad to know who it was he sold them to, so I could call them up and say, "Don't use those greens, cause they aren't clean. I don't know how, I don't know why, but the feds are onto this, I know they are, and if you use those cards they'll nail your fingers to your face."

But if I called would they believe me? They were careful too. Why else did it take a week? They had one of their nothing goons use a card to make sure it had no squeaks or leaks, and it came up clean. Only then did they give the cards to seven big boys, with two held in reserve. Even Organic Crime, the All-seeing Eye, passed those cards same as we did.

I think maybe Dogwalker was a little bit vertical too. I think he knew same as me that something was wrong with this. That's why he kept checking back with the inside man, cause he didn't trust how good it was. That's why he didn't spend any of his share. We'd sit there eating the same old schlock, out of his cut from some leg job or my piece from a data wipe, and every now and then he'd say, "Rich man's food sure tastes good." Or maybe even though he wasn't vertical he still thought maybe I was right when I thought something was wrong. Whatever he thought, though, it just kept getting worse and worse for me, until the morning when we went to see the inside man and the inside man was gone.

Gone clean. Gone like he never existed. His apartment for rent, cleaned out floor to ceiling. A phone call to the fed, and he was on vacation, which meant they had him, he wasn't just moved to another house with his newfound wealth. We stood there in his empty place, his shabby empty hovel that was ten times better than anywhere we ever lived, and Doggy says to me, real quiet, he says, "What was it? What did I do wrong? I thought I was like Hunt, I thought I never made a single mistake in this job, in this one job."

And that was it, right then I knew. Not a week before, not when it would do any good. Right then I finally knew it all, knew what Hunt had done. Jesse Hunt never made *mistakes.* But he was also so paranoid that he haired his bureau to see if the babysitter stole from him. So even though he would never *accidentally* enter the wrong P-word, he was just the kind who would do it *on purpose.* "He doublefingered every time," I says to Dog. "He's so damn careful he does his password wrong the first time every time, and then comes in on his second finger."

"So one time he comes in on the first try, so what?" He says this because he doesn't know computers like I do, being half-glass myself.

"The system knew the pattern, that's what. Jesse H. is so precise he never changed a bit, so when *we* came in on the first try, that set off alarms. It's my fault, Dog, I knew how crazy paranoidical he is, I knew that something was wrong, but not till this minute I didn't know what it was. I should have known it when I got his password, I should have known, I'm sorry, you never should have gotten me into this, I'm sorry, you should have listened to me when I told you something was wrong, I should have known, I'm sorry."

What I done to Doggy that I never meant to do. What I done to him! Anytime, I could have thought of it, it was all there inside my glassy little head, but no, I didn't think of it till after it was way too late. And maybe it's because I didn't want to think of it, maybe it's because I really wanted to be wrong about the green cards, but however it flew, I did what I do, which is to say I'm not the pontiff in his fancy chair, by which I mean I can't be smarter than myself.

Right away he called the gentlebens of Ossified Crime to warn them, but I was already plugged into the library sucking news as fast as I could and so I knew it wouldn't do no good, cause they got all seven of the big boys and their nitwit taster, too, locked up good and tight for card fraud.

And what they said on the phone to Dogwalker made things real clear. "We're dead," says Doggy.

"Give them time to cool," says I.

"They'll never cool," says he. "There's no chance, they'll never forgive this even if they know the whole truth, because look at the names they gave the cards to, it's like they got them for their biggest boys on the borderline, the habibs who bribe presidents of little countries and rake off cash from octopods like Shell and ITT and every now and then kill somebody and walk away clean. Now they're sitting there in jail with the whole life story of the organization in their brains, so they don't care if we meant to do it or not. They're hurting, and the only way they know to make the hurt go away is to pass it on to somebody else. And that's us. They want to make us hurt, and hurt real bad, and for a long long time."

I never saw Dog so scared. That's the only reason we went to the feds ourselves. We didn't ever want to stool, but we needed their protection plan, it was our only hope. So we offered to testify how we did it, not even for immunity, just so they'd change our faces and put us in a safe jail somewhere to work off the sentence and come out alive, you know? That's all we wanted.

But the feds, they laughed at us. They had the inside guy, see, and he was going to get immunity for testifying. "We don't need you," they says to us, "and we don't care if you go to jail or not. It was the big guys we wanted."

"If you let us walk," says Doggy, "then they'll think we set them up."

"Make us laugh," says the feds. "Us work with street poots like you? They know that we don't stoop so low."

"They bought from us," says Doggy. "If we're big enough for them, we're big enough for the dongs."

"Do you believe this?" says one fed to his identical junior officer. "These jollies are begging us to take them into jail. Well listen tight, my jolly boys, maybe we don't want to add you to the taxpayers' expense account, did you think of that? Besides, all we'd give you is time, but on the street, those boys will give you time and a half, and it won't cost us a dime."

So what could we do? Doggy just looks like somebody sucked out six pints, he's so white. On the way out of the fedhouse, he says, "Now we're going to find out what it's like to die."

And I says to him, "Walker, they stuck no gun in your mouth yet, they shove no shiv in your eye. We still breathing, we got legs, so let's *walk* out of here."

"Walk!" he says. "You walk out of G-boro, glasshead, and you bump into trees."

"So what?" says I. "I can plug in and pull out all the data we want about how to live in the woods. Lots of empty land out there. Where do you think the marijuana grows?"

"I'm a city boy," he says. "I'm a city boy." Now we're standing out in front, and he's looking around. "In the city I got a chance, I know the city."

"Maybe in New York or Dallas," says I, "but G-boro's just too small, not even half a million people, you can't lose yourself deep enough here."

"Yeah well," he says, still looking around. "It's none of your business now anyway, Goo Boy. They aren't blaming *you*, they're blaming *me*."

"But it's my fault," says I, "and I'm staying with you to tell them so."

"You think they're going to stop and listen?" says he.

"I'll let them shoot me up with speakeasy so they know I'm telling the truth."

"It's nobody's fault," says he. "And I don't give a twelve-inch poker whose fault it is anyway. You're clean, but if you stay with me you'll get all muddy, too. I don't need you around, and you sure as hell don't need me. Job's over. Done. Get lost."

But I couldn't do that. The same way he couldn't go on walking dogs, I couldn't just run off and leave him to eat my mistake. "They know I was your P-word man," says I. "They'll be after me, too."

"Maybe for a while, Goo Boy. But you transfer your twenty percent into Bobby Joe's Face Shop, so they aren't looking for you to get a refund, and then stay quiet for a week and they'll forget all about you."

He's right but I don't care. "I was in for twenty percent of rich," says I. "So I'm in for fifty percent of trouble."

All of a sudden he sees what he's looking for. "There they are, Goo Boy, the dorks they sent to hit me. In that Mercedes." I look but all I see are electrics. Then his hand is on my back and he gives me a shove that takes me right off the portico and into the bushes, and by the time I crawl out, Doggy's nowhere in sight. For about a minute I'm pissed about getting scratched up in the plants, until I realize he was getting me out of the way, so I wouldn't get shot down or hacked up or lased out, whatever it is they planned to do to him to get even.

I was safe enough, right? I should've walked away, I should've ducked right out of the city. I didn't even have to refund the money. I had enough to go clear out of the country and live the rest of my life where even Occipital Crime couldn't find me.

And I thought about it. I stayed the night in Mama Pimple's flophouse because I knew somebody would be watching my own place. All that night I thought about places I could go. Australia. New Zealand. Or even a foreign place, I could afford a good vocabulary crystal so picking up a new language would be easy.

But in the morning I couldn't do it. Mama Pimple

didn't exactly ask me but she looked so worried and all I could say was, "He pushed me into the bushes and I don't know where he is."

And she just nods at me and goes back to fixing breakfast. Her hands are shaking she's so upset. Because she knows that Dogwalker doesn't stand a chance against Orphan Crime.

"I'm sorry," says I.

"What can you do?" she says. "When they want you, they get you. If the feds don't give you a new face, you can't hide."

"What if they didn't want him?" says I.

She laughs at me. "The story's all over the street. The arrests were in the news, and now everybody knows the big boys are looking for Walker. They want him so bad the whole street can smell it."

"What if they knew it wasn't his fault?" says I. "What if they knew it was an accident? A mistake?"

Then Mama Pimple squints at me—not many people can tell when she's squinting, but I can—and she says, "Only one boy can tell them that so they'll believe it."

"Sure, I know," says I.

"And if that boy walks in and says, Let me tell you why you don't want to hurt my friend Dogwalker—"

"Nobody said life was safe," I says. "Besides, what could they do to me that's worse than what already happened to me when I was nine?"

She comes over and just puts her hand on my head, just lets her hand lie there for a few minutes, and I know what I've got to do.

So I did it. Went to Fat Jack's and told him I wanted to talk to Junior Mint about Dogwalker, and it wasn't thirty seconds before I was hustled on out into the alley and driven somewhere with my face mashed into the floor of the car so I couldn't tell where it was. Idiots didn't know that somebody as vertical as me can tell the number of wheel revolutions and the exact trajectory of every curve. I could've drawn a freehand map of where they took me. But if I let them know that, I'd never come home, and since there was a good chance I'd end up dosed with speakeasy, I went ahead and erased the memory. Good thing I did—that was the first thing they asked me as soon as they had the drug in me.

Gave me a grown-up dose, they did, so I practically told them my whole life story and my opinion of them and everybody and everything else, so the whole session took hours, felt like forever, but at the end they knew, they absolutely knew that Dogwalker was straight with them, and when it was over and I was coming up so I had some control over what I said, I asked them, I begged them, Let Dogwalker live. Just let him go. He'll give back the money, and I'll give back mine, just let him go.

"OK," says the guy.

I didn't believe it.

"No, you can believe me, we'll let him go."

"You got him?"

"Picked him up before you even came in. It wasn't hard."

"And you didn't kill him?"

"Kill him? We had to get the money back first, didn't we, so we needed him alive till morning, and then you came in, and your little story changed our minds, it really did, you made us feel all sloppy and sorry for that poor old pimp."

For a few seconds there I actually believed that it was going to be all right. But then I knew from the way they looked, from the way they acted, I knew the same way I know about passwords.

They brought in Dogwalker and handed me a book. Dogwalker was very quiet and stiff and he didn't look like he recognized me at all. I didn't even have to look at the book to know what it was. They scooped out his brain and replaced it with glass, like me only way over the line, way way over, there was nothing of Dogwalker left inside his head, just glass pipe and goo. The book was a User's Manual, with all the instructions about how to program him and control him.

I looked at him and he was Dogwalker, the same face, the same hair, everything. Then he moved or talked and he was dead, he was somebody else living in Dogwalker's body. And I says to them, "Why? Why didn't you just kill him, if you were going to do this?"

"This one was too big," says the guy. "Everybody in G-boro knew what happened, everybody in the whole country, everybody in the world. Even if it was a mistake, we couldn't let it go. No hard feelings, Goo Boy. He *is* alive. And so are you. And you both stay that way, as long as you follow a few simple rules. Since he's over the line, he has to have an owner, and you're it. You can use him however you want—rent out data storage, pimp him as a jig or a jaw—but he stays with you always. Every day, he's on the street here in G-boro, so we can bring people here and show them what happens to boys who make mistakes. You can even keep your cut from the job, so you don't have to scramble at all if you don't want to. That's how much we like you, Goo Boy. But if he leaves this town or doesn't come out, even one single solitary day, you'll be very sorry for the last six hours of your life. Do you understand?"

I understood. I took him with me. I bought this place, these clothes, and that's how it's been ever since. That's why we go out on the street every day. I read the whole manual, and I figure there's maybe ten percent of Dogwalker left inside. The part that's Dogwalker can't ever get to the surface, can't even talk or move or anything like that, can't ever remember or even consciously think. But maybe he can still wander around inside what used to be his head, maybe he can sample the data stored in all that goo. Maybe someday he'll even run across this story and he'll know what happened to him, and he'll know that I tried to save him.

In the meantime this is my last will and testament. See, I have us doing all kinds of research on Orgasmic Crime, so that someday I'll know enough to reach inside the system and unplug it. Unplug it all, and make those bastards lose everything, the way they took everything away from Dogwalker. Trouble is, some places there ain't no way to look without leaving tracks. Goo is as goo do, I always say. I'll find out I'm not as good as I think I am when somebody comes along and puts a hot steel putz in my face. Knock my brains out when it comes. But there's this, lying in a few hundred places in the system. Three days after I don't lay down my code in a certain program in a certain place, this story pops into view. The fact you're reading this means I'm dead.

Or it means I paid them back, and so I quit suppressing this because I don't care anymore. So maybe this is my swan song, and maybe this is my victory song. You'll never know, will you, mate?

But you'll wonder. I like that. You wondering about us, whoever you are, you thinking about old Goo Boy and Dogwalker, you guessing whether the fangs who scooped Doggy's skull and turned him into self-propelled property paid for it down to the very last delicious little drop.

And in the meantime, I've got this goo machine to take care of. Only ten percent a man, he is, but then I'm only forty percent myself. All added up together we make only half a human. But that's the half that counts. That's the half that still wants things. The goo in me and the goo in him is all just light pipes and electricity. Data without desire. Lightspeed trash. But I have some desires left, just a few, and maybe so does Dogwalker, even fewer. And we'll get what we want. Every speck. Every sparkle. Believe it.

BUT WE TRY NOT TO
ACT LIKE IT

T HERE WAS NO line. Hiram Cloward commented
on it to the pointy-faced man behind the
counter. "There's no line."

"This is the complaint department. We pride ourselves on having few complaints." The pointy-faced
man had a prim little smile that irritated Hiram.
"What's the matter with your television?"

"It shows nothing but soaps, that's what's the matter. And asinine gothics."

"Well—that's programming, sir, not mechanical
at all."

"It's mechanical. I can't turn the damn set off."

"What's your name and social security number?"

"Hiram Cloward. 528-80-693883-7."

"Address?"

"ARF-487-U7b."

"That's singles, sir. Of course you can't turn off
your set."

"You mean because I'm not married I can't turn off my television?"

"According to congressionally authorized scientific studies carried out over a three-year period from 1989 to 1991, it is imperative that persons living alone have the constant companionship of their television sets."

"I like solitude. I also like silence."

"But the Congress passed a *law*, sir, and we can't disobey the *law*—"

"Can't I talk to somebody intelligent?"

The pointy-faced man flared a moment, his eyes burning. But he instantly regained his composure, and said in measured tones, "As a matter of fact, as soon as any complainant becomes offensive or hostile, we immediately refer them to section A-6."

"What's that, the hit squad?"

"It's behind that door."

And Hiram followed the pointing finger to the glass door at the far end of the waiting room. Inside was an office, which was filled with comfortable, homey knickknacks, several chairs, a desk, and a man so offensively nordic that even Hitler would have resented him. "Hello," the Aryan said, warmly.

"Hi."

"Please, sit down." Hiram sat, the courtesy and warmth making him feel even more resentful—did they think they could fool him into believing he was not being grossly imposed upon?

"So you don't like something about your programming," said the Aryan.

"*Your* programming, you mean. It sure as hell isn't mine. I don't know why Bell Television thinks it has the right to impose its idea of fun and entertainment on me twenty-four hours a day, but I'm fed up with it. It was bad enough when there was some variety, but for the last two months I've been getting nothing but soaps and gothics."

"It took you two months to notice?"

"I try to ignore the set. I like to *read.* You can bet that if I had more than my stinking little pension from our loving government, I could pay to have a room where there wasn't a TV so I could have some *peace.*"

"I really can't help your financial situation. And the law's the law."

"Is that all I'm going to hear from you? The law? I could have heard that from the pointy-faced jerk out there."

"Mr. Cloward, looking at your records, I can certainly see that soaps and gothics are not appropriate for you."

"They aren't appropriate," Hiram said, "for anyone with an IQ over eight."

The Aryan nodded. "You feel that people who enjoy soaps and gothics aren't the intellectual equals of people who don't."

"Damn right. I have a Ph.D. in *literature,* for heaven's sake!"

The Aryan was all sympathy. "Of *course* you don't like soaps! I'm sure it's a mistake. We try not to make mistakes, but we're only human—except the computers, of course." It was a joke, but Hiram didn't laugh. The Aryan kept up the small talk as he looked at the computer terminal that he could see and Hiram could not. "We may be the only television company in town, you know, but—"

"But you try not to act like it."

"Yes. Ha. Well, you must have heard our advertising."

"Constantly."

"Well, let's see now. Hiram Cloward, Ph.D. Nebraska 1981. English literature, twentieth century, with a minor in Russian literature. Dissertation on Dostoevski's influence on English-language novelists. A near-perfect class attendance record, and a reputation for arrogance and competence."

"How much do you *know* about me?"

"Only the standard consumer research data. But we do have a bit of a problem."

Hiram waited, but the Aryan merely punched a button, leaned back, and looked at Hiram. His eyes were kindly and warm and intense. It made Hiram uncomfortable.

"Mr. Cloward."

"Yes?"

"You are unemployed."

"Not willingly."

"Few people are willingly unemployed, Mr. Cloward. But you have no job. You also have no family. You also have no friends."

"That's consumer research? What, only people with friends buy Rice Krispies?"

"As a matter of fact, Rice Krispies are favored by solitary people. We have to know who is more likely to be receptive to advertising, and we direct our programming accordingly."

Hiram remembered that he ate Rice Krispies for breakfast almost every morning. He vowed on the spot to switch to something else. Quaker Oats, for instance. Surely they were more gregarious.

"You understand the importance of the Selective Programming Broadcast Act of 1985, yes?"

"Yes."

"It was deemed unfair by the Supreme Court for all programming to be geared to the majority. Minorities were being slighted. And so Bell Television was given the assignment of preparing an individually selected broadcast system so that each individual, in his own home, would have the programming perfect for him."

"I know all this."

"I must go over it again anyway, Mr. Cloward, because I'm going to have to help you understand why there can be no change in your programming."

Hiram stiffened in his chair, his hands flexing. "I knew you bastards wouldn't change."

"Mr. Cloward, we bastards would be delighted to change. But we are very closely regulated by the government to provide the most healthful programming for every American citizen. Now, I will continue my review."

"I'll just go home, if you don't mind."

"Mr. Cloward, we are directed to prepare programming for minorities as small as ten thousand people—but no smaller. Even for minorities of ten thousand the programming is ridiculously expensive—a program seen by so few costs far more per watching-minute to produce than one seen by thirty or forty million. However, you belong to a minority even smaller than ten thousand."

"That makes me feel so special."

"Furthermore, the Consumer Protection Broadcast Act of 1989 and the regulations of the Consumer Broadcast Agency since then have given us very strict guidelines. Mr. Cloward, we cannot show you any program with overt acts of violence."

"Why not?"

"Because you have tendencies toward hostility that are only exacerbated by viewing violence. Similarly, we cannot show you any programs with sex."

Cloward's face turned red.

"You have no sex life whatsoever, Mr. Cloward. Do you realize how dangerous that is? You don't even masturbate. The tension and hostility inside you must be tremendous."

Cloward leaped to his feet. There were limits to what a man had to put up with. He headed for the door.

"Mr. Cloward, I'm sorry." The Aryan followed him to the door. "I don't make these things up. Wouldn't you rather know *why* these decisions are reached?"

Hiram stopped at the door, his hand on the knob. The Aryan was right. Better to know why than to hate them for it.

"How," Hiram asked. "How do they know what I do and do not do within the walls of my home?"

"We don't *know*, of course, but we're pretty sure. We've studied people for years. We know that people who have certain buying patterns and certain living patterns behave in certain ways. And, unfortunately, you have strong destructive tendencies. Repression and denial are your primary means of adaptation to stress, that and, unfortunately, occasional acting out."

"What the hell does all that mean?"

"It means that you lie to yourself until you can't anymore, and then you attack somebody."

Hiram's face was packed with hot blood, throbbing. I must look like a tomato, he told himself, and deliberately calmed himself. I don't care, he thought. They're wrong anyway. Damn scientific tests.

"Aren't there any movies you could program for me?"

"I am sorry, no."

"Not all movies have sex and violence."

The Aryan smiled soothingly. "The movies that don't wouldn't interest you anyway."

"Then turn the damn thing off and let me read!"

"We can't do that."

"Can't you turn it *down*?"

"No."

"I am so sick of hearing all about Sarah Wynn and her damn love life!"

"But isn't Sarah Wynn attractive?" asked the Aryan.

That stopped Hiram cold. He dreamed about Sarah Wynn at night. He said nothing. He had no attraction to Sarah Wynn.

"Isn't she?" the Aryan insisted.

"Isn't who what?"

"Sarah Wynn."

"Who was talking about Sarah Wynn? What about documentaries?"

"Mr. Cloward, you would become extremely hostile if the news programs were broadcast to you. You know that."

"Walter Cronkite's dead. Maybe I'd like them better now."

"You don't care about the news of the real world, Mr. Cloward, do you?"

"No."

"Then you see where we are. Not one iota of our programming is really appropriate for you. But ninety percent of it is downright harmful to you. And we can't turn the television off, because of the Solitude Act. Do you see our dilemma?"

"Do you see mine?"

"Of course, Mr. Cloward. And I sympathize completely. Make some friends, Mr. Cloward, and we'll turn off your television."

And so the interview was over.

For two days Cloward brooded. All the time he did, Sarah Wynn was grieving over her three-days' husband who had just been killed in a car wreck on Wilshire Boulevard, wherever the hell that was. But now the body was scarcely cold and already her old suitors were back, trying to help her, trying to push their love on her. "Can't you let yourself depend on me, just a little?" asked Teddy, the handsome one with lots of money.

"I don't like depending on people," Sarah answered.

"You depended on George." George was the husband's name. The dead one.

"I know," she said, and cried for a moment. Sarah Wynn was good at crying. Hiram Cloward turned another page in *The Brothers Karamazov*.

"You need friends," Teddy insisted.

"Oh, Teddy, I know it," she said, weeping. "Will you be my friend?"

"Who writes this stuff?" Hiram Cloward asked aloud. Maybe the Aryan in the television company offices had been right. Make some friends. Get the damn set turned off whatever the cost.

He got up from his chair and went out into the corridor in the apartment building. Clearly posted on the walls were several announcements:

Chess club 5–9 wed
Encounter groups nightly at 7
Learn to knit 6:30 bring yarn and needles
Games games games in game room (basement)
Just want to chat? Friends of the Family 7:30 to 10:30 nightly

Friends of the Family? Hiram snorted. Family was his maudlin mother and her constant weeping about how hard life was and how no one in her right mind would ever be born a woman if anybody had any choice but there was no choice and marriage was a trap men sprung on women, giving them a few minutes of pleasure for a lifetime of drudgery, and I swear to God if it wasn't for my little baby Hiram I'd ditch that bastard for good, it's for your sake I don't leave, my little baby, because if I leave you'll grow up into a macho bastard like your beerbelly father.

And friends? What friends ever come around when good old Dad is boozing and belting the living crap out of everybody he can get his hands on?

I read. That's what I do. *The Prince and the Pauper. Connecticut Yankee. Pride and Prejudice.* Worlds within worlds within worlds, all so pretty and polite and funny as hell.

Friends of the Family. Worth a shot, anyway.

Hiram went to the elevator and descended eighteen floors to the Fun Floor. Friends of the Family were in quite a large room with alcohol at one end and soda pop at the other. Hiram was surprised to discover that the term *soda pop* had been revived. He walked to the cola sign and asked the woman for a Coke.

"How many cups of coffee have you had today?" she asked.

"Three."

"Then I'm so sorry, but I can't give you a soda pop with caffeine in it. May I suggest Sprite?"

"You may not," Hiram said, clenching his teeth. "We're too damn overprotected."

"Exactly how I feel," said a woman standing beside him, Sprite in hand. "They protect and protect and protect, and what good does it do? People still die, you know."

"I suspected as much," Hiram said, struggling for a smile, wondering if his humor sounded funny or merely sarcastic. Apparently funny. The woman laughed.

"Oh, you're a gem, you are," she said. "What do you do?"

"I'm a detached professor of literature at Princeton."

"But how can you live *here* and work *there*?"

He shrugged. "I don't work there. I said detached. When the new television teaching came in, my PQ was too low. I'm not a screen personality."

"So few of us are," she said sagely, nodding and smiling. "Oh, how I long for the good old days. When ugly men like David Brinkley could deliver the news."

"You remember Brinkley?"

"Actually, no," she said, laughing. "I just remember my mother talking about him." Hiram looked at her appreciatively. Nose not very straight, of course—but that seemed to be the only thing keeping her off TV. Nice voice. Nice nice face. Body.

She put her hand on his thigh.

"What are you doing tonight?" she asked.

"Watching television," he grimaced.

"Really? What do you have?"

"Sarah Wynn."

She squealed in delight. "Oh, how wonderful! We must be kindred spirits then! I have Sarah Wynn, too!"

Hiram tried to smile.

"Can I come up to your apartment?"

Danger signal. Hand moving up thigh. Invitation to apartment. Sex.

"No."

"Why not?"

And Hiram remembered that the only way he could ever get rid of the television was to prove that he wasn't solitary. And fixing up his sex life—*i.e.*, having one—would go a long way toward changing their damn profiles. "Come on," he said, and they left the Friends of the Family without further ado.

Inside the apartment she immediately took off her shoes and blouse and sat down on the old-fashioned sofa in front of the TV. "Oh," she said, "so many books. You really are a professor, aren't you?"

"Yeah," he said, vaguely sensing that the next move was up to him, and not having the faintest idea of what the next move was. He thought back to his only fumbling attempt at sex when he was (what?) thirteen? (no) fourteen and the girl was fifteen and was doing it on a lark. She had walked with him up the creekbed (back when there were creeks and open country) and suddenly she had stopped and unzipped his pants (back when there were zippers) but he was finished before she had hardly started and gave up in disgust and took his pants and ran away. Her name was Diana. He went home without his pants and had no rational explanation and his mother had treated him with loathing and brought it up again and again for years afterward, how a man is a man no matter how you treat him and he'll still get it when he can, who cares about the poor girl. But Hiram was used to that kind of talk. It rolled off him. What haunted him was the uncontrolled shivering of his body, the ecstacy of it, and then the look of disgust on the girl's face. He had thought it was because—well, never mind. Never mind, he thought. I don't think of this anymore.

"Come *on*," said the woman.

"What's your name?" Hiram asked.

She looked at the ceiling. "Agnes, for heaven's sake, come *on*."

He decided that taking off his shirt might be a good idea. She watched, then decided to help.

"No," he said.

"What?"

"Don't touch me."

"Oh, for pete's sake. What's wrong? Impotent?"

Not at all. Not at all. Just uninterested. Is that all right?

"Look, I don't want to play around with a psycho case, all right? I've got better things to do. I make a hundred a whack, that's what I charge, that's standard, right?"

Standard what? Hiram nodded because he didn't dare ask what she was talking about.

"But you obviously, heaven knows how, buddy, you sure as hell obviously don't know what's going on in the world. Twenty bucks. Enough for the ten minutes you've screwed up for me. Right?"

"I don't have twenty," Hiram said.

Her eyes got tight. "A fairy *and* a deadbeat. What a pick. Look, buddy, next time you try a pickup, figure out what you want to do with her first, right?"

She picked up her shoes and blouse and left. Hiram stood there.

"Teddy, no," said Sarah Wynn.

"But I need you. I need you so desperately," said Teddy on the screen.

"It's only been a few days. How can I sleep with another man only a few days after George was killed? Only four days ago we—oh, no, Teddy. Please."

"Then when? How soon? I love you so much."

Drivel, George thought in his analytical mind. But nevertheless obviously based on the Penelope story. No doubt her George, her Odysseus, would return, miraculously alive, ready to sweep her back into wedded bliss. But in the meantime, the suitors: enough suitors to sell fifteen thousand cars and a hundred thousand boxes of Tampax and four hundred thousand packages of Cap'n Crunch.

The nonanalytical part of his mind, however, was not the least bit concerned with Penelope. For some reason he was clasping and unclasping his hands in front of him. For some reason he was shaking. For some reason he fell to his knees at the couch, his hands clasping and unclasping around *Crime and*

Punishment, as his eyes strained to cry but could not.

Sarah Wynn wept.

But she can cry easily, Hiram thought. It's not fair, that she should cry so easily. Spin flax, Penelope.

The alarm went off, but Hiram was already awake. In front of him the television was singing about Dove with lanolin. The products haven't changed, Hiram thought. Never change. They were advertising Dove with lanolin in the little market carts around the base of the cross while Jesus bled to death, no doubt. For softer skin.

He got up, got dressed, tried to read, couldn't, tried to remember what had happened last night to leave him so upset and nervous, but couldn't, and at last he decided to go back to the Aryan at the Bell Television offices.

"Mr. Cloward," said the Aryan.

"You're a psychiatrist, aren't you?" Hiram asked.

"Why, Mr. Cloward, I'm an A-6 complaint representative from Bell Television. What can I do for you?"

"I can't stand Sarah Wynn anymore," Hiram said.

"That's a shame. Things are finally going to work out for her starting in about two weeks."

And in spite of himself, Hiram wanted to ask what was going to happen. It isn't fair for this nordic uberman to know what sweet little Sarah is going to be doing weeks before I do. But he fought down the feeling, ashamed that he was getting caught up in the damn soap.

"Help me," Hiram said.

"How can I help you?"

"You can change my life. You can get the television out of my apartment."

"Why, Mr. Cloward?" the Aryan asked. "It's the

one thing in life that's absolutely free. Except that you get to watch commercials. And you know as well as I do that the commercials are downright entertaining. Why, there are people who actually choose to have double the commercials in their personal programming. We get a thousand requests a day for the latest McDonald's ad. You have no idea."

"I have a very good idea. I want to read. I want to be alone."

"On the contrary, Mr. Cloward, you long not to be alone. You desperately need a friend."

Anger. "And what makes you so damn sure of that?"

"Because, Mr. Cloward, your response is completely typical of your group. It's a group we're very concerned about. We don't have a budget to program for you—there are only about two thousand of you in the country—but a budget wouldn't do us much good because we really don't know what kind of programming you *want*."

"I am not part of any group."

"Oh, you're so much a part of it that you could be called typical. Dominant mother, absent and/or hostile father, no long-term relationships with anybody. No sex life."

"I have a sex life."

"If you have in fact attempted any sexual activity it was undoubtedly with a prostitute and she expected too high a level of sophistication from you. You are easily ashamed, you couldn't cope, and so you have not had intercourse. Correct?"

"What are you! What are you trying to do to me!"

"I *am* a psychoanalyst, of course. Anybody whose complaints can't be handled by our bureaucratic authority figure out in front obviously needs help, not another bureaucrat. I want to help you. I'm your friend."

And suddenly the anger was replaced by the utter incongruity of this nordic masterman wanting to help little Hiram Cloward. The unemployed professor laughed.

"Humor! Very healthy!" said the Aryan.

"What is this? I thought shrinks were supposed to be subtle."

"With some people—notably paranoids, which you are not, and schizoids, which you are not either."

"And what am I?"

"I told you. Denial and repression strategies. Very unhealthy. Acting out—less healthy yet. But you're extremely intelligent, able to do many things. I personally think it's a damn shame you can't teach."

"I'm an excellent teacher."

"Tests with randomly selected students showed that you had an extremely heavy emphasis on esoterica. Only people like you would really enjoy a class from a person like you. There aren't many people like you. You don't fit into many of the normal categories."

"And so I'm being persecuted."

"Don't try to pretend to be paranoid." The Aryan smiled. Hiram smiled back. This is insane. Lewis Carroll, where are you now that we really need you?

"If you're a shrink, then I should talk freely to you."

"If you like."

"I don't like."

"And why not?"

"Because you're so godutterlydamn Aryan, that's why."

The Aryan leaned forward with interest. "Does that bother you?"

"It makes me want to throw up."

"And why is that?"

The look of interest was too keen, too delightful.

Hiram couldn't resist. "You don't know about my experiences in the war, then, is that it?"

"What war? There hasn't been a war recently enough—"

"I was very, very young. It was in Germany. My parents aren't really my parents, you know. They were in Germany with the American embassy. In Berlin in 1938, before the war broke out. My real parents were there, too—German Jews, or half Jews, anyway. My real father—but let that pass, you don't need my whole genealogy. Let's just say that when I was only eleven days old, totally unregistered, my real Jewish father took me to his friend, Mr. Cloward in the American embassy, whose wife had just had a miscarriage. 'Take my child,' he said.

" 'Why?' Cloward asked.

" 'Because my wife and I have a perfect, utterly foolproof plan to kill Hitler. But there is no way for us to survive it.' And so Cloward, my adopted father, took me in.

"And then, the next day, he read in the papers about how my real parents had been killed in an 'accident' in the street. He investigated—and discovered that just by chance, while my parents were on their way to carry out their foolproof plan, some brown shirts in the street had seen them. Someone pointed them out as Jews. They were bored—so they attacked them. Had no idea they were saving Hitler's life, of course. These nordic mastermen started beating my mother, forcing my father to watch as they stripped her and raped her and then disemboweled her. My father was then subjected to experimental use of the latest model testicle-crusher until he bit off his own tongue in agony and bled to death. I don't like nordic types." Hiram sat back, his eyes full of tears and emotion, and realized that he had actually been able to cry—not much, but it was hopeful.

"Mr. Cloward," said the Aryan, "you were born in Missouri in 1951. Your parents of record are your natural parents."

Hiram smiled. "But it was one hell of a Freudian fantasy, wasn't it? My mother raped, my father emasculated to death, myself divorced from my true heritage, etc., etc."

The Aryan smiled. "You should be a writer, Mr. Cloward."

"I'd rather read. Please, let me read."

"I can't stop you from reading."

"Turn off Sarah Wynn. Turn off the mansions from which young girls flee from the menace of a man who turns out to be friendly and loving. Turn off the commercials for cars and condoms."

"And leave you alone to wallow in cataleptic fantasies among your depressing Russian novels?"

Hiram shook his head. Am I begging? he wondered. Yes, he decided. "I'm begging. My Russian novels aren't depressing. They're exalting, uplifting, overwhelming."

"It's part of your sickness, Mr. Cloward, that you long to be overwhelmed."

"Every time I read Dostoevski, I feel fulfilled."

"You have read everything by Dostoevski twenty times over. And everything by Tolstoy a dozen times."

"Every time I read Dostoevski is the first time!"

"We can't leave you alone."

"I'll kill myself!" Hiram shouted. "I can't live like this much longer!"

"Then make friends," the Aryan said simply. Hiram gasped and panted, gathering his rage back under control. This is not happening. I am not angry. Put it away, put it back, get control, smile. Smile at the Aryan.

"You're my friend, right?" Hiram asked.

"If you'll let me," the Aryan answered.

"I'll let you," Hiram said. Then he got up and left the office.

On the way home he passed a church. He had often seen the church before. He had little interest in religion—it had been too thoroughly dissected for him in the novels. What Twain had left alive, Dostoevski had withered and Pasternak had killed. But his mother was a passionate Presbyterian. He went into the church.

At the front of the building was a huge television screen. On it a very charismatic young man was speaking. The tones were subdued—only those in the front could hear it. Those in the back seemed to be meditating. Cloward knelt at a bench to meditate, too.

But he couldn't take his eyes off the screen. The young man stepped aside, and an older man took his place, intoning something about Christ. Hiram could hear the word *Christ*, but no others.

The walls were decorated with crosses. Row on row of crosses. This was a Protestant church—none of the crosses contained a figure of Jesus bleeding. But Hiram's imagination supplied him nonetheless. Jesus, his hands and wrists nailed to the cross, his feet pegged to the cross, his throat at the intersection of the beams.

Why the cross, after all? The intersection of two utterly opposite lines, perpendiculars that can only touch at one point. The epitome of the life of man, passing through eternity without a backward glance at those encountered along the way, each in his own, endlessly divergent direction. The cross. But not at all the symbol of today, Hiram decided. Today we are in spheres. Today we are curves, not lines, bending back on ourselves, touching everybody again and again, wrapped up inside little balls, none of us daring to be at the outside. Pull me in, we cry, pull me and keep me safe, don't let me fall out, don't let me fall off the edge of the world.

But the world has an edge now, and we can all see it, Hiram decided. We know where it is, and we can't bear to let anyone find his own way of staying on top.

Or do I want to stay on top?

The age of crosses is over. Now the age of spheres. Balls.

"We are your friends," said the old man on the screen. "We can help you."

There is a grandeur, Hiram answered silently, about muddling through alone.

"Why be alone when Jesus can take your burden?" said the man on the screen.

If I were alone, Hiram answered, there would be no burden to bear.

"Pick up your cross, fight the good fight," said the man on the screen.

If only, Hiram answered, I could find my cross to pick it up.

Then Hiram realized that he still could not hear the voice from the television. Instead he had been supplying his own sermon, out loud. Three people near him in the back of the church were watching him. He smiled sheepishly, ducked his head in apology, and left. He walked home whistling.

Sarah Wynn's voice greeted him. "Teddy. Teddy! What have we done? Look what we've done."

"It was beautiful," Teddy said. "I'm glad of it."

"Oh, Teddy! How can I ever forgive myself?" And Sarah wept.

Hiram stood transfixed, watching the screen. Penelope had given in. Penelope had left her flax and fornicated with a suitor! This is wrong, he thought.

"This is wrong," he said.

"I love you, Sarah," Teddy said.

"I can't bear it, Teddy," she answered. "I feel that in my heart I have murdered George! I have betrayed him!"

Penelope, is there no virtue in the world? Is there no Artemis, hunting? Just Aphrodite, bedding down every hour on the hour with every man, god, or sheep that promised forever and delivered a moment. The bargains are never fulfilled, never, Hiram thought.

At that moment on the screen, George walked in. "My dear," he exclaimed. "My dear Sarah! I've been wandering with amnesia for days! It was a hitchhiker who was burned to death in my car! I'm home!"

And Hiram screamed and screamed and screamed.

The Aryan found out about it quickly, at the same time that he got an alarming report from the research teams analyzing the soaps. He shook his head, a sick feeling in the pit of his stomach. Poor Mr. Cloward. Ah, what agony we do in the name of protecting people, the Aryan thought.

"I'm sorry," he said to Hiram. But Hiram paid him no attention. He just sat on the floor, watching the television set. As soon as the report had come in, of course, all the soaps—especially Sarah Wynn's—had gone off the air. Now the game shows were on, a temporary replacement until errors could be corrected.

"I'm so sorry," the Aryan said, but Hiram tried to shrug him away. A black woman had just traded the box for the money in the envelope. It was what Hiram would have done, and it paid off. Five thousand dollars instead of a donkey pulling a cart with a monkey in it. She had just avoided being zonked.

"Mr. Cloward, I thought the problem was with you. But it wasn't at all. I mean, you were marginal, all right. But we didn't realize what Sarah Wynn was doing to people."

Sarah schmarah, Hiram said silently, watching the screen. The black woman was bounding up and down in delight.

"It was entirely our fault. There are thousands of marginals just like you who were seriously damaged by Sarah Wynn. We had no idea how powerful the identification was. We had no idea."

Of course not, thought Hiram. You didn't read enough. You didn't know what the myths do to people. But now was the Big Deal of the Day, and Hiram shook his head to make the Aryan go away.

"Of course the Consumer Protection Agency will pay you a lifetime compensation. Three times your present salary and whatever treatment is possible."

At last Hiram's patience ended. "Go away!" he said. "I have to see if the black woman there is going to get the car!"

"I just can't decide," the black woman said.

"Door number three!" Hiram shouted. "Please, God, door number three!"

The Aryan watched Hiram silently.

"Door number two!" the black woman finally decided. Hiram groaned. The announcer smiled.

"Well," said the announcer. "Is the car behind door number *two*? Let's just see!"

The curtain opened, and behind it was a man in a hillbilly costume strumming a beat-up looking banjo. The audience moaned. The man with the banjo sang "Home on the Range." The black woman sighed.

They opened the curtains, and there was the car behind door number three. "I knew it," Hiram said, bitterly. "They never listen to me. Door number three, I say, and they never do it."

The Aryan turned to leave.

"I told you, didn't I?" Hiram asked, weeping.

"Yes," the Aryan said.

"I knew it. I knew it all along. I was *right*." Hiram sobbed into his hands.

"Yeah," the Aryan answered, and then he left to sign all the necessary papers for the commitment. Now Cloward fit into a category. No one can exist outside one for long, the Aryan realized. We are creating a new man. *Homo categoricus*. The classified man.

But the papers didn't have to be signed after all. Instead Hiram went into the bathroom, filled the tub, and joined the largest category of all.

"Damn," the Aryan said, when he heard about it.

I Put My Blue Genes On

IT HAD TAKEN three weeks to get there—longer than any man in living memory had been in space, and there were four of us crammed into the little Hunter III skipship. It gave us a hearty appreciation for the pioneers, who had had to crawl across space at a tenth of the speed of light. No wonder only three colonies ever got founded. Everybody else must have eaten each other alive after the first month in space.

Harold had taken a swing at Amauri the last day, and if we hadn't hit the homing signal I would have ordered the ship turned around to go home to Núncamais, which was mother and apple pie to everybody but me—I'm from Pennsylvania. But we got the homing signal and set the computer to scanning the old maps, and after a few hours found ourselves in stationary orbit over Prescott, Arizona.

At least that's what the geologer said, and computers can't lie. It didn't look like what the old books *said* Arizona should look like.

But there was the homing signal, broadcasting in Old English: "God bless America, come in, safe landing guaranteed." The computer assured us that in Old English the word *guarantee* was *not* obscene, but rather had something to do with a statement being particularly trustworthy—we had a chuckle over that one.

But we were excited, too. When great-great-great-great to the umpteenth power grandpa and grandma upped their balloons from old Terra Firma eight hundred years ago, it had been to escape the ravages of microbiological warfare that was just beginning (a few germs in a sneak attack on Madagascar, quickly spreading to epidemic proportions, and South Africa holding the world ransom for the antidote; quick retaliation with virulent cancer; you guess the rest). And even from a couple of miles out in space, it was pretty obvious that the war hadn't stopped there. And yet there was this homing signal.

"Obviamente automática," Amauri observed.

"*Que* máquina, que ñão pofa em tantos anos, bichinha! Não acredito!" retorted Harold, and I was afraid I might have a rerun of the day before.

"English," I said. "Might as well get used to it. We'll have to speak it for a few days, at least."

Vladimir sighed. "Merda."

I laughed. "All right, you can keep your scatological comments in lingua deporto."

"Are you so sure there's anybody alive down there?" Vladimir asked.

What could I say? That I felt it in my bones? So I just threw a sponge at him, which scattered drinking water all over the cabin, and for a few minutes we had a waterfight. I know, discipline, discipline. But we're not a land army up here, and what the hell. I'd rather have my crew acting like crazy children than like crazy grown-ups.

Actually, I didn't believe that at the level of technology our ancestors had reached in 1992 they could build a machine that would keep running until 2810. Somebody had to be alive down there—or else they'd gotten smart. Again, the surface of old Terra didn't give many signs that anybody had gotten smart.

So somebody was alive down there. And that was exactly what we had been sent to find out.

They complained when I ordered monkeysuits.

"That's old Mother *Earth* down there!" Harold argued. For a halibut with an ike of 150 he sure could act like a baiano sometimes.

"Show me the cities," I answered. "Show me the millions of people running around taking the sun in their rawhide summer outfits."

"And there may be germs," Amauri added, in his snottiest voice, and immediately I had another argument going between two men brown enough to know better.

"We will follow," I said in my nasty captain's voice, "standard planetary procedure, whether it's Mother Earth or mother—"

And at that moment the monotonous homing signal changed.

"Please respond, please identify, please respond, or we'll blast your asses out of the sky."

We responded. And soon afterward found ourselves in monkeysuits wandering around in thick pea soup up to our navels (if we could have located our navels without a map, surrounded as they were with lifesaving devices) waiting for somebody to open a door.

A door opened and we picked ourselves up off a

very hard floor. Some of the pea soup had fallen down
the hatch with us. A gas came into the sterile chamber where we waited, and pretty soon the pea soup
settled down and turned into mud.

"Mariajoseijesus!" Amauri muttered. "Aquela
merda *vivia!*"

"English," I muttered into the monkey mouth,
"and clean up your language."

"That crap was alive," Amauri said, rephrasing
and cleaning up his language.

"And now it isn't, but we are." It was hard to be
patient.

For all we knew, what passed for humanity here
liked eating spacemen. Or sacrificing them to some
local deity. We passed a nervous four hours in that
cubicle. And I had already laid about five hopeless
escape plans—when a door opened, and a person appeared.

He was dressed in a white farmersuit, or at least
close to it. He was very short, but smiled pleasantly
and beckoned. Proof positive. Living human beings.
Mission successful. *Now* we know there was no
cause for rejoicing, but at that moment we rejoiced.
Backslapping, embracing our little host (afraid of
crushing him for a moment), and then into the labyrinth of U.S. MB Warfare Post 004.

They were all very small—not more than 140 centimeters tall—and the first thought that struck me
was how much humanity had grown since then. The
stars must agree with us, I thought.

Till quiet, methodical Vladimir, looking, as always, white as a ghost, pointedly turned a doorknob
and touched a lightswitch (it actually was *mechanical*). They were both above eye level for our little
friends. So it wasn't us colonists who had grown—
it was our cousins from old Gaea who had shrunk.

We tried to catch them up on history, but all they

cared about was their own politics. "Are you American?" they kept asking.

"I'm from Pennsylvania," I said, "but these humble-butts are from Núncamais."

They didn't understand.

"Núncamais. It means 'never again.' In lingua deporto."

Again puzzled. But they asked another question.

"Where did your colony *come from?*" One-track minds.

"Pennsylvania was settled by Americans from Hawaii. We lay no bets as to why they named the damned planet Pennsylvania."

One of the little people piped up, "That's obvious. Cradle of liberty. And *them?*"

"From Brazil," I said.

They conferred quietly on that one, and then apparently decided that while Brazilian ancestry wasn't a capital offense, it didn't exactly confer human status. From then on, they made no attempt to talk to my crew. Just watched them carefully, and talked to me.

Me they loved.

"God bless America," they said.

I felt agreeable. "God bless America," I answered.

Then, again in unison, they made an obscene suggestion as to what I should do with the Russians. I glanced at my compatriots and fellow travelers and shrugged. I repeated the little folks' wish for the Russians' sexual bliss.

Fact time. I won't bore by repeating all the clever questioning and probing that elicited the following information. Partly because it didn't take any questioning. They seemed to have been rehearsing for years what they would say to any visitors from outer space, particularly the descendants of the long-lost colonists. It went this way:

Germ warfare had begun in earnest about three years after we left. Three very cleverly designed cancer viruses had been loosed on the world, apparently by no one at all, since both the Russians and the Americans denied it and the Chinese were all dead. That was when the scientists knuckled down and set to work.

Recombinant DNA had been a rough enough science when my ancestors took off for the stars—and we hadn't developed it much since then. When you're developing raw planets you have better things to do with your time. But under the pressure of warfare, the science of do-it-yourself genetics had a field day on planet Earth.

"We are constantly developing new strains of viruses and bacteria," they said. "And constantly we are bombarded by the Russians' latest weapons." They were hard-pressed. There weren't many of them in that particular MB Warfare Post, and the enemy's assaults were clever.

And finally the picture became clear. To all of us at once. It was Harold who said, "Fossa-me, mãe! You mean for eight hundred *years* you bunnies've been down here?"

They didn't answer until I asked the question— more politely, too, since I had noticed a certain set to those inscrutable jaws when Harold called them bunnies. Well, they *were* bunnies, white as white could be, but it was tasteless for Harold to call them that, particularly in front of Vladimir, who had more than a slight tendency toward white skin himself.

"Have you Americans been trapped down here ever since the war began?" I asked, trying to put awe into my voice, and succeeding. Horror isn't that far removed from awe, anyway.

They beamed with what I took for pride. And I was beginning to be able to interpret some of their facial expressions. As long as I had good words for America, I was all right.

"Yes, Captain Kane Kanea, we and our ancestors have been here from the beginning."

"Doesn't it get a little cramped?"

"Not for American soldiers, Captain. For the right to life, liberty, and the pursuit of happiness we would sacrifice anything." I didn't ask how much liberty and happiness-pursuing were possible in a hole in the rock. Our hero went on: "We fight on that millions may live, free, able to breathe the clean air of America unoppressed by the lashes of Communism."

And then they broke into a few choice hymns about purple mountains and yellow waves with a rousing chorus of God blessing America. It all ended with a mighty shout: "Better dead than red." When it was over we asked them if we could sleep, since according to our ship's time it was well past bedding-down hour.

They put us in a rather small room with three cots in it that were far too short for us. Didn't matter. We couldn't possibly be comfortable in our monkeysuits anyway.

Harold wanted to talk in lingua deporto as soon as we were alone, but I managed to convince him without even using my monkeysuit's discipliner button that we didn't want them to think we were trying to keep any secrets. We all took it for granted that they were monitoring us.

And so our conversation was the sort of conversation that one doesn't mind having overheard by a bunch of crazy patriots.

Amauri: "I am amazed at their great love for America, persisting so many centuries." Translation: "What the hell got these guys so nuts about something as dead as the ancient U.S. empire?"

Me: "Perhaps it is due to such unwavering loyalty
to the flag, God, country, and liberty" (I admit I was
laying it on thick, but better to be safe, etc.) "that
they have been able to survive so long." Translation:
"Maybe being crazy fanatics is all that's kept them
alive in this hole."

Harold: "I wonder how long we can stay in this
bastion of democracy before we must reluctantly go
back to our colony of the glorious American dream."
Translation: "What are the odds they don't let us go?
After all, they're so loony they might think we're
spies or something."

Vladimir: "I only hope we can learn from them.
Their science is infinitely beyond anything we have
hitherto developed with our poor resources." Translation: "We're not going anywhere until I have a
chance to do *my* job and check out the local flora
and fauna. Eight hundred years of recombining DNA
has got to have something we can take back home
to Núncamais."

And so the conversation went until we were sick
of the flowers and perfume that kept dropping out of
our mouths. Then we went to sleep.

The next day was guided tour day, Russian attack
day, and damn near good-bye to the crew of the good
ship Pollywog.

The guided tour kept us up hill and down dale
for most of the morning. Vladimir was running the
tracking computer from his monkeysuit. Mine was
too busy analyzing the implications of all their comments while Amauri was absorbing the science and
Harold was trying to figure out how to pick his nose
with mittens on. Harold was along for the ride—a
weapons expert, just in case. Thank God.

We began to be able to tell one little person from
another. George Washington Steiner was our usual

guide. The big boss, who had talked to us through most of the history lesson the day before, was Andrew Jackson Wallichinsky. And the guy who led the singing was Richard Nixon Dixon. The computer told us those were names of beloved American presidents, with surnames added.

And my monkeysuit's analysis also told us that the music leader was the *real* big boss, while Andy Jack Wallichinsky was merely the director of scientific research. Seems that the politicians ran the brains, instead of vice versa.

Our guide, G.W. Steiner, was very proud of his assignment. He showed us everything. I mean, even with the monkeysuit keeping three-fourths of the gravity away from me, my feet were sore by lunchtime (a quick sip of recycled xixi and cocó). And it was impressive. Again, I give it unto you in abbreviated form:

Even though the installation was technically airtight, in fact the enemy viruses and bacteria could get in quite readily. It seems that early in the twenty-first century the Russians had stopped making any kind of radio broadcasts. (I know, that sounds like a non sequitur. Patience, patience.) At first the Americans in 004 had thought they had won. And then, suddenly, a new onslaught of another disease. At this time the 004 researchers had never been *personally* hit by any diseases—the airtight system was working fine. But their commander at that time, Rodney Fletcher, had been very suspicious.

"He thought it was a commie trick," said George Washington Steiner. I began to see the roots of super-patriotism in 004's history.

So Rodney Fletcher set the scientists to working on strengthening the base personnel's antibody system. They plugged away at it for two weeks and came up with three new strains of bacteria that selectively devoured practically anything that wasn't supposed to be in the human body. Just in time, too, because then that new disease hit. It wasn't stopped by the airtight system, because instead of being a virus, it was just two little amino acids and a molecule of lactose, put together *just so*. It fit right through the filters. It sailed right through the antibiotics. It entered right into the lungs of every man, woman, and child in 004. And if Rodney Fletcher hadn't been a paranoid, they all would have died. As it was, only about half lived.

Those two amino acids and the lactose molecule had the ability to fit right into *that* spot on a human DNA and then make the DNA replicate that way. Just one little change—and pretty soon nerves just stopped working.

Those two amino acids and the lactose molecule system worked just well enough to slow down the disease's progress until a plug could be found that fit even better into that spot on the DNA, keeping the Russians' little devices out. (Can they be called viruses? Can they be called alive? I'll leave it to the godcallers and the philosophers to decide that.)

Trouble was, the plugs also caused all the soldiers' babies to grow up to be very short with a propensity for having their teeth fall out and their eyes go blind at the age of thirty. G.W. Steiner was very proud of the fact that they had managed to correct for the eyes after four generations. He smiled and for the first time we really noticed that his teeth weren't like ours.

"We make them out of certain bacteria that gets very hard when a particular virus is exposed to it. My own great-great-grandmother invented it," Steiner said. "We're always coming up with new and useful tools."

I asked to see how they did this trick, which brings us full circle to what we saw on the guided tour that day. We saw the laboratories where eleven researchers were playing clever little games with DNA. I didn't understand any of it, but my monkeysuit assured me that the computer was getting it all.

We also saw the weapons delivery system. It was very clever. It consisted of setting a culture dish full of a particular nasty weapon in a little box, closing the door to the box, and then pressing a button that opened another door to the box that led outside.

"We let the wind take it from there," said Steiner. "We figure it takes about a year for a new weapon to reach Russia. But by then it's grown to a point that it's irresistible."

I asked him what the bacteria lived on. He laughed. "Anything," he said. It turns out that their basic breeding stock is a bacterium that can photosynthesize and dissolve any form of iron, both at the same time. "Whatever else we change about a particular weapon, we don't change that," Steiner said. "Our weapons can travel anywhere without hosts. Quarantines don't do any good."

Harold had an idea. I was proud of him. "If these little germs can dissolve steel, George, why the hell aren't they in here dissolving this whole installation?"

Steiner looked like he had just been hoping we'd ask that question.

"When we developed our basic breeder stock, we also developed a mold that inhibits the bacteria from reproducing and eating. The mold only grows on metal and the spores die if they're away from both mold and metal for more than one-seventy-seventh of a second. That means that the mold grows all the way around this installation—and nowhere else. My fourteenth great-uncle William Westmoreland Hannamaker developed the mold."

"Why," I asked, "do you keep mentioning your blood relationship to these inventors? Surely after eight hundred years here everybody's related?"

I thought I was asking a simple question. But G.W. Steiner looked at me coldly and turned away, leading us to the next room.

We found bacteria that processed other bacteria that processed still other bacteria that turned human excrement into very tasty, nutritious food. We took their word for the tasty. I know, we were still eating recycled us through the tubes in our suit. But at least we knew where *ours* had been.

They had bacteria that without benefit of sunlight processed carbon dioxide and water back into oxygen and starch. So much for photosynthesis.

And we got a list of what shelf after shelf of weapons could do to an unprepared human body. If somebody ever broke all those jars on Núncamais or Pennsylvania or Kiev, everybody would simply disappear, completely devoured and incorporated into the life-systems of bacteria and viruses and trained amino-acid sets.

No sooner did I think of that, than I said it. Only I didn't get any farther than the word *Kiev*.

"Kiev? One of the colonies is named Kiev?"

I shrugged. "There are only three planets colonized. Kiev, Pennsylvania, and Núncamais."

"*Russian* ancestry?"

Oops, I thought. Oops is an all-purpose word standing for every bit of profanity, blasphemy, and pornographic and scatological exculpation I could think of.

The guided tour ended right then.

Back in our bedroom, we became aware that we

had somehow dissolved our hospitality. After a while, Harold realized that it was my fault.

"Captain, by damn, if you hadn't told them about Kiev we wouldn't be locked in here like this!"

I agreed, hoping to pacify him, but he didn't calm down until I used the discipliner button in my monkeysuit.

Then we consulted the computers.

Mine reported that in all we had been told, two areas had been completely left out: While it was obvious that in the past the little people had done extensive work on human DNA, there had been no hint of any work going on in that field today. And though we had been told of all kinds of weapons that had been flung among the Russians on the other side of the world, there had been no hint of any kind of limited effect antipersonnel weapon *here.*

"Oh," Harold said. "There's nothing to stop us from walking out of here anytime we can knock the door down. And I can knock the door down anytime I want to," he said, playing with the buttons on his monkeysuit. I urged him to wait until all the reports were done.

Amauri informed us that he had gleaned enough information from their talk and his monkeyeyes that we could go home with the entire science of DNA recombination hidden away in our computer.

And then Vladimir's suit played out a holomap of Post 004.

The bright green, infinitesimally thin lines marked walls, doors, passages. We immediately recognized the corridors we had walked in throughout the morning, located the laboratories, found where we were imprisoned. And then we noticed a rather larger area in the middle of the holomap that seemed empty.

"Did you see a room like that?" I asked. The others shook their heads. Vladimir asked the holomap if we had been in it. The suit answered in its whispery monkeyvoice: "No. I have only delineated the unpenetrated perimeter and noted apertures that perhaps give entry."

"So they didn't let us in there," Harold said. "I knew the bastards were hiding something."

"And let's make a guess," I said. "That room either has something to do with antipersonnel weapons, or it has something to do with human DNA research."

We sat and pondered the revelations we had just had, and realized they didn't add up to much. Finally Vladimir spoke up. Trust a half-bunny to come up with the idea where three browns couldn't. Just goes to show you that a racial theory is a bunch of waggy-woggle.

"Antipersonnel hell," Vladimir said. "They don't need antipersonnel. All they have to do is open a little hole in our suits and let the germs come through."

"Our suits close immediately," Amauri said, but then corrected himself. "I guess it doesn't take long for a virus to get through, does it?"

Harold didn't get it. "Let one of those bunnies try to lay a knife on me, and I'll split him from ass to armpit."

We ignored him.

"What makes you think there are germs in here? Our suits don't measure that," I pointed out.

Vladimir had already thought of that. "Remember what they said. About the Russians getting those little amino-acid monsters in here."

Amauri snorted. "Russians."

"Yeah, right," Vladimir said, "but keep the voice down, viado."

Amauri turned red, started to say, "Quem é que

cê chama de viado!"—but I pushed the discipliner button. No time for any of that crap.

"Watch your language, Vladimir. We got enough problems."

"Sorry, Amauri, Captain," Vladimir said. "I'm a little wispy, you know?"

"So's everybody."

Vladimir took a breath and went on. "Once those bugs got in here, 004 must have been pretty thoroughly permeable. The, uh, Russians must've kept pumping more variations on the same into Post 004."

"So why aren't they all dead?"

"What I think is that a lot of these people *have* been killed—but the survivors are ones whose bodies took readily to those plugs they came up with. The plugs are regular parts of their body chemistry now. They'd have to be, wouldn't they? They told us they were passed on in the DNA transmitted to the next generation."

I got it. So did Amauri, who said, "So they've had seven or eight centuries to select for adaptability."

"Why not?" Vladimir asked. "Didn't you notice? Eleven researchers on developing new weapons. And only two on developing new defenses. They can't be *too* worried."

Amauri shook his head. "Oh, Mother Earth. Whatever got into you?"

"Just caught a cold," Vladimir said, and then laughed. "A virus. Called humanity."

We sat around looking at the holomap for a while. I found four different routes from where we were to the secret area—if we wanted to get there. I also found three routes to the exit. I pointed them out to the others.

"Yeah," Harold said. "Trouble is, who knows if those doors really lead into that unknown area? I mean, what the hell, three of the four doors might lead to the broom closets or service stations."

A good point.

We just sat there, wondering whether we should head for the Pollywog or try to find out what was in the hidden area, when the Russian attack made up our minds for us. There was a tremendous bang. The floor shook, as if some immense dog had just picked up Post 004 and given it a good shaking. When it stopped the lights flickered and went out.

"Golden opportunity," I said into the monkeymouth. The others agreed. So we flashed on the lights from our suits and pointed them at the door. Harold suddenly felt very important. He went to the door and ran his magic flipper finger all the way around the door. Then he stepped back and flicked a lever on his suit.

"Better turn your backs," he said. "This can flash pretty bright."

Even looking at the back wall the explosion blinded me for a few seconds. The world looked a little green when I turned around. The door was in shreds on the floor, and the doorjamb didn't look too healthy.

"Nice job, Harold," I said.

"Graças a deus," he answered, and I had to laugh. Odd how little religious phrases refused to die, even with an irreverent filho de punta like Harold.

Then I remembered that I was in charge of ordergiving. So I gave.

The second door we tried led into the rooms we wanted to see. But just as we got in, the lights came on.

"Damn. They've got the station back in order," Amauri said. But Vladimir just pointed down the corridor.

The pea soup had gotten in. It was oozing sluggishly toward us.

"Whatever the Russians did, it must have opened up a big hole in the station." Vladimir pointed his laser finger at the mess. Even on full power, it only made a little spot steam. The rest just kept coming.

"Anyone for swimming?" I asked. No one was. So I hustled them all into the not-so-hidden room.

There were some little people in there, cowering in the darkness. Harold wrapped them in cocoons and stuck them in a corner. So we had time to look around.

There wasn't that much to see, really. Standard lab equipment, and then thirty-two boxes, about a meter square. They were under sunlamps. We looked inside.

The animals were semisolid looking. I didn't touch one right then, but the sluggish way it sent out pseudopodia, I concluded that the one I was watching, at least, had a rather crusty skin—with jelly inside. They were all a light brown—even lighter than Vladimir's skin. But there were little green spots here and there. I wondered if they photosynthesized.

"Look what they're floating in," Amauri said, and I realized that it was pea soup.

"They've developed a giant amoeba that lives on all other microorganisms, I guess," Vladimir said. "Maybe they've trained it to carry bombs. Against the Russians."

At that moment Harold began firing his arsenal, and I noticed that the little people were gathered at the door to the lab, looking agitated. A few at the front were looking dead.

Harold probably would have killed all of them, except that we were still standing next to a box with a giant amoeba in it. When he screamed, we looked and saw the creature fastened against his leg. Even as we watched, Harold fell, the bottom half of his leg dropping away as the amoeba continued eating up his thigh.

We watched just long enough for the little people to grab hold of us in sufficient numbers that resistance would have been ridiculous. Besides, we couldn't take our eyes off Harold.

At about the groin, the amoeba stopped eating. It didn't matter. Harold was dead anyway—we didn't know what disease got him, but as soon as his suit had cracked he started vomiting into his suit. There were pustules all over his face. In short, Vladimir's guess about the virus content of Post 004 had been pretty accurate.

And now the amoeba formed itself into a pentagon. Five very smooth sides, the creature sitting in a clump on the gaping wound that had once been a pelvis. Suddenly, with a brief convulsion, all the sides bisected, forming sharp angles, so that now there were ten sides to the creature. A hairline crack appeared down the middle. And then, like jelly sliced in the middle and finally deciding to split, the two halves slumped away on either side. They quickly formed into two new pentagons, and then they relaxed into pseudopodia again, and continued devouring Harold.

"Well," Amauri said. "They *do* have an antipersonnel weapon."

When he spoke, the spell of stillness was broken, and the little people had us spread on tables with sharp-pointed objects pointed at us. If any one of those punctured a suit even for a moment, we would be dead. We held very still.

Richard Nixon Dixon, the top halibut, interrogated us himself. It all started with a lot of questions about the Russians, when we had visited them, why we had decided to serve them instead of the Americans, etc. We kept insisting that they were full of crap.

But when they threatened to open a window into Vladimir's suit, I decided enough was enough.

"Tell 'em!" I shouted into the monkeymouth, and Vladimir said, "All right," and the little people leaned back to listen.

"There *are* no Russians," Vladimir said.

The little people got ready to carve holes.

"No, wait, it's true! After we got your homing signal, before we landed, we made seven orbital passes over the entire planet. There is absolutely no human life anywhere but here!"

"Commie lies," Richard Nixon Dixon said.

"God's own truth!" I shouted. "Don't touch him, man! He's telling the truth! The only thing out there over this whole damn planet is that pea soup! It covers every inch of land and every inch of water, except a few holes at the poles."

Dixon began to feel a little confused, and the little people murmured. I guess I sounded sincere.

"If there aren't any people," Dixon said, "where do the Russian attacks come from?"

Vladimir answered that one. For a bunny, he was quick on the uptake. "Spontaneous recombination! You and the Russians got new strains of every microbe developing like crazy. All the people, all the animals, all the *plants* were killed. And only the microbes lived. But you've been introducing new strains constantly, tough competitors for all those beasts out there. The ones that couldn't adapt died. And now that's all that's left—the ones who adapt. Constantly."

Andrew Jackson Wallichinsky, the head researcher, nodded. "It sounds plausible."

"If there's anything we've learned about commies

in the last thousand years," Richard Nixon Dixon said, "it's that you can't trust 'em any farther than you can spit."

"Well," Andy Jack said, "it's easy enough to test them."

Dixon nodded. "Go ahead."

So three of the little people went to the boxes and each came back with an amoeba. In a minute it was clear that they planned to set them on us. Amauri screamed. Vladimir turned white. I would have screamed but I was busy trying to swallow my tongue.

"Relax," Andy Jack said. "They won't hurt you."

"Acredito!" I shouted. "Like it didn't hurt Harold!"

"Harold was killing people. These won't harm you. Unless you were lying."

Great, I thought. Like the ancient test for witches. Throw them in the water, if they drown they're innocent, if they float they're guilty so kill 'em.

But *maybe* Andy Jack was telling the truth and they wouldn't hurt us. And if we refused to let them put those buggers on us they'd "know" we had been lying and punch holes in our monkeysuits.

So I told the little people to put one on me only. They didn't need to test us all.

And then I put my tongue between my teeth, ready to bite down hard and inhale the blood when the damn thing started eating me. Somehow I thought I'd feel better about going honeyduck if I helped myself along.

They set the thing on my shoulder. It didn't penetrate my monkeysuit. Instead it just oozed up toward my head.

It slid over my faceplate and the world went dark.

"Kane Kanea," said a faint vibration in the faceplate.

"Meu deus," I muttered.

The amoeba could talk. But I didn't have to speak to answer it. A question would come through the vibration of the faceplate. And then I would lie there and—it knew my answer. Easy as pie. I was so scared I urinated twice during the interview. But my imperturbable monkeysuit cleaned it all up and got it ready for breakfast, just like normal.

And at last the interview was over. The amoeba slithered off my faceplate and returned to the waiting arms of one of the little people, who carried it back to Andy Jack and Ricky Nick. The two men put their hands on the thing, and then looked at us in surprise.

"You're telling the truth. There are no Russians."

Vladimir shrugged. "Why would we lie?"

Andy Jack started toward me, carrying the writhing monster that had interviewed me.

"I'll kill myself before I let that thing touch me again."

Andy Jack stopped in surprise. "You're still afraid of that?"

"It's intelligent," I said. "It read my mind."

Vladimir looked startled, and Amauri muttered something. But Andy Jack only smiled. "Nothing mysterious about that. It can read and interpret the electromagnetic fields of your brain, coupled with the amitron flux in your thyroid gland."

"What *is* it?" Vladimir asked.

Andy Jack looked very proud. "This one is my son."

We waited for the punch line. It didn't come. And suddenly we realized that we had found what we had been looking for—the result of the little people's research into recombinant human DNA.

"We've been working on these for years. Finally we got it right about four years ago," Andy Jack said. "They were our last line of defense. But now that we know the Russians are dead—well, there's no reason for them to stay in their nests."

And the man reached down and laid the amoeba into the pea soup that was now about sixty centimeters deep on the floor. Immediately it flattened out on the surface until it was about a meter in diameter. I remembered the whispering voice through my faceplate.

"It's too flexible to have a brain," Vladimir said.

"It doesn't have one," Andy Jack answered. "The brain functions are distributed throughout the body. If it were cut in forty pieces, each piece would have enough memory and enough mindfunction to continue to live. It's indestructible. And when several of them get together, they set up a sympathetic field. They become very bright, then."

"Head of the class and everything, I'm sure," Vladimir said. He couldn't hide the loathing in his voice. Me, I was trying not to be sick.

So this is the next stage of evolution, I thought. Man screws up the planet till it's fit for nothing but microbes—and then changes himself so that he can live on a diet of bacteria and viruses.

"It's really the perfect step in evolution," Andy Jack said. "This fellow can adapt to new species of parasitic bacteria and viruses almost by reflex. Control the makeup of his own DNA consciously. Manipulate the DNA of other organisms by absorbing them through the semipermeable membranes of specialized cells, altering them, and setting them free again."

"Somehow it doesn't make me want to feed it or change its diapers."

Andy Jack laughed lightly. "Since they reproduce by fission, they're never infant. Oh, if the piece were too small, it would take a while to get back to adult competence again. But otherwise, in the normal run of things, it's always an adult."

Then Andy Jack reached down, let his son wrap itself around his arm, and then walked back to where Richard Nixon Dixon stood watching. Andy Jack put the arm that held the amoeba around Dixon's shoulder.

"By the way, sir," Andy Jack said. "With the Russians dead, the damned war is over, sir."

Dixon looked startled. "And?"

"We don't need a commander anymore."

Before Dixon could answer, the amoeba had eaten through his neck and he was quite dead. Rather an abrupt coup, I thought, and looked at the other little people for a reaction. No one seemed to mind. Apparently their superpatriotic militarism was only skin deep. I felt vaguely relieved. Maybe they had something in common with me after all.

They decided to let us go, and we were glad enough to take them up on the offer. On the way out, they showed us what had caused the explosion in the last "Russian" attack. The mold that protected the steel surface of the installation had mutated slightly in one place, allowing the steel-eating bacteria to enter into a symbiotic relationship. It just happened that the mutation occurred at the place where the hydrogen storage tanks rested against the wall. When a hole opened, one of the first amino-acid sets that came through with the pea soup was one that combines radically with raw hydrogen. The effect was a three-second population explosion. It knocked out a huge chunk of Post 004.

We were glad, when we got back to our skipship, that we had left dear old Pollywog floating some forty meters off the ground. Even so, there had been some damage. One of the airborne microbes had a penchant for lodging in hairline cracks and reproducing rapidly, widening microscopic gaps in the structure of the ship. Nevertheless, Amauri judged us fit for takeoff.

We didn't kiss anybody good-bye.

So now I've let you in on the true story of our visit to Mother Earth back in 2810. The parallel with our current situation should be obvious. If we let Pennsylvania get soaked into this spongy little war between Kiev and Núncamais, we'll deserve what we get. Because those damned antimatter convertors will do things that make germ warfare look as pleasant as sniffing pinkweeds.

And if anything human survives the war, it sure as hell won't look like anything we call human now.

And maybe that doesn't matter to anybody these days. But it matters to me. I don't like the idea of amoebas for grandchildren, and having an antimatter great-nephew thrills me less. I've been human all my life, and I like it.

So I say, turn on our repressors and sit out the damned war. Wait until they've disappeared each other, and then go about the business of keeping humanity alive—and human.

So much for the political tract. If you vote for war, though, I can promise you there'll be more than one skipship heading for the wild black yonder. We've colonized before, and we can do it again. In case no one gets the hint, that's a call for volunteers, if, as, and when. Over.

Not over. On the first printing of this program, I got a lot of inquiries as to why we didn't report all this when we got back home. The answer's simple. On Núncamais it's a capital crime to alter a ship's log. But we had to.

As soon as we got into space from Mother Earth,

Vladimir had the computer present all its findings, all its data, and all its conclusions about recombinant DNA. And then he erased it all.

I probably would have stopped him if I'd known what he was doing in advance. But once it was done, Amauri and I realized that he was right. That kind of merda didn't belong in the universe. And then we systematically covered our tracks. We erased all reference to Post 004, eradicated any hint of a homing signal. All we left in the computer was the recording of our overflight, showing nothing but pea soup from sea to soupy sea. It was tricky, but we also added a serious malfunction of the EVA lifesupport gear on the way home—which cost us the life of our dear friend and comrade, Harold.

And then we recorded in the ship's log, "Planet unfit for human occupancy. No human life found."

Hell. It wasn't even a lie.

IN THE DOGHOUSE
(WITH JAY A. PARRY)

As Mlikluln awoke, he felt the same depression that he had felt as he went to sleep ninety-seven years ago. And though he knew it would only make his depression worse, he immediately scanned backward as his ship decelerated, hunting for the star that had been the sun. He couldn't find it. Which meant that even with acceleration and deceleration time, the light from the nova—or supernova—had not yet reached the system he was heading for.

Sentimentality be damned, he thought savagely as he turned his attention to the readouts on the upcoming system. So the ice cliffs will melt, and the sourland will turn to huge, planet-spanning lakes. So the atmosphere will fly away in the intense heat. Who cares? Humanity was safe.

As safe as bodiless minds can be, resting in their own supporting mindfields somewhere in space, waiting for the instantaneous message that *here* is a planet with bodies available, *here* is a home for the millions for whom there had been no spaceships, *here* we can once again—

Once again what?

No matter how far we search, Mklikluln reminded himself, we have no hope of finding those graceful, symmetrical, hexagonally delicate bodies we left behind to burn.

Of course, Mklikluln still had his, but only for a while.

Thirteen true planetary bodies, two of which co-orbited as binaries in the third position. Ignoring the gas giants and the crusty pebbles outside the habitable range, Mklikluln got increasingly more complex readouts on the binary and the single in the fourth orbit, a red midget.

The red was dead, the smaller binary even worse, but the blue-green larger binary was ideal. Not because it matched the conditions on Mklikluln's home world—that would be impossible. But because it had life. And not only life—intelligent life.

Or at least fairly bright life. Energy output in the sub- and supravisible spectra exceeded reflection from the star (No, I must try to think of it as the *sun*) by a significant degree. Energy clearly came from a breakdown of carbon compounds, just what current theory (current? ninety-seven-year-old) had assumed would be the logical energy base of a developing world in this temperature range. The professors would be most gratified.

And after several months of maneuvering his craft, he was in stationary orbit around the larger binary. He began monitoring communications on the supravisible wavelengths. He learned the language quickly, though of course he couldn't have produced it with his own body, and sighed a little when he realized that the aliens, like his own people, called their little star "the sun," their minor binary "the moon," and their own humble, overhot planet "earth" (terra, mund, etc.). The array of languages was impressive—to think that people would go to all the trouble of thinking out hundreds of completely different ways of communicating for the sheer love of the logical exercise was amazing—what minds they must have!

For a moment he fleetingly thought of taking over for his people's use the bipedal bodies of the dominant intelligent race; but law was law, and his people would commit mass suicide if they realized—as they would surely realize—that they had gained their bodies at the expense of another intelligent race. One could think of such bipedals as being almost human, right down to the whimsical sense of humor that so reminded Mklikluln of his wife (Ah, Glundnindn, and you the pilot who volunteered to plunge into the sun, scooping out the sample that killed you, but saved us!); but he refused to mourn.

The dominant race was out. Similar bipedals were too small in population, too feared or misunderstood by the dominant race. Other animals with appropriate populations didn't have body functions that could easily support intelligence without major revisions—and many were too weak to survive unaided, too short of lifespan to allow civilization.

And so he narrowed down the choices to two quadrupeds, of very different sorts, of course, but well within the limits of choice: both had full access to the domiciles of the dominant race; both had adequate body structure to support intellect; both had potential means of communicating; both had sufficient population to hold all the encapsulated minds waiting in the space between the stars.

Mklikluln did the mental equivalent of flipping a coin—would have flipped a coin, in fact, except that he had neither hand nor coin nor adequate gravity for flipping.

The choice made—for the noisy one of greater intelligence that already had the love of most members of the master race—he set about making plans on how to introduce the transceivers that would call his people. (The dominant race must not know what is happening; and it can't be done without the cooperation of the dominant race.)

Mklikluln's six points vibrated just a little as he thought.

'

Abu was underpaid, underfed, underweight, and within about twelve minutes of the end of his lifespan. He was concentrating on the first problem, however, as the fourth developed.

"Why am I being paid less than Faisel, who sits on his duff by the gate while I walk back and forth in front of the cells all day?" he righteously said—under his breath, of course, in case his supervisor should overhear him. "Am I not as good a Muslim? Am I not as smart? Am I not as loyal to the Party?"

And as he was immersed in righteous indignation at man's inhumanity, not so much to mankind as to Abu ibn Assur, a great roaring sound tore through the desert prison, followed by a terrible, hot, dry, sand-stabbing wind. Abu screamed and covered his eyes—too late, however, and the sand ripped them open, and the hot air dried them out.

That was why he didn't see the hole in the outside wall of cell 23, which held a political prisoner condemned to die the next morning for having murdered his wife—normally not a political crime, except when the wife was also the daughter of somebody who could make phone calls and get people put in prison.

That was why he didn't see his supervisor come in,

discover cell 23 empty, and then aim his submachine gun at Abu as the first step to setting up the hapless guard as the official scapegoat for this fiasco. Abu did, however, hear and feel the discharge of the gun, and wondered vaguely what had happened as he died.

Mklikluln stretched the new arms and legs (the fourness of the body, the two-sidedness, the overwhelming sexuality of it—all were amazing, all were delightful) and walked around his little spacecraft. And the fiveness and tenness of the fingers and toes! (What we could have done with fingers and toes! except that we might not have developed thoughttalk, then, and would have been tied to the vibration of air as are these people.) Inside the ship he could see his own body melting as the hot air of the Kansas farmland raised the temperature above the melting point of ice.

He had broken the law himself, but could see no way around it. Necessary as his act had been, and careful as he had been to steal the body of a man doomed anyway to die, he knew that his own people would try him, convict him, and execute him for depriving an intelligent being of life.

But in the meantime, it was a new body and a whole range of sensations. He moved the tongue over the teeth. He made the buzzing in his throat that was used for communication. He tried to speak.

It was impossible. Or so it seemed, as the tongue and lips and jaw tried to make the Arabic sounds the reflex pathways were accustomed to, while Mklikluln tried to speak in the language that had dominated the airwaves.

He kept practicing as he carefully melted down his ship (though it was transparent to most electromagnetic spectra, it might still cause comment if found) and by the time he made his way into the nearby city, he was able to communicate fairly well. Well enough, anyway, to contract with the Kansas City Development Corporation for the manufacture of the machine he had devised; with Farber, Farber, and Maynard to secure patents on every detail of the machinery; and with Sidney's carpentry shop to manufacture the doghouses.

He sold enough diamonds to pay for the first 2,000 finished models. And then he hit the road, humming the language he had learned from the radio. "It's the real thing, Coke is," he sang to himself. "Mr. Transmission will put in commission the worst transmissions in town."

The sun set as he checked into a motel outside Manhattan, Kansas. "How many?" asked the clerk.

"One," said Mklikluln.

"Name?"

"Robert," he said, using a name he had randomly chosen from among the many thousands mentioned on the airwaves. "Robert Redford."

"Ha-ha," said the clerk. "I bet you get teased about that a lot."

"Yeah. But I get in to see a lot of important people."

The clerk laughed. Mklikluln smiled. Speaking was fun. For one thing, you could lie. An art his people had never learned to cultivate.

"Profession?"

"Salesman."

"Really, Mr. Redford? What do you sell?"

Mklikluln shrugged, practicing looking mildly embarrassed. "Doghouses," he said.

Royce Jacobsen pulled open the front door of his swelteringly hot house and sighed. A salesman.

"We don't want any," he said.

"Yes you do," said the man, smiling.

Royce was a little startled. Salesmen usually didn't argue with potential customers—they usually whined. And those that did argue rarely did it with such calm self-assurance. The man was an ass, Royce decided. He looked at the sample case. On the side were the letters spelling out: "Doghouses Unlimited."

"We don't got a dog," Royce said.

"But you *do* have a very warm house, I believe," the salesman said.

"Yeah. Hotter'n Hades, as the preachers say. Ha." The laugh would have been bigger than one *Ha*, but Royce was hot and tired and it was only a salesman.

"But you have an air conditioner."

"Yeah," Royce said. "What I don't have is a permit for more than a hundred bucks worth of power from the damnpowercompany. So if I run the air conditioner more than one day a month, I get the refrigerator shut down, or the stove, or some other such thing."

The salesman looked sympathetic.

"It's guys like me," Royce went on, "who always get the short end of the stick. You can bet your boots that the mayor gets all the air conditioning he wants. You can bet your boots *and* your overalls, as the farmers say, ha ha, that the president of the damnpowercompany takes three hot showers a day and three cold showers a night and leaves his windows open in the winter, too, you can bet on it."

"Right," said the salesman. "The power companies own this whole country. They own the whole world, you know? Think it's any different in England? In Japan? They got the gas, and so they get the gold."

"Yeah," Royce agreed. "You're my kind of guy.

You come right in. House is hot as Hades, as the preachers say, ha ha ha, but it sure beats standing in the sun."

They sat on a beat-up looking couch and Royce explained exactly what was wrong with the damn-powercompany and what he thought of the damn-powercompany's executives and in what part of their anatomy they should shove their quotas, bills, rates, and periods of maximum and minimum use. "I'm sick to death of having to take a shower at 2:00 A.M!" Royce shouted.

"Then do something about it!" the salesman rejoindered.

"Sure. Like what?"

"Like buy a doghouse from me."

Royce thought that was funny. He laughed for a good long while.

But then the salesman started talking very quietly, showing him pictures and diagrams and cost analysis papers that proved—what?

"That the solar energy utilizer built into this doghouse can power your entire house, all day every day, with four times as much power as you could use if you turned on all your home appliances all day every day, for exactly zero once you pay me this simple one-time fee."

Royce shook his head, though he coveted the doghouse. "Can't. Illegal. I think they passed a law against solar energy thingies back in '85 or '86, to protect the power companies."

The salesman laughed. "How much protection do the power companies need?"

"Sure," Royce answered, "it's me that needs protection. But the meter reader—if I stop using power, he'll report me, they'll investigate—"

"That's why we don't put your whole house on it. We just put the big power users on it, and gradually take more off the regular current until you're paying what, maybe fifteen dollars a month. Right? Only instead of fifteen dollars a month and cooking over a fire and sweating to death in a hot house, you've got the air conditioner running all day, the heater running all day in the winter, showers whenever you want them, and you can open the refrigerator as often as you like."

Royce still wasn't sure.

"What've you got to lose?" the salesman asked.

"My sweat," Royce answered. "You hear that? My sweat. Ha ha ha ha."

"That's why we build them into doghouses—so that nobody'll suspect anything."

"Sure, why not?" Royce asked. "Do it. I'm game. I didn't vote for the damncongressman who voted in that stupid law anyway."

The air conditioner hummed as the guests came in. Royce and his wife, Junie, ushered them into the living room. The television was on in the family room and the osterizer was running in the kitchen. Royce carelessly flipped on a light. One of the women gasped. A man whispered to his wife. Royce and Junie carelessly began their conversation—as Royce *left the door open.*

A guest noticed it—Mr. Detweiler from the bowling team. He said, "Hey!" and leaped from the chair toward the door.

Royce stopped him, saying, "Never mind, never mind, I'll get it in a minute. Here, have some peanuts." And the guests all watched the door in agony as Royce passed the peanuts around, then (finally!) went to the door to close it.

"Beautiful day outside," Royce said, holding the door open a few minutes longer.

Somebody in the living room mentioned a name

of the deity. Somebody else countered with a one word discussion of defecation. Royce was satisfied that the point had been made. He shut the door.

"Oh, by the way," he said. "I'd like you to meet a friend of mine. His name is Robert Redford."

Gasp, gasp, of course you're joking, Robert Redford, what a laugh, sure.

"Actually, his name *is* Robert Redford, but he isn't, of course, the all time greatest star of stage, screen, and the Friday Night Movie, as the disc jockeys say, ha ha. He is, in short, my friends, a doghouse salesman."

Mklikluln came in then, and shook hands all around.

"He looks like an Arab," a woman whispered.

"Or a Jew," her husband whispered back. "Who can tell?"

Royce beamed at Mklikluln and patted him on the back. "Redford here is the best salesman I ever met."

"Must be, if he sold you a doghouse, and you not even got a dog," said Mr. Detweiler of the bowling league, who could sound patronizing because he was the only one in the bowling league who had ever had a perfect game.

"Nevethemore, as the raven said, ha ha ha, I want you all to see my doghouse." And so Royce led the way past a kitchen where all the lights were on, where the refrigerator was standing open ("Royce, the fridge is open!" "Oh, I guess one of the kids left it that way." "I'd kill one of my kids that did something like that!"), where the stove *and* microwave *and* osterizer *and* hot water were all running at once. Some of the women looked faint.

And as the guests tried to rush through the back door all at once, to conserve energy, Royce said,

"Slow down, slow down, what's the panic, the house on fire? Ha ha ha." But the guests still hurried through.

On the way out to the doghouse, which was located in the dead center of the backyard, Detweiler took Royce aside.

"Hey, Royce, old buddy. Who's your touch with the damnpowercompany? How'd you get your quota upped?"

Royce only smiled, shaking his head. "Quota's the same as ever, Detweiler." And then, raising his voice just a bit so that everybody in the backyard could hear, he said, "I only pay fifteen bucks a month for power as it is."

"Woof woof," said a small dog chained to the hook on the doghouse.

"Where'd the dog come from?" Royce whispered to Mklikluln.

"Neighbor was going to drown 'im," Mklikluln answered. "Besides, if you don't have a dog the power company's going to get suspicious. It's cover."

Royce nodded wisely. "Good idea, Redford. I just hope this party's a good idea. What if somebody talks?"

"Nobody will," Mklikluln said confidently.

And then Mklikluln began showing the guests the finer points of the doghouse.

When they finally left, Mklikluln had twenty-three appointments during the next two weeks, checks made out to Doghouses Unlimited for $221.23, including taxes, and many new friends. Even Mr. Detweiler left smiling, his check in Mklikluln's hand, even though the puppy had pooped on his shoe.

"Here's your commission," Mklikluln said as he wrote out a check for three hundred dollars to Royce

Jacobsen. "It's more than we agreed, but you earned it," he said.

"I feel a little funny about this," Royce said. "Like I'm conspiring to break the law or something."

"Nonsense," Mklikluln said. "Think of it as a Tupperware party."

"Sure," Royce said after a moment's thought. "It's not as if I actually did any selling myself, right?"

Within a week, however, Detweiler, Royce, and four other citizens of Manhattan, Kansas, were on their way to various distant cities of the United States, Doghouses Unlimited briefcases in their hands.

And within a month, Mklikluln had a staff of three hundred in seven cities, building doghouses and installing them. And into every doghouse went a frisky little puppy. Mklikluln did some figuring. In about a year, he decided. One year and I can call my people.

"What's happened to power consumption in Manhattan, Kansas?" asked Bill Wilson, up-and-coming young executive in the statistical analysis section of Central Kansas Power, otherwise known as the damnpowercompany.

"It's gotten lower," answered Kay Block, relic of outdated affirmative action programs in Central Kansas Power, who had reached the level of records examiner before the ERA was repealed to make our bathrooms safe for mankind.

Bill Wilson sneered, as if to say, "That much I knew, woman." And Kay Block simpered, as if to say, "Ah, the boy has an IQ after all, eh?"

But they got along well enough, and within an hour they had the alarming statistic that power consumption in the city of Manhattan, Kansas, was down by forty percent.

"What was consumption in the previous trimester?"

Normal. Everything normal.

"Forty percent is ridiculous," Bill fulminated.

"Don't fulminate at me," Kay said, irritated at her boss for raising his voice. "Go yell at the people who unplugged their refrigerators!"

"No," Bill said. "*You* go yell at people who unplugged their refrigerators. Something's gone wrong there, and if it isn't crooked meter readers, it's people who've figured out a way to jimmy the billing system."

After two weeks of investigation, Kay Block sat in the administration building of Kansas State University (9–2 last football season, coming *that* close to copping the Plains Conference pennant for '98) refusing to admit that her investigation had turned up a big fat zero. A random inspection of thirty-eight meters showed no tampering at all. A complete audit of the local branch office's books showed no doctoring at all. And a complete examination of KSU's power consumption figures showed absolutely nothing. No change in consumption—no change in billing system—and yet a sharp drop in electricity use.

"The drop in power use may be localized," Kay suggested to the white-haired woman from the school who was babysitting her through the process. "The stadium surely uses as much light as ever—so the drop must be somewhere else, like in the science labs."

The white-haired woman shook her head. "That may be so, but the figures you see are the figures we've got."

Kay sighed and looked out the window. Down from the window was the roof of the new Plant Science Building. She looked at it as her mind struggled vainly to find something meaningful in the data she had. Somebody was cheating—but how?

There was a doghouse on the roof of the Plant Science Building.

"What's a doghouse doing on the roof of that building?" asked Kay.

"I would assume," said the white-haired woman, "for a dog to live in."

"On the roof?"

The white-haired woman smiled. "Fresh air, perhaps," she said.

Kay looked at the doghouse awhile longer, telling herself that the only reason she was suspicious was because she was hunting for *anything* unusual that could explain the anomalies in the Manhattan, Kansas, power usage pattern.

"I want to see that doghouse," she said.

"Why?" asked the white-haired lady. "Surely you don't think a generator could hide in a doghouse! Or solar-power equipment! Why, those things take whole buildings!"

Kay looked carefully at the white-haired woman and decided that she protested a bit too much. "I insist on seeing the doghouse," she said again.

The white-haired woman smiled again. "Whatever you want, Miss Block. Let me call the custodian so he can unlock the door to the roof."

After the phone call they went down the stairs to the main floor of the administration building, across the lawns, and then up the stairs to the roof of the Plant Science Building. "What's the matter, no elevators?" Kay asked sourly as she panted from the exertion of climbing the stairs.

"Sorry," the white-haired woman said. "We don't build elevators into buildings anymore. They use too much power. Only the power company can afford elevators these days."

The custodian was at the door of the roof, looking very apologetic.

"Sorry if old Rover's been causin' trouble ladies. I keep him up on the roof nowadays, ever since the break-in attempt through the roof door last spring. Nobody's tried to jimmy the door since."

"Arf," said a frisky, cheerful looking mix between an elephant and a Labrador retriever (just a quick guess, of course) that bounded up to them.

"Howdy, Rover old boy," said the custodian. "Don't bite nobody."

"Arf," the dog answered, trying to wiggle out of his skin and looking as if he might succeed. "Gur-rarf."

Kay examined the roof door from the outside. "I don't see any signs of anyone jimmying at the door," she said.

"Course not," said the custodian. "The burglars was seen from the administration building before they could get to the door."

"Oh," said Kay. "Then why did you need to put a dog up here?"

"Cause what if the burglars hadn't been seen?" the custodian said, his tone implying that only a moron would have asked such a question.

Kay looked at the doghouse. It looked like every other doghouse in the world. It looked like cartoons of doghouses, in fact, it was so ordinary. Simple arched door. Pitched roof with gables and eaves. All it lacked was a water dish and piles of doggy-do and old bones. No doggy-do?

"What a talented dog," Kay commented. "He doesn't even go to the bathroom."

"Uh," answered the custodian, "he's really house-broken. He just won't go until I take him down from here to the lawn, will ya Rover?"

Kay surveyed the wall of the roof-access building they had come through. "Odd. He doesn't even mark the walls."

"I told you. He's really housebroken. He wouldn't think of mucking up the roof here."

"Arf," said the dog as it urinated on the door and then defecated in a neat pile at Kay's feet. "Woof woof woof," he said proudly.

"All that training," Kay said, "and it's all gone to waste."

Whether the custodian's answer was merely describing what the dog had done or had a more emphatic purpose was irrelevant. Obviously the doghouse was not normally used for a dog. And if that was true, what was a doghouse doing on the roof of the Plant Science Building?

The damnpowercompany brought civil actions against the city of Manhattan, Kansas, and a court injunction insisted that all doghouses be disconnected from all electric wiring systems. The city promptly brought countersuit against the damnpowercompany (a very popular move) and appealed the court injunction.

The damnpowercompany shut off all the power in Manhattan, Kansas.

Nobody in Manhattan, Kansas, noticed, except the branch office of the damnpowercompany, which now found itself the only building in the city without electricity.

The "Doghouse War" got quite a bit of notoriety. Feature articles appeared in magazines about Doghouses Unlimited and its elusive founder, Robert Redford, who refused to be interviewed and in fact could not be found. All five networks did specials on the cheap energy source. Statistics were gathered showing that not only did seven percent of the American public *have* doghouses, but also that 99.8 percent of the American public *wanted* to have doghouses. The 0.2 percent represented, presumably, power company stockholders and executives. Most politicians could add, or had aides who could, and the prospect of elections coming up in less than a year made the result clear.

The antisolar power law was repealed.

The power companies' stock plummeted on the stock market.

The world's most unnoticed depression began.

With alarming rapidity an economy based on expensive energy fell apart. The OPEC monolith immediately broke up, and within five months petroleum had fallen to 38¢ a barrel. Its only value was in plastics and as a lubricant, and the oil producing nations had been overproducing for those needs.

The reason the depression wasn't much noticed was because Doghouses Unlimited easily met the demand for their product. Scenting a chance for profit, the government slapped a huge export tax on the doghouses. Doghouses Unlimited retaliated by publishing the complete plans for the doghouse and declaring that foreign companies would not be sued for manufacturing it.

The U.S. government just as quickly removed the huge tax, whereupon Doghouses Unlimited announced that the plans it had published were not complete, and continued to corner the market around the world.

As government after government, through subterfuge, bribery, or, in a few cases, popular revolt, were forced to allow Doghouses Unlimited into their countries, Robert Redford (the doghouse one) became even more of a household word than Robert Redford (the old-time actor). Folk legends which had formerly been ascribed to Kuan Yu, Paul Bunyan, or Gautama Buddha became, gradually, attached to Robert Doghouse Redford.

And, at last, every family in the world that wanted

one had a cheap energy source, an unlimited energy source, and everybody was happy. So happy that they shared their newfound plenty with all God's creatures, feeding birds in the winter, leaving bowls of milk for stray cats, and putting dogs in the doghouses.

Mklikluln rested his chin in his hands and reflected on the irony that he had, quite inadvertently, saved the world for the bipedal dominant race, solely as a byproduct of his campaign to get a good home for every dog. But good results are good results, and humanity—either his own or the bipedals—couldn't condemn him completely for his murder of an Arab political prisoner the year before.

"What will happen when you come?" he asked his people, though of course none of them could hear him. "I've saved the world—but when these creatures, bright as they are, come in contact with our infinitely superior intelligence, won't it destroy them? Won't they suffer in humiliation to realize that we are so much more powerful than they; that we can span galactic distances at the speed of light, communicate telepathically, separate our minds and allow our bodies to die while we float in space unscathed, and then, at the beck of a simple machine, come instantaneously and inhabit the bodies of animals completely different from our former bodies?"

He worried—but his responsibility to his own people was clear. If this bipedal race was so proud they could not cope with inferiority, that was not Mklikluln's problem.

He opened the top drawer of his desk in the San Diego headquarters of Doghouses Unlimited, his latest refuge from the interview seekers, and pushed a button on a small box.

From the box, a powerful burst of electromagnetic energy went out to the eighty million doghouses in southern California. Each doghouse relayed the same signal in an unending chain that gradually spread all over the world—wherever doghouses could be found.

When the last doghouse was linked to the network, all the doghouses simultaneously transmitted something else entirely. A signal that only sneered at lightspeed and that crossed light-years almost instantaneously. A signal that called millions of encapsulated minds that slept in their mindfields until they heard the call, woke, and followed the signal back to its source, again at speeds far faster than poor pedestrian light.

They gathered around the larger binary in the third orbit from their new sun, and listened as Mklikluln gave a full report. They were delighted with his work, and commended him highly, before convicting him of murder of an Arabian political prisoner and ordering him to commit suicide. He felt very proud, for the commendation they had given him was rarely awarded, and he smiled as he shot himself.

And then the minds slipped downward toward the doghouses that still called to them.

"Argworfgyardworfl," said Royce's dog as it bounded excitedly through the backyard.

"Dog's gone crazy," Royce said, but his two sons laughed and ran around with the dog as it looped the yard a dozen times, only to fall exhausted in front of the doghouse.

"Griffwigrofrf," the dog said again, panting happily. It trotted up to Royce and nuzzled him.

"Cute little bugger," Royce said.

The dog walked over to a pile of newspapers waiting for a paper drive, pulled the top newspaper off the stack, and began staring at the page.

"I'll be humdingered," said Royce to Junie, who was bringing out the food for their backyard picnic supper. "Dog looks like he's readin' the paper."

"Here, Robby!" shouted Royce's oldest son, Jim. "Here, Robby! Chase a stick."

The dog, having learned how to read and write from the newspaper, chased the stick, brought it back, and instead of surrendering it to Jim's outstretched hand, began to write with it in the dirt.

"Hello, man," wrote the dog. "Perhaps you are surprised to see me writing."

"Well," said Royce, looking at what the dog had written. "Here, Junie, will you look at that. This is some dog, eh?" And he patted the dog's head and sat down to eat. "Now I wonder, is there anybody who'd pay to see a dog do that?"

"We mean no harm to your planet," wrote the dog.

"Jim," said Junie, slapping spoonfuls of potato salad onto paper plates, "you make sure that dog doesn't start scratching around in the petunias."

"C'mere, Robby," said Jim. "Time to tie you up."

"Wrowrf," the dog answered, looking a bit perturbed and backing away from the chain.

"Daddy," said Jim, "the dog won't come when I call anymore."

Impatiently, Royce got up from his chair, his mouth full of chicken salad sandwich. "Doggonit, Jim, if you don't control the dog we'll just have to get rid of it. We only got it for you kids anyway!" And Royce grabbed the dog by the collar and dragged it to where Jimmy held the other end of the chain.

Clip.

"Now you learn to obey, dog, cause if you don't I don't care what tricks you can do, I'll sell ya."

"Owrf."

"Right. Now you remember that."

The dog watched them with sad, almost frightened

eyes all through dinner. Royce began to feel a little guilty, and gave the dog a leftover ham.

That night Royce and Junie seriously discussed whether to show off the dog's ability to write, and decided against it, since the kids loved the dog and it was cruel to use animals to perform tricks. They were, after all, very enlightened people.

And the next morning they discovered that it was a good thing they'd decided that way—because all anyone could talk about was their dog's newfound ability to write, or unscrew garden hoses, or lay and start an entire fire from a cold empty fireplace to a bonfire. "I got the most talented dog in the world," crowed Detweiler, only to retire into grim silence as everyone else in the bowling team bragged about his own dog.

"Mine goes to the bathroom in the toilet now, and flushes it, too!" one boasted.

"And mine can fold an entire laundry, after washing her little paws so nothing gets dirty."

The newspapers were full of the story, too, and it became clear that the sudden intelligence of dogs was a nationwide—a worldwide—phenomenon. Aside from a few superstitious New Guineans, who burned their dogs to death as witches, and some Chinese who didn't let their dogs' strange behavior stop them from their scheduled appointment with the dinnerpot, most people were pleased and proud of the change in their pets.

"Worth twice as much to me now," boasted Bill Wilson, formerly an up-and-coming executive with the damnpowercompany. "Not only fetches the birds, but plucks 'em and cleans 'em and puts 'em in the oven."

And Kay Block smiled and went home to her mastiff, which kept her good company and which she loved very, very much.

* * *

"In the five years since the sudden rise in dog intelligence," said Dr. Wheelwright to his class of graduate students in animal intelligence, "we have learned a tremendous amount about how intelligence arises in animals. The very suddenness of it has caused us to take a second look at evolution. Apparently mutations can be much more complete than we had supposed, at least in the higher functions. Naturally, we will spend much of this semester studying the research on dog intelligence, but for a brief overview:

"At the present time it is believed that dog intelligence surpasses that of the dolphin, though it still falls far short of man's. However, while the dolphin's intelligence is nearly useless to us, the dog can be trained as a valuable, simple household servant, and at last it seems that man is no longer alone on his planet. To which animal such a rise in intelligence will happen next, we cannot say, any more than we can be certain that such a change *will* happen to any other animal."

Question from the class.

"Oh, well, I'm afraid it's like the big bang theory. We can guess and guess at the cause of certain phenomena, but since we can't repeat the event in a laboratory, we will never be quite sure. However, the best guess at present is that some critical mass of total dog population in a certain ratio to the total mass of dog brain was reached that pushed the entire species over the edge into a higher order of intelligence. This change, however, did not affect *all* dogs equally—primarily it affected dogs in civilized areas, leading many to speculate on the possibility that continued exposure to man was a contributing factor. However, the very fact that many dogs, mostly in uncivilized parts of the world, were *not* affected destroys completely the idea that cosmic radiation or some other influence from outer space was responsible for the change. In the first place, any such influence would have been detected by the astronomers constantly watching every wavelength of the night sky, and in the second place, such an influence would have affected all dogs equally."

Another question from a student.

"Who knows? But I doubt it. Dogs, being incapable of speech, though many have learned to write simple sentences in an apparently mnemonic fashion somewhere between the blind repetition of parrots and the more calculating repetition at high speeds by dolphins—um, how did I get into this sentence? I can't get out!"

Student laughter.

"Dogs, I was saying, are incapable of another advance in intelligence, particularly an advance bringing them to equal intellect with man, because they cannot communicate verbally and because they lack hands. They are undoubtedly at their evolutionary peak. It is only fortunate that so many circumstances combined to place man in the situation he has reached. And we can only suppose that somewhere, on some other planet, some other species might have an even more fortunate combination leading to even higher intelligence. But let us hope not!" said the professor, scratching the ears of his dog, B. F. Skinner. "Right, B. F.? Because man may not be able to cope with the presence of a more intelligent race!"

Student laughter.

"Owrowrf," said B. F. Skinner, who had once been called Hihiwnkn on a planet where white hexagons had telepathically conquered time and space; hexagons who had only been brought to this pass by a solar process they had not quite learned how to control. What he wished he could say was, "Don't worry, professor. Humanity will never be fazed by a higher intelligence. It's too damn proud to notice."

But instead he growled a little, lapped some water from a bowl, and lay down in a corner of the lecture room as the professor droned on.

It snowed in September in Kansas in the autumn of the year 2000, and Jim (Don't call me Jimmy anymore, I'm grown up) was out playing with his dog Robby as the first flakes fell.

Robby had been uprooting crabgrass with his teeth and paws, a habit much encouraged by Royce and Junie, when Jim yelled, "Snow!" and a flake landed on the grass in front of the dog. The flake melted immediately, but Robby watched for another, and another, and another. And he saw the whiteness of the flakes, and the delicate six-sided figures so spare and strange and familiar and beautiful, and he wept.

"Mommy!" Jim called out. "It looks like Robby's crying!"

"It's just water in his eyes," Junie called back from the kitchen, where she stood washing radishes in front of an open window. "Dogs don't cry."

But the snow fell deep all over the city that night, and many dogs stood in the snow watching it fall, sharing an unspoken reverie.

"Can't we?" again and again the thought came from a hundred, a thousand minds.

"No, no, no," came the despairing answer. For without fingers of *some* kind, how could they ever build the machines that would let them encapsulate again and leave this planet?

And in their despair, they cursed for the millionth time that fool Mklikluln, who had got them into this.

"Death was too good for the bastard," they agreed,

and in a worldwide vote they removed the commendation they had voted him. And then they all went back to having puppies and teaching them everything they knew.

The puppies had it easier. They had never known their ancestral home, and to them snowflakes were merely fun, and winter was merely cold. And instead of standing out in the snow, they curled up in the warmth of their doghouses and slept.

THE ORIGINIST

LEYEL FORSKA SAT before his lector display, reading through an array of recently published scholarly papers. A holograph of two pages of text hovered in the air before him. The display was rather larger than most people needed their pages to be, since Leyel's eyes were no younger than the rest of him. When he came to the end he did not press the PAGE key to continue the article. Instead he pressed NEXT.

The two pages he had been reading slid backward about a centimeter, joining a dozen previously discarded articles, all standing in the air over the lector. With a soft beep, a new pair of pages appeared in front of the old ones.

Deet spoke up from where she sat eating breakfast. "You're only giving the poor soul *two pages* before you consign him to the wastebin?"

"I'm consigning him to oblivion," Leyel answered cheerfully. "No, I'm consigning him to hell."

"What? Have you rediscovered religion in your old age?"

"I'm creating one. It has no heaven, but it has a terrible everlasting hell for young scholars who think they can make their reputation by attacking my work."

"Ah, you have a theology," said Deet. "Your work is holy writ, and to attack it is blasphemy."

"I welcome *intelligent* attacks. But this young tube-headed professor from—yes, of course, Minus University—"

"Old Minus U?"

"He thinks he can refute me, destroy me, lay me in the dust, and all he has bothered to cite are studies published within the last thousand years."

"The principle of millennial depth is still widely used—"

"The principle of millennial depth is the confession of modern scholars that they are not willing to spend as much effort on research as they do on academic politics. I shattered the principle of millennial depth thirty years ago. I proved that it was—"

"Stupid and outmoded. But my dearest darling sweetheart Leyel, you did it by spending part of the immeasurably vast Forska fortune to search for inaccessible and forgotten archives in every section of the Empire."

"Neglected and decaying. I had to reconstruct half of them."

"It would take a thousand universities' library budgets to match what you spent on research for 'Human Origin on the Null Planet.'"

"But once I spent the money, all those archives were open. They *have* been open for three decades. The *serious* scholars all use them, since millennial depth yields nothing but predigested, preexcreted muck. They search among the turds of rats who have devoured elephants, hoping to find ivory."

"So colorful an image. My breakfast tastes much better now." She slid her tray into the cleaning slot and glared at him. "Why are you so snappish? You used to read me sections from their silly little papers and we'd laugh. Lately you're just nasty."

Leyel sighed. "Maybe it's because I once dreamed of changing the galaxy, and every day's mail brings more evidence that the galaxy refuses to change."

"Nonsense. Hari Seldon has promised that the Empire will fall any day now."

There. She had said Hari's name. Even though she had too much tact to speak openly of what bothered him, she was hinting that Leyel's bad humor was because he was still waiting for Hari Seldon's answer. Maybe so—Leyel wouldn't deny it. It *was* annoying that it had taken Hari so long to respond. Leyel had expected a call the day Hari got his application. At least within the week. But he wasn't going to give her the satisfaction of admitting that the waiting bothered him. "The Empire will be killed by its own refusal to change. I rest my case."

"Well, I hope you have a wonderful morning, growling and grumbling about the stupidity of everyone in origin studies—except your esteemed self."

"Why are you teasing me about my vanity today? I've always been vain."

"I consider it one of your most endearing traits."

"At least I make an effort to live up to my own opinion of myself."

"That's nothing. You even live up to *my* opinion of you." She kissed the bald spot on the top of his head as she breezed by, heading for the bathroom.

Leyel turned his attention to the new essay at the front of the lector display. It was a name he didn't recognize. Fully prepared to find pretentious writing and puerile thought, he was surprised to find himself becoming quite absorbed. This woman had been following a trail of primate studies—a field so long neglected that there simply *were* no papers within the range of millennial depth. Already he knew she was his kind of scholar. She even mentioned the fact that she was using archives opened by the Forska Research Foundation. Leyel was not above being pleased at this tacit expression of gratitude.

It seemed that the woman—a Dr. Thoren Magolissian—had been following Leyel's lead, searching for the *principles* of human origin rather than wasting time on the irrelevant search for one particular planet. She had uncovered a trove of primate research from three millennia ago, which was based on chimpanzee and gorilla studies dating back to seven thousand years ago. The earliest of these had referred to original research so old it may have been conducted before the founding of the Empire—but those most ancient reports had not yet been located. They probably didn't exist any more. Texts abandoned for more than five thousand years were very hard to restore; texts older than eight thousand years were simply unreadable. It was tragic, how many texts had been "stored" by librarians who never checked them, never refreshed or recopied them. Presiding over vast archives that had lost every scrap of readable information. All neatly catalogued, of course, so you knew *exactly* what it was that humanity had lost forever.

Never mind.

Magolissian's article. What startled Leyel was her conclusion that primitive language capability seemed to be inherent in the primate mind. Even in primates incapable of speech, other symbols could easily be learned—at least for simple nouns and verbs—and the nonhuman primates could come up with sentences and ideas that had never been spoken to them. This meant that mere production of language, per se, was prehuman, or at least not the determining factor of humanness.

It was a dazzling thought. It meant that the difference between humans and nonhumans—the real origin of humans in recognizably human form—was postlinguistic. Of course this came as a direct contradiction of one of Leyel's own assertions in an early paper—he had said that "since language is what separates human from beast, historical linguistics may provide the key to human origins"—but this was the sort of contradiction he welcomed. He wished he could shout at the other fellow, make him look at Magolissian's article. See? This is how to do it! Challenge my assumption, not my conclusion, and do it with new evidence instead of trying to twist the old stuff. Cast a light in the darkness, don't just churn up the same old sediment at the bottom of the river.

Before he could get into the main body of the article, however, the house computer informed him that someone was at the door of the apartment. It was a message that crawled along the bottom of the lector display. Leyel pressed the key that brought the message to the front, in letters large enough to read. For the thousandth time he wished that sometime in the decamillennia of human history, somebody had invented a computer capable of *speech*.

"Who is it?" Leyel typed.

A moment's wait, while the house computer interrogated the visitor.

The answer appeared on the lector: "Secure courier with a message for Leyel Forska."

The very fact that the courier had got past house security meant that it was genuine—and important. Leyel typed again. "From?"

Another pause. "Hari Seldon of the Encyclopedia Galactica Foundation."

Leyel was out of his chair in a moment. He got to the door even before the house computer could open it, and without a word took the message in his hands. Fumbling a bit, he pressed the top and bottom of the black glass lozenge to prove by fingerprint that it was he, by body temperature and pulse that he was alive to receive it. Then, when the courier and her bodyguards were gone, he dropped the message into the chamber of his lector and watched the page appear in the air before him.

At the top was a three-dimensional version of the logo of Hari's Encyclopedia Foundation. Soon to be my insignia as well, thought Leyel. Hari Seldon and I, the two greatest scholars of our time, joined together in a project whose scope surpasses anything ever attempted by any man or group of men. The gathering together of all the knowledge of the Empire in a systematic, easily accessible way, to preserve it through the coming time of anarchy so that a new civilization can quickly rise out of the ashes of the old. Hari had the vision to foresee the need. And I, Leyel Forska, have the understanding of all the old archives that will make the Encyclopedia Galactica possible.

Leyel started reading with a confidence born of experience; had he ever really desired anything and been denied?

My dear friend:

I was surprised and honored to see an application from you and insisted on writing your answer personally. It is gratifying beyond measure that you believe in the Foundation enough to apply to take part. I can truthfully tell you that we have received no application from any other scholar of your distinction and accomplishment.

Of course, thought Leyel. There *is* no other scholar of my stature, except Hari himself, and perhaps Deet, once her current work is published. At least we have no equals by the standards that Hari and I have always recognized as valid. Hari created the science of psychohistory. I transformed and revitalized the field of originism.

And yet the tone of Hari's letter was wrong. It sounded like—flattery. That was it. Hari was softening the coming blow. Leyel knew before reading it what the next paragraph would say.

Nevertheless, Leyel, I must reply in the negative. The Foundation on Terminus is designed to collect and preserve knowledge. Your life's work has been devoted to expanding it. You are the opposite of the sort of researcher we need. Far better for you to remain on Trantor and continue your inestimably valuable studies, while lesser men and women exile themselves on Terminus.

Your servant,
Hari

Did Hari imagine Leyel to be so vain he would read these flattering words and preen himself contentedly? Did he think Leyel would believe that this was the real reason his application was being denied? Could Hari Seldon misknow a man so badly?

Impossible. Hari Seldon, of all people in the Empire, knew how to know other people. True, his great work in psychohistory dealt with large masses of people, with populations and probabilities. But Hari's fascination with populations had grown out of his interest in and understanding of individuals. Besides, he and Hari had been friends since Hari first arrived on Trantor. Hadn't a grant from Leyel's own research fund financed most of Hari's original research? Hadn't they held long conversations in the early days, tossing ideas back and forth, each helping the other hone his thoughts? They may not have seen each other much in the last—what, five years? Six?—but they were adults, not children. They didn't need constant visits in order to remain friends. And this was not the letter a true friend would send to Leyel Forska. Even if, doubtful as it might seem, Hari Seldon really meant to turn him down, he would not suppose for a moment that Leyel would be content with a letter like *this*.

Surely Hari would have known that it would be like a taunt to Leyel Forska. "Lesser men and women," indeed! The Foundation on Terminus was so valuable to Hari Seldon that he had been willing to risk death on charges of treason in order to launch the project. It was unlikely in the extreme that he would populate Terminus with second-raters. No, this was the form letter sent to placate prominent scholars who were judged unfit for the Foundation. Hari would have known Leyel would immediately recognize it as such.

There was only one possible conclusion. "Hari could not have written this letter," Leyel said.

"Of course he could," Deet told him, blunt as always. She had come out of the bathroom in her dressing gown and read the letter over his shoulder.

"If *you* think so then I truly *am* hurt," said Leyel. He got up, poured a cup of peshat, and began to sip it. He studiously avoided looking at Deet.

"Don't pout, Leyel. Think of the problems Hari is facing. He has so little time, so much to do. A hundred thousand people to transport to Terminus, most

of the resources of the Imperial Library to duplicate—"

"He already *had* those people—"

"All in six months since his trial ended. No wonder we haven't seen him, socially or professionally,
in—years. A decade!"

"You're saying that he no longer knows me? Unthinkable."

"I'm saying that he knows you very well. He knew
you would recognize his message as a form letter.
He also knew that you would understand at once
what this meant."

"Well, then, my dear, he overestimated me. I do
not understand what it means, unless it means he
did not send it himself."

"Then you're getting old, and I'm ashamed of you.
I shall deny we are married and pretend you are my
idiot uncle whom I allow to live with me out of
charity. I'll tell the children they were illegitimate.
They'll be very sad to learn they won't inherit a bit
of the Forska estate."

He threw a crumb of toast at her. "You are a cruel
and disloyal wench, and I regret raising you out of
poverty and obscurity. I only did it for pity, you
know."

This was an old tease of theirs. She had commanded a decent fortune in her own right, though of
course Leyel's dwarfed it. And, technically, he *was*
her uncle, since her stepmother was Leyel's older
half sister Zenna. It was all very complicated. Zenna
had been born to Leyel's mother when she was married to someone else—before she married Leyel's father. So while Zenna was well dowered, she had no
part in the Forska fortune. Leyel's father, amused at
the situation, once remarked, "Poor Zenna. Lucky
you. My semen flows with gold." Such are the iro-
nies that come with great fortune. Poor people don't

have to make such terrible distinctions between their children.

Deet's father, however, assumed that a Forska was a Forska, and so, several years after Deet had married Leyel, he decided that it wasn't enough for his daughter to be married to uncountable wealth, he ought to do the same favor for himself. He *said*, of course, that he loved Zenna to distraction, and cared nothing for fortune, but only Zenna believed him. Therefore she married him. Thus Leyel's half sister became Deet's stepmother, which made Leyel his wife's stepuncle—and his own stepuncle-in-law. A dynastic tangle that greatly amused Leyel and Deet.

Leyel of course compensated for Zenna's lack of inheritance with a lifetime stipend that amounted to ten times her husband's income each year. It had the happy effect of keeping Deet's old father in love with Zenna.

Today, though, Leyel was only half teasing Deet. There were times when he needed her to confirm him, to uphold him. As often as not she contradicted him instead. Sometimes this led him to rethink his position and emerge with a better understanding— thesis, antithesis, synthesis, the dialectic of marriage, the result of being espoused to one's intellectual equal. But sometimes her challenge was painful, unsatisfying, infuriating.

Oblivious to his underlying anger, she went on. "Hari assumed that you would take his form letter for what it is—a definite, final no. He isn't hedging, he's not engaging in some bureaucratic deviousness, he isn't playing politics with you. He isn't stringing you along in hopes of getting more financial support from you—if that were it you know he'd simply ask."

"I already know what he *isn't* doing."

"What he *is* doing is turning you down with finality. An answer from which there is no appeal. He gave you credit for having the wit to understand that."

"How convenient for you if I believe that."

Now, at last, she realized he was angry. "What's that supposed to mean?"

"You can stay here on Trantor and continue your work with all your bureaucratic friends."

Her face went cold and hard. "I told you. I am quite happy to go to Terminus with you."

"Am I supposed to believe that, even now? Your research in community formation within the Imperial bureaucracy cannot possibly continue on Terminus."

"I've already done the most important research. What I'm doing with the Imperial Library staff is a test."

"Not even a scientific one, since there's no control group."

She looked annoyed. "I'm the one who told *you* that."

It was true. Leyel had never even heard of control groups until she taught him the whole concept of experimentation. She had found it in some very old child-development studies from the 3100s G.E. "Yes, I was just agreeing with you," he said lamely.

"The point is, I can write my book as well on Terminus as anywhere else. And yes, Leyel, you *are* supposed to believe that I'm happy to go with you, because I said it, and therefore it's so."

"I believe that you believe it. I also believe that in your heart you are very glad that I was turned down, and you don't want me to pursue this matter any further so there'll be no chance of your having to go to the godforsaken end of the universe."

Those had been her words, months ago, when he first proposed applying to join the Seldon Foundation. "We'd have to go to the godforsaken end of the universe!" She remembered now as well as he did. "You'll hold that against me forever, won't you! I think I deserve to be forgiven my first reaction. I did consent to go, didn't I?"

"Consent, yes. But you never wanted to."

"Well, Leyel, that's true enough. I never *wanted* to. Is that your idea of what our marriage means? That I'm to subsume myself in you so deeply that even your desires become my own? I thought it was enough that from time to time we consent to sacrifice for each other. I never expected you to *want* to leave the Forska estates and come to Trantor when I needed to do my research here. I only asked you to *do* it—whether you wanted to or not—because *I* wanted it. I recognized and respected your sacrifice. I am very angry to discover that *my* sacrifice is despised."

"*Your* sacrifice remains unmade. We are still on Trantor."

"Then by all means, go to Hari Seldon, plead with him, humiliate yourself, and then realize that what I told you is true. He doesn't want you to join his Foundation and he will not allow you to go to Terminus."

"Are you so certain of that?"

"No, I'm not *certain*. It merely seems likely."

"I *will* go to Terminus, if he'll have me. I hope I don't have to go alone."

He regretted the words as soon as he said them. She froze as if she had been slapped, a look of horror on her face. Then she turned and ran from the room. A few moments later, he heard the chime announcing that the door of their apartment had opened. She was gone.

No doubt to talk things over with one of her friends. Women have no sense of discretion. They cannot keep domestic squabbles to themselves. She will tell them all the awful things I said, and they'll cluck and tell her it's what she must expect from a husband, husbands demand that their wives make all the sacrifices, you poor thing, poor poor Deet. Well, Leyel didn't begrudge her this barnyard of sympathetic hens. It was part of human nature, he knew, for women to form a perpetual conspiracy against the men in their lives. That was why women have always been so certain that men also formed a conspiracy against *them*.

How ironic, he thought. Men have no such solace. Men do not bind themselves so easily into communities. A man is always aware of the possibility of betrayal, of conflicting loyalties. Therefore when a man *does* commit himself truly, it is a rare and sacred bond, not to be cheapened by discussing it with others. Even a marriage, even a *good* marriage like theirs—*his* commitment might be absolute, but he could never trust hers so completely.

Leyel had buried himself within the marriage, helping and serving and loving Deet with all his heart. She was wrong, completely wrong about his coming to Trantor. He hadn't come as a sacrifice, against his will, solely because she wanted to come. On the contrary: because she wanted so much to come, he *also* wanted to come, changing even his desires to coincide with hers. She commanded his very heart, because it was impossible for him not to desire anything that would bring her happiness.

But she, no, she could not do that for him. If *she* went to Terminus, it would be as a noble sacrifice. She would never let him forget that she hadn't wanted to. To him, their marriage was his very soul. To Deet, their marriage was just a friendship with sex. Her soul belonged as much to these other women as to him. By dividing her loyalties, she fragmented them; none were strong enough to sway her deepest desires. Thus he discovered what he supposed all faithful men eventually discover—that no human relationship is ever anything but tentative. There is no such thing as an unbreakable bond between people. Like the particles in the nucleus of the atom. They are bound by the strongest forces in the universe, and yet they can be shattered, they can break.

Nothing can last. Nothing is, finally, what it once seemed to be. Deet and he had had a perfect marriage until there came a stress that exposed its imperfection. Anyone who thinks he has a perfect marriage, a perfect friendship, a perfect trust of any kind, he only believes this because the stress that will break it has not yet come. He might die with the illusion of happiness, but all he has proven is that sometimes death comes before betrayal. If you live long enough, betrayal will inevitably come.

Such were the dark thoughts that filled Leyel's mind as he made his way through the maze of the city of Trantor. Leyel did not seal himself inside a private car when he went about in the planet-wide city. He refused the trappings of wealth; he insisted on experiencing the life of Trantor as an ordinary man. Thus his bodyguards were under strict instructions to remain discreet, interfering with no pedestrians except those carrying weapons, as revealed by a subtle and instantaneous scan.

It was much more expensive to travel through the city this way, of course—every time he stepped out the door of his simple apartment, nearly a hundred high-paid bribeproof employees went into action. A weaponproof car would have been much cheaper. But Leyel was determined not to be imprisoned by his wealth.

So he walked through the corridors of the city, riding cabs and tubes, standing in lines like anyone else. He felt the great city throbbing with life around him. Yet such was his dark and melancholy mood today that the very life of the city filled him with a sense of betrayal and loss. Even you, great Trantor, the Imperial City, even you will be betrayed by the people who made you. Your empire will desert you, and you will become a pathetic remnant of yourself, plated with the metal of a thousand worlds and asteroids as a reminder that once the whole galaxy promised to serve you forever, and now you are abandoned. Hari Seldon had seen it. Hari Seldon understood the changeability of humankind. He knew that the great empire would fall, and so—unlike the government, which depended on things remaining the same forever—Hari Seldon could actually take steps to ameliorate the Empire's fall, to prepare on Terminus a womb for the rebirth of human greatness. Hari was creating the future. It was unthinkable that he could mean to cut Leyel Forska out of it.

The Foundation, now that it had legal existence and Imperial funding, had quickly grown into a busy complex of offices in the four-thousand-year-old Putassuran Building. Because the Putassuran was originally built to house the Admiralty shortly after the great victory whose name it bore, it had an air of triumph, of monumental optimism about it—rows of soaring arches, a vaulted atrium with floating bubbles of light rising and dancing in channeled columns of air. In recent centuries the building had served as a site for informal public concerts and lectures, with the offices used to house the Museum Authority. It had come empty only a year before Hari Seldon was granted the right to form his Foundation, but it seemed as though it had been built for this very purpose. Everyone was hurrying this way and that, always seeming to be on urgent business, and yet also happy to be part of a noble cause. There had been no noble causes in the Empire for a long, long time.

Leyel quickly threaded his way through the maze that protected the Foundation's director from casual interruption. Other men and women, no doubt, had tried to see Hari Seldon and failed, put off by this functionary or that. Hari Seldon is a very busy man. Perhaps if you make an appointment for later. Seeing him today is out of the question. He's in meetings all afternoon and evening. Do call before coming next time.

But none of this happened to Leyel Forska. All he had to do was say, "Tell Mr. Seldon that Mr. Forska wishes to continue a conversation." However much awe they might have of Hari Seldon, however they might intend to obey his orders not to be disturbed, they all knew that Leyel Forska was the universal exception. Even Linge Chen would be called out of a meeting of the Commission of Public Safety to speak with Forska, especially if Leyel went to the trouble of coming in person.

The ease with which he gained entry to see Hari, the excitement and optimism of the people, of the building itself, had encouraged Leyel so much that he was not at all prepared for Hari's first words.

"Leyel, I'm surprised to see you. I thought you would understand that my message was final."

It was the worst thing that Hari could possibly have said. Had Deet been right after all? Leyel studied Hari's face for a moment, trying to see some sign of change. Was all that had passed between them through the years forgotten now? Had Hari's friendship never been real? No. Looking at Hari's face, a bit more lined and wrinkled now, Leyel saw still the same earnestness, the same plain honesty that had always been there. So instead of expressing the rage and disappointment that he felt, Leyel answered carefully, leaving the way open for Hari to change his mind. "I understood that your message was deceptive, and therefore could not be final."

Hari looked a little angry. "Deceptive?"

"I know which men and women you've been taking into your Foundation. They are not second-raters."

"Compared to you they are," said Hari. "They're academics, which means they're clerks. Sorters and interpreters of information."

"So am I. So are all scholars today. Even *your* inestimable theories arose from sorting through a trillion bytes of data and interpreting it."

Hari shook his head. "I didn't just sort through data. I had an idea in my head. So did you. Few others do. You and I are expanding human knowledge. Most of the rest are only digging it up in one place and piling it in another. That's what the Encyclopedia Galactica *is*. A new pile."

"Nevertheless, Hari, you know and I know that this is not the real reason you turned me down. And don't tell me that it's because Leyel Forska's presence on Terminus would call undue attention to the project. You already have so much attention from the government that you can hardly breathe."

"You are unpleasantly persistent, Leyel. I don't like even having this conversation."

"That's too bad, Hari. I want to be part of your project. I would contribute to it more than any other person who might join it. I'm the one who plunged back into the oldest and most valuable archives and exposed the shameful amount of data loss that had arisen from neglect. I'm the one who launched the computerized extrapolation of shattered documents that your Encyclopedia—"

"Absolutely depends on. Our work would be impossible without your accomplishments."

"And yet you turned me down, and with a crudely flattering note."

"I didn't mean to give offense, Leyel."

"You also didn't mean to tell the truth. But you *will* tell me, Hari, or I'll simply go to Terminus anyway."

"The Commission of Public Safety has given my Foundation absolute control over who may or may not come to Terminus."

"Hari. You know perfectly well that all I have to do is hint to some lower-level functionary that I want to go to Terminus. Chen will hear of it within minutes, and within an hour he'll grant me an exception to your charter. If I did that, and if you fought it, you'd lose your charter. You *know* that. If you want me not to go to Terminus, it isn't enough to forbid me. You must persuade me that I ought not to be there."

Hari closed his eyes and sighed. "I don't think you're willing to be persuaded, Leyel. Go if you must."

For a moment Leyel wondered if Hari was giving in. But no, that was impossible, not so easily. "Oh, yes, Hari, but then I'd find myself cut off from everybody else on Terminus except my own serving people. Fobbed off with useless assignments. Cut out of the real meetings."

"That goes without saying," said Hari. "You are not part of the Foundation, you will not be, you cannot be. And if you try to use your wealth and influence to force your way in, you will succeed only in annoying the Foundation, not in joining it. Do you understand me?"

Only too well, thought Leyel in shame. Leyel knew perfectly well the limitations of power, and it was beneath him to have tried to bluster his way into getting something that could only be given freely. "Forgive me, Hari. I wouldn't have tried to force you. You know I don't do that sort of thing."

"I know you've never done it since we've been friends, Leyel. I was afraid that I was learning something new about you." Hari sighed. He turned away for a long moment, then turned back with a different look on his face, a different kind of energy in his voice. Leyel knew that look, that vigor. It meant Hari was taking him more deeply into his confidence. "Leyel, you have to understand, I'm not just creating an encyclopedia on Terminus."

Immediately Leyel grew worried. It had taken a great deal of Leyel's influence to persuade the government not to have Hari Seldon summarily exiled when he first started disseminating copies of his treatises about the impending fall of the Empire. They were sure Seldon was plotting treason, and had even put him on trial, where Seldon finally persuaded them that all he wanted to do was create the Encyclopedia Galactica, the repository of all the wisdom of the Empire. Even now, if Seldon confessed some ulterior motive, the government would move against him. It was to be assumed that the Pubs—Public Safety Office—were recording this entire conversation. Even Leyel's influence couldn't stop them if they had a confession from Hari's own mouth.

"No, Leyel, don't be nervous. My meaning is plain enough. For the Encyclopedia Galactica to succeed, I have to create a thriving city of scholars on Terminus. A colony full of men and women with fragile egos and unstemmable ambition, all of them trained in vicious political infighting at the most dangerous

and terrible schools of bureaucratic combat in the
Empire—the universities."

"Are you actually telling me you won't let me
join your Foundation because I never attended one
of those pathetic universities? My self-education is
worth ten times their lockstep force-fed pseudo-
learning."

"Don't make your antiuniversity speech to me,
Leyel. I'm saying that one of my most important
concerns in staffing the Foundation is compatibility.
I won't bring anyone to Terminus unless I believe
he—or *she*—would be happy there."

The emphasis Hari put on the word *she* suddenly
made everything clearer. "This isn't about me at all,
is it?" Leyel said. "It's about Deet."

Hari said nothing.

"You know she doesn't want to go. You know she
prefers to remain on Trantor. And that's why you
aren't taking me! Is that it?"

Reluctantly, Hari conceded the point. "It does
have something to do with Deet, yes."

"Don't you know how much the Foundation
means to me?" demanded Leyel. "Don't you know
how much I'd give up to be part of your work?"

Hari sat there in silence for a moment. Then he
murmured, "Even Deet?"

Leyel almost blurted out an answer. Yes, of course,
even Deet, anything for this great work.

But Hari's measured gaze stopped him. One thing
Leyel had known since they first met at a conference
back in their youth was that Hari would not stand
for another man's self-deception. They had sat next
to each other at a presentation by a demographer
who had a considerable reputation at the time. Leyel
watched as Hari destroyed the poor man's thesis
with a few well-aimed questions. The demographer
was furious. Obviously he had not seen the flaws

in his own argument—but now that they had been shown to him, he refused to admit that they were flaws at all.

Afterward, Hari had said to Leyel, "I've done him a favor."

"How, by giving him someone to hate?" said Leyel.

"No. Before, he believed his own unwarranted conclusions. He had deceived himself. Now he doesn't believe them."

"But he still propounds them."

"So—now he's more of a liar and less of a fool. I have improved his private integrity. His public morality I leave up to him."

Leyel remembered this and knew that if he told Hari he could give up Deet for any reason, even to join the Foundation, it would be worse than a lie. It would be foolishness.

"It's a terrible thing you've done," said Leyel. "You know that Deet is part of myself. I can't give her up to join your Foundation. But now for the rest of our lives together I'll know that I could have gone, if not for her. You've given me wormwood and gall to drink, Hari."

Hari nodded slowly. "I hoped that when you read my note you'd realize I didn't want to tell you more. I hoped you wouldn't come to me and ask. I can't lie to you, Leyel. I wouldn't if I could. But I did withhold information, as much as possible. To spare us both problems."

"It didn't work."

"It isn't Deet's fault, Leyel. It's who she is. She belongs on Trantor, not on Terminus. And you belong with her. It's a fact, not a decision. We'll never discuss this again."

"No," said Leyel.

They sat there for a long minute, gazing steadily

at each other. Leyel wondered if he and Hari would ever speak again. No. Never again. I don't ever want to see you again, Hari Seldon. You've made me regret the one unregrettable decision of my life—Deet. You've made me wish, somewhere in my heart, that I'd never married her. Which is like making me wish I'd never been born.

Leyel got up from his chair and left the room without a word. When he got outside, he turned to the reception room in general, where several people were waiting to see Seldon. "Which of you are mine?" he asked.

Two women and one man stood up immediately. "Fetch me a secure car and a driver."

Without a glance at each other, one of them left on the errand. The others fell in step beside Leyel. Subtlety and discretion were over for the moment. Leyel had no wish to mingle with the people of Trantor now. He only wanted to go home.

Hari Seldon left his office by the back way and soon found his way to Chandrakar Matt's cubicle in the Department of Library Relations. Chanda looked up and waved, then effortlessly slid her chair back until it was in the exact position required. Hari picked up a chair from the neighboring cubicle and, again without showing any particular care, set it exactly where it had to be.

Immediately the computer installed inside Chanda's lector recognized the configuration. It recorded Hari's costume of the day from three angles and superimposed the information on a long-stored holoimage of Chanda and Hari conversing pleasantly. Then, once Hari was seated, it began displaying the hologram. The hologram exactly matched the positions of the real Hari and Chanda, so that infrared sensors would show no discrepancy between image and fact. The only thing different was the faces—the movement of lips, blinking of eyes, the expressions. Instead of matching the words Hari and Chanda were actually saying, they matched the words being pushed into the air outside the cubicle— a harmless, randomly chosen series of remarks that took into account recent events so that no one would suspect that it was a canned conversation.

It was one of Hari's few opportunities for candid conversation that the Pubs would not overhear, and he and Chanda protected it carefully. They never spoke long enough or often enough that the Pubs would wonder at their devotion to such empty conversations. Much of their communication was subliminal—a sentence would stand for a paragraph, a word for a sentence, a gesture for a word. But when the conversation was done, Chanda knew where to go from there, what to do next; and Hari was reassured that his most important work was going on behind the smokescreen of the Foundation.

"For a moment I thought he might actually leave her."

"Don't underestimate the lure of the Encyclopedia."

"I fear I've wrought too well, Chanda. Do you think someday the Encyclopedia Galactica might actually exist?"

"It's a good idea. Good people are inspired by it. It wouldn't serve its purpose if they weren't. What should I tell Deet?"

"Nothing, Chanda. The fact that Leyel is staying, that's enough for her."

"If he changes his mind, will you actually let him go to Terminus?"

"If he changes his mind, then he *must* go, because if he would leave Deet, he's not the man for us."

"Why not just tell him? Invite him?"

"He must become part of the Second Foundation without realizing it. He must do it by natural inclination, not by a summons from me, and above all not by his own ambition."

"Your standards are so high, Hari, it's no wonder so few measure up. Most people in the Second Foundation don't even know that's what it is. They think they're librarians. Bureaucrats. They think Deet is an anthropologist who works among them in order to study them."

"Not so. They once thought that, but now they think of Deet as one of them. As one of the *best* of them. She's defining what it means to be a librarian. She's making them proud of the name."

"Aren't you ever troubled, Hari, by the fact that in the practice of your art—"

"My *science.*"

"Your meddlesome magical *craft,* you old wizard, you don't fool *me* with all your talk of science. I've seen the scripts of the holographs you're preparing for the vault on Terminus."

"That's all a pose."

"I can just imagine you saying those words. Looking perfectly satisfied with yourself. 'If you care to smoke, I wouldn't mind . . . Pause for chuckle . . . Why should I? I'm not really here.' Pure showmanship."

Hari waved off the idea. The computer quickly found a bit of dialogue to fit his gesture, so the false scene would not seem false. "No, I'm *not* troubled by the fact that in the practice of my *science* I change the lives of human beings. Knowledge has always changed people's lives. The only difference is that I *know* I'm changing them—and the changes I introduce are planned, they're under control. Did the man who invented the first artificial light—what was it,

animal fat with a wick? A light-emitting diode?—
did he realize what it would do to humankind, to be
given power over night?"

As always, Chanda deflated him the moment he
started congratulating himself. "In the first place, it
was almost certainly a woman, and in the second
place, she knew exactly what she was doing. It allowed her to find her way through the house at night.
Now she could put her nursing baby in another bed,
in another room, so she could get some sleep at night
without fear of rolling over and smothering the
child."

Hari smiled. "If artificial light was invented by a
woman, it was certainly a prostitute, to extend her
hours of work."

Chanda grinned. She did not laugh—it was too
hard for the computer to come up with jokes to explain laughter. "We'll watch Leyel carefully, Hari.
How will we know when he's ready, so we can begin
to count on him for protection and leadership?"

"When you already count on him, then he's ready.
When his commitment and loyalty are firm, when
the goals of the Second Foundation are already in his
heart, when he acts them out in his life, then he's
ready."

There was a finality in Hari's tone. The conversation was nearly over.

"By the way, Hari, you were right. No one has
even questioned the omission of any important psychohistorical data from the Foundation library on
Terminus."

"Of course not. Academics never look outside
their own discipline. That's another reason why I'm
glad Leyel isn't going. *He* would notice that the only
psychologist we're sending is Bor Alurin. Then I'd
have to explain more to him than I want. Give my

love to Deet, Chanda. Tell her that her test case is going very well. She'll end up with a husband *and* a community of scientists of the mind."

"Artists. Wizards. Demigods."

"Stubborn misguided women who don't know science when they're doing it. All in the Imperial Library. Till next time, Chanda."

If Deet had asked him about his interview with Hari, if she had commiserated with him about Hari's refusal, his resentment of her might have been uncontainable, he might have lashed out at her and said something that could never be forgiven. Instead, she was perfectly herself, so excited about her work and so beautiful, even with her face showing all the sag and wrinkling of her sixty years, that all Leyel could do was fall in love with her again, as he had so many times in their years together.

"It's working beyond anything I hoped for, Leyel. I'm beginning to hear stories that I created months and years ago, coming back as epic legends. You remember the time I retrieved and extrapolated the accounts of the uprising at Misercordia only three days before the Admiralty needed them?"

"Your finest hour. Admiral Divart still talks about how they used the old battle plots as a strategic guideline and put down the Tellekers' strike in a single three-day operation without loss of a ship."

"You have a mind like a trap, even if you *are* old."

"Sadly, all I can remember is the past."

"Dunce, that's all *anyone* can remember."

He prompted her to go on with her account of today's triumph. "It's an epic legend now?"

"It came back to me without my name on it, and bigger than life. As a reference. Rinjy was talking with some young librarians from one of the inner provinces who were on the standard interlibrary tour, and one of them said something about how you could stay in the Imperial Library on Trantor all your life and never see the real world at all."

Leyel hooted. "Just the thing to say to Rinjy!"

"Exactly. Got her dander up, of course, but the important thing is, she immediately told them the story of how a librarian, *all on her own*, saw the similarity between the Misercordia uprising and the Tellekers' strike. She knew no one at the Admiralty would listen to her unless she brought them all the information at once. So she delved back into the ancient records and found them in deplorable shape—the original data had been stored in glass, but that was forty-two centuries ago, and no one had refreshed the data. None of the secondary sources actually showed the battle plots or ship courses— Misercordia had mostly been written about by biographers, not military historians—"

"Of course. It was Pol Yuensau's first battle, but he was just a pilot, not a commander—"

"I know *you* remember, my intrusive pet. The point is what Rinjy *said* about this mythical librarian."

"You."

"I was standing right there. I don't think Rinjy knew it was me, or she would have said something— she wasn't even in the same division with me then, you know. What matters is that Rinjy heard a version of the story and by the time she told it, it was transformed into a magic hero tale. The prophetic librarian of Trantor."

"What does *that* prove? You *are* a magic hero."

"The way she told it, I did it all on my own initiative—"

"You did. You were assigned to do document extrapolation, and you just happened to start with Misercordia."

"But in Rinjy's version, I had *already* seen its usefulness with the Tellekers' strike. She said the librarian sent it to the Admiralty and only then did they realize it was the key to bloodless victory."

"Librarian saves the Empire."

"Exactly."

"But you did."

"But I didn't *mean* to. And Admiralty requested the information—the only really extraordinary thing was that I had already finished two weeks of document restoration—"

"Which you did brilliantly."

"Using programs you had helped design, thank you very much, O Wise One, as you indirectly praise yourself. It was sheer coincidence that I could give them exactly what they wanted within five minutes of their asking. But now it's a hero story within the community of librarians. In the Imperial Library itself, and now spreading outward to all the other libraries."

"This is so anecdotal, Deet. I don't see how you can publish this."

"Oh, I don't intend to. Except perhaps in the introduction. What matters to me is that it proves my theory."

"It has no statistical validity."

"It proves it to *me*. I know that my theories of community formation are true. That the vigor of a community depends on the allegiance of its members, and the allegiance can be created and enhanced by the dissemination of epic stories."

"She speaks the language of academia. I should be writing this down, so you don't have to think up all those words again."

"Stories that make the community seem more important, more central to human life. Because Rinjy could tell this story, it made her more proud to be a librarian, which increased her allegiance to the community and gave the community more power within her."

"You are possessing their souls."

"And they've got mine. Together our souls are possessing each other."

There was the rub. Deet's role in the library had begun as applied research—joining the library staff in order to confirm her theory of community formation. But that task was impossible to accomplish without in fact becoming a committed part of the library community. It was Deet's dedication to serious science that had brought them together. Now that very dedication was stealing her away. It would hurt her more to leave the library than it would to lose Leyel.

Not true. Not true at all, he told himself sternly. Self-pity leads to self-deception. Exactly the opposite is true—it would hurt her more to lose Leyel than to leave her community of librarians. That's why she consented to go to Terminus in the first place. But could he blame her for being glad that she didn't have to choose? Glad that she could have both?

Yet even as he beat down the worst of the thoughts arising from his disappointment, he couldn't keep some of the nastiness from coming out in his conversation. "How will you know when your experiment is over?"

She frowned. "It'll never be *over*, Leyel. They're all really librarians—I don't pick them up by the tails like mice and put them back in their cages when the experiment's done. At some point I'll simply stop, that's all, and write my book."

"Will you?"

"Write the book? I've written books before, I think I can do it again."

"I meant, will you stop?"

"When, now? Is this some test of my love for you, Leyel? Are you jealous of my friendships with Rinjy and Animet and Fin and Urik?"

No! Don't accuse me of such childish, selfish feelings!

But before he could snap back his denial, he knew that his denial would be false.

"Sometimes I am, yes, Deet. Sometimes I think you're happier with them."

And because he had spoken honestly, what could have become a bitter quarrel remained a conversation. "But I *am*, Leyel," she answered, just as frankly. "It's because when I'm with them, I'm creating something new, I'm creating something *with them*. It's exciting, invigorating, I'm discovering new things every day, in every word they say, every smile, every tear someone sheds, every sign that being one of *us* is the most important thing in their lives."

"I can't compete with that."

"No, you can't, Leyel. But you complete it. Because it would all mean nothing, it would be more frustrating than exhilarating if I couldn't come back to you every day and tell you what happened. You always understand what it means, you're always excited for me, you validate my experience."

"I'm your audience. Like a parent."

"Yes, old man. Like a husband. Like a child. Like the person I love most in all the world. You are my root. I make a brave show out there, all branches and bright leaves in the sunlight, but I come here to suck the water of life from your soil."

"Leyel Forska, the font of capillarity. You are the tree, and I am the dirt."

"Which happens to be full of fertilizer." She kissed him. A kiss reminiscent of younger days. An invitation, which he gladly accepted.

A softened section of floor served them as an impromptu bed. At the end, he lay beside her, his arm across her waist, his head on her shoulder, his lips brushing the skin of her breast. He remembered when her breasts were small and firm, perched on her chest like small monuments to her potential. Now when she lay on her back they were a ruin, eroded by age so they flowed off her chest to either side, resting wearily on her arms.

"You are a magnificent woman," he whispered, his lips tickling her skin.

Their slack and flabby bodies were now capable of greater passion than when they were taut and strong. Before, they were all potential. That's what we love in youthful bodies, the teasing potential. Now hers is a body of accomplishment. Three fine children were the blossoms, then the fruit of this tree, gone off and taken root somewhere else. The tension of youth could now give way to a relaxation of the flesh. There were no more promises in their lovemaking. Only fulfillment.

She murmured softly in his ear, "That was a ritual, by the way. Community maintenance."

"So I'm just another experiment?"

"A fairly successful one. I'm testing to see if this little community can last until one of us drops."

"What if you drop first? Who'll write the paper then?"

"You will. But you'll sign my name to it. I want the Imperial medal for it. Posthumously. Glue it to my memorial stone."

"I'll wear it myself. If you're selfish enough to leave all the real work to me, you don't deserve anything better than a cheap replica."

She slapped his back. "You are a nasty selfish old man, then. The real thing or nothing."

He felt the sting of her slap as if he deserved it. A nasty selfish old man. If she only knew how right she was. There had been a moment in Hari's office when he'd almost said the words that would deny all that there was between them. The words that would cut her out of his life. Go to Terminus without her! I would be more myself if they took my heart, my liver, my brain.

How could I have thought I wanted to go to Terminus, anyway? To be surrounded by academics of the sort I most despise, struggling with them to get the encyclopedia properly designed. They'd each fight for their petty little province, never catching the vision of the whole, never understanding that the encyclopedia would be valueless if it were compartmentalized. It would be a life in hell, and in the end he'd lose, because the academic mind was incapable of growth or change.

It was here on Trantor that he could still accomplish something. Perhaps even solve the question of human origin, at least to his own satisfaction—and perhaps he could do it soon enough that he could get his discovery included in the Encyclopedia Galactica before the Empire began to break down at the edges, cutting Terminus off from the rest of the Galaxy.

It was like a shock of static electricity passing through his brain; he even saw an afterglow of light around the edges of his vision, as if a spark had jumped some synaptic gap.

"What a sham," he said.

"Who, you? Me?"

"Hari Seldon. All this talk about his Foundation to create the Encyclopedia Galactica."

"Careful, Leyel." It was almost impossible that the Pubs could have found a way to listen to what went on in Leyel Forska's own apartments. Almost.

"He told me twenty years ago. It was one of his first psychohistorical projections. The Empire will crumble at the edges first. He projected it would happen within the next generation. The figures were crude then. He must have it down to the year now. Maybe even the month. Of course he put his Foundation on Terminus. A place so remote that when the edges of the Empire fray, it will be among the first threads lost. Cut off from Trantor. Forgotten at once!"

"What good would *that* do, Leyel? They'd never hear of any new discoveries then."

"What you said about us. A tree. Our children like the fruit of that tree."

"I never said that."

"I thought it, then. He is dropping his Foundation out on Terminus like the fruit of Empire. To grow into a new Empire by and by."

"You frighten me, Leyel. If the Pubs ever heard you say that—"

"That crafty old fox. That sly, deceptive—he never actually lied to me, but of course he couldn't send me there. If the Forska fortune was tied up with Terminus, the Empire would never lose track of the place. The edges might fray elsewhere, but never there. Putting me on Terminus would be the undoing of the *real* project." It was such a relief. Of course Hari couldn't tell him, not with the Pubs listening, but it had nothing to do with him or Deet. It wouldn't have to be a barrier between them after all. It was just one of the penalties of being the keeper of the Forska fortune.

"Do you really think so?" asked Deet.

"I was a fool not to see it before. But Hari was a fool too if he thought I wouldn't guess it."

"Maybe he expects you to guess everything."

"Oh, nobody could ever come up with *everything* Hari's doing. He has more twists and turns in his brain than a hyperpath through core space. No matter how you labor to pick your way through, you'll always find Hari at the end of it, nodding happily and congratulating you on coming this far. He's ahead of us all. He's already planned everything, and the rest of us are doomed to follow in his footsteps."

"Is it doom?"

"Once I thought Hari Seldon was God. Now I know he's much less powerful than that. He's merely Fate."

"No, Leyel. Don't say that."

"Not even Fate. Just our guide through it. He sees the future, and points the way."

"Rubbish." She slid out from under him, got up, pulled her robe from its hook on the wall. "My old bones get cold when I lie about naked."

Leyel's legs were trembling, but not with cold. "The future is his, and the present is yours, but the past belongs to me. I don't know how far into the future his probability curves have taken him, but I can match him, step for step, century for century into the past."

"Don't tell me you're going to solve the question of origin. You're the one who proved it wasn't worth solving."

"I proved that it wasn't important or even possible to find the planet of origin. But I also said that we could still discover the natural laws that accounted for the origin of man. Whatever forces created us as human beings must still be present in the universe."

"I did read what you wrote, you know. You said it would be the labor of the next millennium to find the answer."

"Just now. Lying here, just now, I saw it, just out of reach. Something about your work and Hari's work, and the tree."

"The tree was about me needing you, Leyel. It wasn't about the origin of humanity."

"It's gone. Whatever I saw for a moment there, it's

gone. But I can find it again. It's there in your work, and Hari's Foundation, and the fall of the Empire, and the damned pear tree."

"I never said it was a pear tree."

"I used to play in the pear orchard on the grounds of the estate in Holdwater. To me the word 'tree' always means a pear tree. One of the deep-worn ruts in my brain."

"I'm relieved. I was afraid you were reminded of pears by the shape of these ancient breasts when I bend over."

"Open your robe again. Let me see if I think of pears."

Leyel paid for Hari Seldon's funeral. It was not lavish. Leyel had meant it to be. The moment he heard of Hari's death—not a surprise, since Hari's first brutal stroke had left him half-paralyzed in a wheelchair— he set his staff to work on a memorial service appropriate to honor the greatest scientific mind of the millennium. But word arrived, in the form of a visit from Commissioner Rom Divart, that any sort of public services would be . . .

"Shall we say, inappropriate?"

"The man was the greatest genius I've ever heard of! He virtually invented a branch of science that clarified things that—he made a science out of the sort of thing that soothsayers and—and—*economists* used to do!"

Rom laughed at Leyel's little joke, of course, because he and Leyel had been friends forever. Rom was the only friend of Leyel's childhood who had never sucked up to him or resented him or stayed cool toward him because of the Forska fortune. This was, of course, because the Divart holdings were, if anything, slightly greater. They had played together unencumbered by strangeness or jealousy or awe.

They even shared a tutor for two terrible, glorious years, from the time Rom's father was murdered until the execution of Rom's grandfather, which caused so much outrage among the nobility that the mad Emperor was stripped of power and the Imperium put under the control of the Commission of Public Safety. Then, as the youthful head of one of the great families, Rom had embarked on his long and fruitful career in politics.

Rom said later that for those two years it was Leyel who taught him that there was still some good in the world; that Leyel's friendship was the only reason Rom hadn't killed himself. Leyel always thought this was pure theatrics. Rom was a born actor. That's why he so excelled at making stunning entrances and playing unforgettable scenes on the grandest stage of all—the politics of the Imperium. Someday he would no doubt exit as dramatically as his father and grandfather had.

But he was not all show. Rom never forgot the friend of his childhood. Leyel knew it, and knew also that Rom's coming to deliver this message from the Commission of Public Safety probably meant that Rom had fought to make the message as mild as it was. So Leyel blustered a bit, then made his little joke. It was his way of surrendering gracefully.

What Leyel didn't realize, right up until the day of the funeral, was exactly *how* dangerous his friendship with Hari Seldon had been, and how stupid it was for him to associate himself with Hari's name now that the old man was dead. Linge Chen, the Chief Commissioner, had not risen to the position of greatest power in the Empire without being fiercely suspicious of potential rivals and brutally efficient about eliminating them. Hari had maneuvered Chen into a position such that it was more dangerous to kill the old man than to give him his Foundation on

Terminus. But now Hari was dead, and apparently Chen was watching to see who mourned.

Leyel did—Leyel and the few members of Hari's staff who had stayed behind on Trantor to maintain contact with Terminus up to the moment of Hari's death. Leyel should have known better. Even alive, Hari wouldn't have cared who came to his funeral. And now, dead, he cared even less. Leyel didn't believe his friend lived on in some ethereal plane, watching carefully and taking attendance at the services. No, Leyel simply felt he had to be there, felt he had to speak. Not for Hari, really. For himself. To continue to be himself, Leyel had to make some kind of public gesture toward Hari Seldon and all he had stood for.

Who heard? Not many. Deet, who thought his eulogy was too mild by half. Hari's staff, who were quite aware of the danger and winced at each of Leyel's list of Hari's accomplishments. Naming them—and emphasizing that only Seldon had the vision to do these great works—was inherently a criticism of the level of intelligence and integrity in the Empire. The Pubs were listening, too. They noted that Leyel clearly agreed with Hari Seldon about the certainty of the Empire's fall—that in fact as a galactic empire it had probably already fallen, since its authority was no longer coextensive with the Galaxy.

If almost anyone else had said such things, to such a small audience, it would have been ignored, except to keep him from getting any job requiring a security clearance. But when the head of the Forska family came out openly to affirm the correctness of the views of a man who had been tried before the Commission of Public Safety—that posed a greater danger to the Commission than Hari Seldon.

For, as head of the Forska family, if Leyel Forska

wanted, he could be one of the great players on the political stage, could have a seat on the Commission along with Rom Divart and Linge Chen. Of course, that would also have meant constantly watching for assassins—either to avoid them or to hire them—and trying to win the allegiance of various military strongmen in the farflung reaches of the Galaxy. Leyel's grandfather had spent his life in such pursuits, but Leyel's father had declined, and Leyel himself had thoroughly immersed himself in science and never so much as inquired about politics.

Until now. Until he made the profoundly political act of paying for Hari Seldon's funeral and then *speaking* at it. What would he do next? There were a thousand would-be warlords who would spring to revolt if a Forska promised what would-be emperors so desperately needed: a noble sponsor, a mask of legitimacy, and *money*.

Did Linge Chen really believe that Leyel meant to enter politics at his advanced age? Did he really think Leyel posed a threat?

Probably not. If he *had* believed it, he would surely have had Leyel killed, and no doubt all his children as well, leaving only one of his minor grandchildren, whom Chen would carefully control through the guardians he would appoint, thereby acquiring control of the Forska fortune as well as his own.

Instead, Chen only believed that Leyel *might* cause trouble. So he took what were, for him, mild steps.

That was why Rom came to visit Leyel again, a week after the funeral.

Leyel was delighted to see him. "Not on somber business this time, I hope," he said. "But such bad luck—Deet's at the library again, she practically lives there now, but she'd want to—"

"Leyel." Rom touched Leyel's lips with his fingers.

So it *was* somber business after all. Worse than somber. Rom recited what had to be a memorized speech.

"The Commission of Public Safety has become concerned that in your declining years—"

Leyel opened his mouth to protest, but again Rom touched his lips to silence him.

"That in your declining years, the burdens of the Forska estates are distracting you from your exceptionally important scientific work. So great is the Empire's need for the new discoveries and understanding your work will surely bring us, that the Commission of Public Safety has created the office of Forska Trustee to oversee all the Forska estates and holdings. You will, of course, have unlimited access to these funds for your scientific work here on Trantor, and funding will continue for all the archives and libraries you have endowed. Naturally, the Commission has no desire for you to thank us for what is, after all, our duty to one of our noblest citizens, but if your well-known courtesy required you to make a brief public statement of gratitude it would not be inappropriate."

Leyel was no fool. He knew how things worked. He was being stripped of his fortune and being placed under arrest on Trantor. There was no point in protest or remonstrance, no point even in trying to make Rom feel guilty for having brought him such a bitter message. Indeed, Rom himself might be in great danger—if Leyel so much as hinted that he expected Rom to come to his support, his dear friend might also fall. So Leyel nodded gravely, and then carefully framed his words of reply.

"Please tell the Commissioners how grateful I am for their concern on my behalf. It has been a long, long time since anyone went to the trouble of easing my burdens. I accept their kind offer. I am especially glad because this means that now I can pursue my studies unencumbered."

Rom visibly relaxed. Leyel wasn't going to cause trouble. "My dear friend, I will sleep better knowing that you are always here on Trantor, working freely in the library or taking your leisure in the parks."

So at least they weren't going to confine him to his apartment. No doubt they would never let him off-planet, but it wouldn't hurt to ask. "Perhaps I'll even have time now to visit my grandchildren now and then."

"Oh, Leyel, you and I are both too old to enjoy hyperspace any more. Leave that for the youngsters—they can come visit you whenever they want. And sometimes they can stay home, while their parents come to see you."

Thus Leyel learned that if any of his children came to visit him, *their* children would be held hostage, and vice versa. Leyel himself would never leave Trantor again.

"So much the better," said Leyel. "I'll have time to write several books I've been meaning to publish."

"The Empire waits eagerly for every scientific treatise you publish." There was a slight emphasis on the word "scientific." "But I hope you won't bore us with one of those tedious autobiographies."

Leyel agreed to the restriction easily enough. "I *promise*, Rom. You know better than anyone else exactly how boring my life has always been."

"Come now. *My* life's the boring one, Leyel, all this government claptrap and bureaucratic bushwa. You've been at the forefront of scholarship and learning. Indeed, my friend, the Commission hopes you'll honor us by giving us first look at every word that comes out of your scriptor."

"Only if you promise to read it carefully and point out any mistakes I might make." No doubt the Commission intended only to censor his work to remove political material—which Leyel had never included anyway. But Leyel had already resolved never to publish anything again, at least as long as Linge Chen was Chief Commissioner. The safest thing Leyel could do now was to disappear, to let Chen forget him entirely—it would be egregiously stupid to send occasional articles to Chen, thus reminding him that Leyel was still around.

But Rom wasn't through yet. "I must extend that request to Deet's work as well. We really want first look at it—do tell her so."

"Deet?" For the first time Leyel almost let his fury show. Why should Deet be punished because of Leyel's indiscretion? "Oh, she'll be too shy for that, Rom—she doesn't think her work is *important* enough to deserve any attention from men as busy as the Commissioners. They'll think you only want to see her work because she's my wife—she's always annoyed when people patronize her."

"You must insist, then, Leyel," said Rom. "I assure you, her studies of the functions of the Imperial bureaucracy have long been interesting to the Commission for their own sake."

Ah. Of course. Chen would never have allowed a report on the workings of government to appear without making sure it wasn't dangerous. Censorship of Deet's writings wouldn't be Leyel's fault after all. Or at least not entirely.

"I'll tell her that, Rom. She'll be flattered. But won't you stay and tell her yourself? I can bring you a cup of peshat, we can talk about old times—"

Leyel would have been surprised if Rom had stayed. No, this interview had been at least as hard on Rom as it had been on him. The very fact that Rom had been forced into being the Commission's messenger to his childhood friend was a humiliating reminder that the Chens were in the ascendant over the Divarts. But as Rom bowed and left, it occurred to Leyel that Chen might have made a mistake. Humiliating Rom this way, forcing him to place his dearest friend under arrest like this—it might be the straw to break the camel's back. After all, though no one had ever been able to find out who hired the assassin who killed Rom's father, and no one had ever learned who denounced Rom's grandfather, leading to his execution by the paranoid Emperor Wassiniwak, it didn't take a genius to realize that the House of Chen had profited most from both events.

"I wish I could stay," said Rom. "But duty calls. Still, you can be sure I'll think of you often. Of course, I doubt I'll think of you as you are *now*, you old wreck. I'll remember you as a boy, when we used to tweak our tutor—remember the time we recoded his lector, so that for a whole week explicit pornography kept coming up on the display whenever the door of his room opened?"

Leyel couldn't help laughing. "You never forget anything, do you!"

"The poor fool. He never figured out that it was us! Old times. Why couldn't we have stayed young forever?" He embraced Leyel and then swiftly left.

Linge Chen, you fool, you have reached too far. Your days are numbered. None of the Pubs who were listening in on their conversation could possibly know that Rom and Leyel had never teased their tutor—and that they had never done anything to his lector. It was just Rom's way of letting Leyel know that they were still allies, still keeping secrets together—and that someone who had authority over both of them was going to be in for a few nasty surprises.

It gave Leyel chills, thinking about what might

come of all this. He loved Rom Divart with all his heart, but he also knew that Rom was capable of biding his time and then killing swiftly, efficiently, coldly. Linge Chen had just started his latest six-year term of office, but Leyel knew he'd never finish it. And the next Chief Commissioner would not be a Chen.

Soon, though, the enormity of what had been done to him began to sink in. He had always thought that his fortune meant little to him—that he would be the same man with or without the Forska estates. But now he began to realize that it wasn't true, that he'd been lying to himself all along. He had known since childhood how despicable rich and powerful men could be—his father had made sure he saw and understood how cruel men became when their money persuaded them they had a right to use others however they wished. So Leyel had learned to despise his own birthright, and, starting with his father, had pretended to others that he could make his way through the world solely by wit and diligence, that he would have been exactly the same man if he had grown up in a common family, with a common education. He had done such a good job of acting as if he didn't care about his wealth that he came to believe it himself.

Now he realized that Forska estates had been an invisible part of himself all along, as if they were extensions of his body, as if he could flex a muscle and cargo ships would fly, he could blink and mines would be sunk deep into the earth, he could sigh and all over the Galaxy there would be a wind of change that would keep blowing until everything was exactly as he wanted it. Now all those invisible limbs and senses had been amputated. Now he was crippled—he had only as many arms and legs and eyes as any other human being.

At last he was what he had always pretended to be. An ordinary, powerless man. He hated it.

For the first hours after Rom left, Leyel pretended he could take all this in stride. He sat at the lector and spun through the pages smoothly—without anything on the pages registering in his memory. He kept wishing Deet were there so he could laugh with her about how little this hurt him; then he would be glad that Deet was not there, because one sympathetic touch of her hand would push him over the edge, make it impossible to contain his emotion.

Finally he could not help himself. Thinking of Deet, of their children and grandchildren, of all that had been lost to them because he had made an empty gesture to a dead friend, he threw himself to the softened floor and wept bitterly. Let Chen listen to recordings of what the spy beam shows of this! Let him savor his victory! I'll destroy him somehow, my staff is still loyal to me, I'll put together an army, I'll hire assassins of my own, I'll make contact with Admiral Sipp, and then Chen will be the one to sob, crying out for mercy as I disfigure him the way he has mutilated me—

Fool.

Leyel rolled over onto his back, dried his face on his sleeve, then lay there, eyes closed, calming himself. No vengeance. No politics. That was Rom's business, not Leyel's. Too late for him to enter the game now—and who would help him, anyway, now that he had already lost his power? There was nothing to be done.

Leyel didn't really want to do anything, anyway. Hadn't they guaranteed that his archives and libraries would continue to be funded? Hadn't they guaranteed him unlimited research funds? And wasn't that all he had cared about anyway? He had long since turned over all the Forska operations to his subordinates—Chen's trustee would simply do the same job. And Leyel's children wouldn't suffer much—he had raised them with the same values that he had grown up with, and so they all pursued careers unrelated to the Forska holdings. They were true children of their father and mother—they wouldn't have any self-respect if they didn't earn their own way in the world. No doubt they'd be disappointed by having their inheritance snatched away. But they wouldn't be destroyed.

I am not ruined. All the lies that Rom told are really true, only they didn't realize it. All that matters in my life, I still have. I really *don't* care about my fortune. It's just the *way* I lost it that made me so furious. I can go on and be the same person I always was. This will even give me an opportunity to see who my true friends are—to see who still honors me for my scientific achievements, and who despises me for my poverty.

By the time Deet got home from the library—late, as was usual these days—Leyel was hard at work, reading back through all the research and speculation on protohuman behavior, trying to see if there was anything other than half-assed guesswork and pompous babble. He was so engrossed in his reading that he spent the first fifteen minutes after she got home telling her of the hilarious stupidities he had found in the day's reading, and then sharing a wonderful, impossible thought he had had.

"What if the human species isn't the only branch to evolve on our family tree? What if there's some other primate species that looks exactly like us, but can't interbreed with us, that functions in a completely different way, and we don't even know it, we all think everybody's just like us, but here and there all over the Empire there are whole towns, cities, maybe even worlds of people who secretly aren't human at all."

"But Leyel, my overwrought husband, if they look just like us and act just like us, then they *are* human."

"But they *don't* act exactly like us. There's a difference. A completely different set of rules and assumptions. Only they don't know that we're different, and we don't know that *they're* different. Or even if we suspect it, we're never sure. Just two different species, living side by side and never guessing it."

She kissed him. "You poor fool, that isn't speculation, it already exists. You have just described the relationship between males and females. Two completely different species, completely unintelligible to each other, living side by side and thinking they're really the same. The fascinating thing, Leyel, is that the two species persist in marrying each other and having babies, sometimes of one species, sometimes of the other, and the whole time they can't understand why they can't understand each other."

He laughed and embraced her. "You're right, as always, Deet. If I could once understand women, then perhaps I'd know what it is that makes men human."

"Nothing could possibly make men human," she answered. "Every time they're just about to get it right, they end up tripping over the damned Y chromosome and turning back into beasts." She nuzzled his neck.

It was then, with Deet in his arms, that he whispered to her what had happened when Rom visited that day. She said nothing, but held him tightly for the longest time. Then they had a very late supper and went about their nightly routines as if nothing had changed.

Not until they were in bed, not until Deet was

softly snoring beside him, did it finally occur to Leyel that Deet was facing a test of her own. Would she still love him, now that he was merely Leyel Forska, scientist on a pension, and not Lord Forska, master of worlds? Of course she would *intend* to. But just as Leyel had never been aware of how much he depended on his wealth to define himself, so also she might not have realized how much of what she loved about him was his vast power; for even though he didn't flaunt it, it had always been there, like a solid platform underfoot, hardly noticed except now, when it was gone, when their footing was unsure.

Even before this, she had been slipping away into the community of women in the library. She would drift away even faster now, not even noticing it as Leyel became less and less important to her. No need for anything as dramatic as divorce. Just a little gap between them, an empty space that might as well be a chasm, might as well be the abyss. My fortune was a part of me, and now that it's gone, I'm no longer the same man she loved. She won't even know that she doesn't love me any more. She'll just get busier and busier in her work, and in five or ten years when I die of old age, she'll grieve—and then suddenly she'll realize that she isn't half as devastated as she thought she'd be. In fact, she won't be devastated at all. And she'll get on with her life and won't even remember what it was like to be married to me. I'll disappear from all human memory then, except perhaps for a few scientific papers and the libraries.

I'm like the information that was lost in all those neglected archives. Disappearing bit by bit, unnoticed, until all that's left is just a little bit of noise in people's memories. Then, finally, nothing. Blank.

Self-pitying fool. That's what happens to everyone, in the long run. Even Hari Seldon—someday he'll be forgotten, sooner rather than later, if Chen has his way. We all die. We're all lost in the passage of time. The only thing that lives on after us is the new shape we've given to the communities we lived in. There are things that are known because I said them, and even though people have forgotten who said it, they'll go on knowing. Like the story Rinjy was telling—she had forgotten, if she ever knew it, that Deet was the librarian in the original tale. But still she remembered the tale. The community of librarians was different because Deet had been among them. They would be a little different, a little braver, a little stronger, because of Deet. She had left traces of herself in the world.

And then, again, there came that flash of insight, that sudden understanding of the answer to a question that had long been troubling him.

But in the moment that Leyel realized that he held the answer, the answer slipped away. He couldn't remember it. You're asleep, he said silently. You only dreamed that you understood the origin of humanity. That's the way it is in dreams—the truth is always so beautiful, but you can never hold on to it.

"How is he taking it, Deet?"

"Hard to say. Well, I think. He was never much of a wanderer anyway."

"Come now, it can't be that simple."

"No. No, it isn't."

"Tell me."

"The social things—those were easy. We rarely went anyway, but now people don't invite us. We're politically dangerous. And the few things we had scheduled got canceled or, um, postponed. You know—we'll call you as soon as we have a new date."

"He doesn't mind this?"

"He *likes* that part. He always hated those things.

But they've canceled his speeches. And the lecture series on human ecology."

"A blow."

"He pretends not to mind. But he's brooding."

"Tell me."

"Works all day, but he doesn't read it to me any more, doesn't make me sit down at the lector the minute I get home. I think he isn't writing anything."

"Doing nothing?"

"No. Reading. That's all."

"Maybe he just needs to do research."

"You don't know Leyel. He *thinks* by writing. Or talking. He isn't doing either."

"Doesn't talk to you?"

"He answers. I try to talk about things here at the library, his answers are—what? Glum. Sullen."

"He resents your work?"

"That's not possible. Leyel has always been as enthusiastic about my work as about his own. And he won't talk about his own work, either. I ask him, and he says nothing."

"Not surprising."

"So it's all right?"

"No. It's just not surprising."

"What is it? Can't you tell me?"

"What good is telling you? It's what we call ILS—Identity Loss Syndrome. It's identical to the passive strategy for dealing with loss of body parts."

"ILS. What happens in ILS?"

"Deet, come on, you're a scientist. What do you expect? You've just described Leyel's behavior, I tell you that it's called ILS, you want to know what ILS is, and what am I going to do?"

"Describe Leyel's behavior back to me. What an idiot I am."

"Good, at least you can laugh."

"Can't you tell me what to expect?"

"Complete withdrawal from you, from everybody. Eventually he becomes completely antisocial and starts to strike out. Does something self-destructive—like making public statements against Chen, that'd do it."

"No!"

"Or else he severs his old connections, gets away from you, and reconstructs himself in a different set of communities."

"This would make him happy?"

"Sure. Useless to the Second Foundation, but happy. It would also turn you into a nasty-tempered old crone, not that you aren't one already, mind you."

"Oh, you think Leyel's the only thing keeping me human?"

"Pretty much, yes. He's your safety valve."

"Not lately."

"I know."

"Have I been so awful?"

"Nothing that we can't bear. Deet, if we're going to be fit to govern the human race someday, shouldn't we first learn to be good to each other?"

"Well, I'm glad to provide you all with an opportunity to test your patience."

"You should be glad. We're doing a fine job so far, wouldn't you say?"

"Please. You were teasing me about the prognosis, weren't you?"

"Partly. Everything I said was true, but you know as well as I do that there are as many different ways out of a B-B syndrome as there are people who have them."

"Behavioral cause, behavioral effect. No little hormone shot, then?"

"Deet. He doesn't know who he is."

"Can't I help him?"

"Yes."

"What? What can I do?"

"This is only a guess, since I haven't talked to him."

"Of course."

"You aren't home much."

"I can't *stand* it there, with him brooding all the time."

"Fine. Get him out with you."

"He won't go."

"Push him."

"We barely talk. I don't know if I even have any leverage over him."

"Deet. You're the one who wrote, 'Communities that make few or no demands on their members cannot command allegiance. All else being equal, members who feel most needed have the strongest allegiance.' "

"You memorized that?"

"Psychohistory *is* the psychology of populations, but populations can only be quantified as communities. Seldon's work on statistical probabilities only worked to predict the future within a generation or two until you first published your community theories. That's because statistics *can't* deal with cause and effect. Stats tell you what's happening, never why, never the result. Within a generation or two, the present statistics evaporate, they're meaningless, you have whole new populations with new configurations. Your community theory gave us a way of predicting which communities would survive, which would grow, which would fade. A way of looking across long stretches of time and space."

"Hari never told me he was using community theory in any important way."

"How could he tell you that? He had to walk a

tightrope—publishing enough to get psychohistory taken seriously, but not so much that anybody outside the Second Foundation could ever duplicate or continue his work. Your work was a key—but he couldn't say so."

"Are you just saying this to make me feel better?"

"Sure. That's why I'm saying it. But it's also true— since lying to you wouldn't make you feel better, would it? Statistics are like taking cross sections of the trunk of a tree. It can tell you a lot about its history. You can figure how healthy it is, how much volume the whole tree has, how much is root and how much is branch. But what it *can't* tell you is where the tree will branch, and which branches will become major, which minor, and which will rot and fall off and die."

"But you can't *quantify* communities, can you? They're just stories and rituals that bind people together—"

"You'd be surprised what we can quantify. We're very good at what we do, Deet. Just as you are. Just as Leyel is."

"*Is* his work important? After all, human origin is only a historical question."

"Nonsense, and you know it. Leyel has stripped away the historical issues and he's searching for the scientific ones. The principles by which human life, as we understand it, is differentiated from nonhuman. If he finds that—don't you see, Deet? The human race is re-creating itself all the time, on every world, in every family, in every individual. We're born animals, and we teach each other how to be human. Somehow. It matters that we find out how. It matters to psychohistory. It matters to the Second Foundation. It matters to the human race."

"So—you aren't just being kind to Leyel."

"Yes, we are. You are, too. Good people are kind."

"Is that all? Leyel is just one man who's having trouble?"

"We need him. He isn't important just to you. He's important to *us*."

"Oh. Oh."

"Why are you crying?"

"I was so afraid—that I was being selfish—being so worried about him. Taking up your time like this."

"Well, if that doesn't—I thought you were beyond surprising me."

"Our problems were just—our problems. But now they're not."

"Is that so important to you? Tell me, Deet—do you really value this community so much?"

"Yes."

"More than Leyel?"

"No! But enough—that I felt *guilty* for caring so much about him."

"Go home, Deet. Just go home."

"What?"

"That's where you'd rather be. It's been showing up in your behavior for two months, ever since Hari's death. You've been nasty and snappish, and now I know why. You *resent* us for keeping you away from Leyel."

"No, it was my choice, I—"

"Of course it was your choice! It was your *sacrifice* for the good of the Second Foundation. So now I'm telling you—healing Leyel is more important to Hari's plan than keeping up with your day-to-day responsibilities here."

"You're not removing me from my position, are you?"

"No. I'm just telling you to ease up. And get Leyel out of the apartment. Do you understand me? Demand it! Reengage him with *you*, or we've all lost him."

"Take him *where*?"

"I don't know. Theater. Athletic events. Dancing."

"We don't *do* those things."

"Well, what *do* you do?"

"Research. And then talk about it."

"Fine. Bring him here to the library. Do research with him. Talk about it."

"But he'll meet people here. He'd certainly meet *you*."

"Good. Good. I like that. Yes, let him come here."

"But I thought we had to keep the Second Foundation a secret from him until he's ready to take part."

"I didn't say you should introduce me as First Speaker."

"No, no, of course you didn't. What am I thinking of? Of course he can meet you, he can meet everybody."

"Deet, listen to me."

"Yes, I'm listening."

"It's all right to love him, Deet."

"I know that."

"I mean, it's all right to love him more than you love us. More than you love any of us. More than you love all of us. There you are, crying again."

"I'm so—"

"Relieved."

"How do you understand me so well?"

"I only know what you show me and what you tell me. It's all we ever know about each other. The only thing that helps is that nobody can ever lie for long about who they really are. Not even to themselves."

For two months Leyel followed up on Magolissian's paper by trying to find some connection between language studies and human origins. Of course this meant weeks of wading through old, useless point-of-origin studies, which kept indicating that Trantor was the focal point of language throughout the history of the Empire, even though *nobody* seriously put forth Trantor as the planet of origin. Once again, though, Leyel rejected the search for a particular planet; he wanted to find out regularities, not unique events.

Leyel hoped for a clue in the fairly recent work—only two thousand years old—of Dagawell Kispitorian. Kispitorian came from the most isolated area of a planet called Artashat, where there were traditions that the original settlers came from an earlier world named Armenia, now uncharted. Kispitorian grew up among mountain people who claimed that long ago, they spoke a completely different language. In fact, the title of Kispitorian's most interesting book was *No Man Understood Us*; many of the folk tales of these people began with the formula "Back in the days when no man understood us . . ."

Kispitorian had never been able to shake off this tradition of his upbringing, and as he pursued the field of dialect formation and evolution, he kept coming across evidence that at one time the human species spoke not one but many languages. It had always been taken for granted that Galactic Standard was the up-to-date version of the language of the planet of origin—that while a few human groups might have developed dialects, civilization was impossible without mutually intelligible speech. But Kispitorian had begun to suspect that Galactic Standard did not become the universal human language until *after* the formation of the Empire—that, in fact, one of the first labors of the Imperium was to stamp out all other competing languages. The mountain people of Artashat believed that their language had been stolen from them. Kispitorian eventually devoted his life to proving they were right.

He worked first with names, long recognized as the most conservative aspect of language. He found that there were many separate naming traditions, and it was not until about the year 6000 G.E. that all were finally amalgamated into one Empire-wide stream. What was interesting was that the farther back he went, the *more* complexity he found.

Because certain worlds tended to have unified traditions, and so the simplest explanation of this was the one he first put forth—that humans left their home world with a unified language, but the normal forces of language separation caused each new planet to develop its own offshoot, until many dialects became mutually unintelligible. Thus, different languages would not have developed until humanity moved out into space; this was one of the reasons why the Galactic Empire was necessary to restore the primeval unity of the species.

Kispitorian called his first and most influential book *Tower of Confusion*, using the widespread legend of the Tower of Babble as an illustration. He supposed that this story might have originated in that pre-Empire period, probably among the rootless traders roaming from planet to planet, who had to deal on a practical level with the fact that no two worlds spoke the same language. These traders had preserved a tradition that when humanity lived on one planet, they all spoke the same language. They explained the linguistic confusion of their own time by recounting the tale of a great leader who built the first "tower," or starship, to raise mankind up into heaven. According to the story, "God" punished these upstart people by confusing their tongues, which forced them to disperse among the different worlds. The story presented the confusion of tongues as the *cause* of the dispersal instead of its result, but cause-reversal was a commonly recognized feature of myth. Clearly this legend preserved a historical fact.

So far, Kispitorian's work was perfectly acceptable to most scientists. But in his forties he began to go off on wild tangents. Using controversial algorithms—on calculators with a suspiciously high level of processing power—he began to tear apart Galactic Standard itself, showing that many words revealed completely separate phonetic traditions, incompatible with the mainstream of the language. They could not comfortably have evolved within a population that regularly spoke either Standard or its primary ancestor language. Furthermore, there were many words with clearly related meanings that showed they had once diverged according to standard linguistic patterns and then were brought together later, with different meanings or implications. But the time scale implied by the degree of change was far too great to be accounted for in the period between humanity's first settlement of space and the formation of the Empire. Obviously, claimed Kispitorian, there had been many different languages *on the planet of origin*; Galactic Standard was the *first* universal human language. Throughout all human history, separation of language had been a fact of life; only the Empire had had the pervasive power to unify speech.

After that, Kispitorian was written off as a fool, of course—his own Tower of Babble interpretation was now used against him as if an interesting illustration had now become a central argument. He very narrowly escaped execution as a separatist, in fact, since there was an unmistakable tone of regret in his writing about the loss of linguistic diversity. The Imperium did succeed in cutting off all his funding and jailing him for a while because he had been using a calculator with an illegal level of memory and processing power. Leyel suspected that Kispitorian got off easy at that—working with language as he did, getting the results he got, he might well have developed a calculator so intelligent that it could understand and produce human speech, which, if discovered, would have meant either the death penalty or a lynching.

No matter now. Kispitorian insisted to the end that his work was pure science, making no value judgments on whether the Empire's linguistic unity was a Good Thing or not. He was merely reporting that the natural condition of humanity was to speak many different languages. And Leyel believed that he was right.

Leyel could not help but feel that by combining Kispitorian's language studies with Magolissian's work with language-using primates he could come up with something important. But what was the connection? The primates had never developed their *own* languages—they only learned nouns and verbs presented to them by humans. So they could hardly have developed diversity of language. What connection could there be? Why would diversity ever have developed? Could it have something to do with why humans became human?

The primates used only a tiny subset of Standard. For that matter, so did most people—most of the two million words in Standard were used only by a few professionals who actually needed them, while the common vocabulary of humans throughout the Galaxy consisted of a few thousand words.

Oddly, though, it was that small subset of Standard that was the *most* susceptible to change. Highly esoteric scientific or technical papers written in 2000

G.E. were still easily readable. Slangy, colloquial passages in fiction, especially in dialogue, became almost unintelligible within five hundred years. The language shared by the most different communities was the language that changed the most. But over time, that mainstream language always changed *together*. It made no sense, then, for there ever to be linguistic diversity. Language changed most when it was most unified. Therefore when people were most divided, their language should remain most similar.

Never mind, Leyel. You're out of your discipline. Any competent linguist would know the answer to that.

But Leyel knew that wasn't likely to be true. People immersed in one discipline rarely questioned the axioms of their profession. Linguists all took for granted the fact that the language of an isolated population is invariably more archaic, less susceptible to change. Did they understand why?

Leyel got up from his chair. His eyes were tired from staring into the lector. His knees and back ached from staying so long in the same position. He wanted to lie down, but knew that if he did, he'd fall asleep. The curse of getting old—he could fall asleep so easily, yet could never stay asleep long enough to feel well rested. He didn't *want* to sleep now, though. He wanted to think.

No, that wasn't it. He wanted to *talk*. That's how his best and clearest ideas always came, under the pressure of conversation, when someone else's questions and arguments forced him to think sharply. To make connections, invent explanations. In a contest with another person, his adrenaline flowed, his brain made connections that would never otherwise be made.

Where was Deet? In years past, he would have been talking this through with Deet all day. All week. She would know as much about his research as he did, and would constantly say "Have you thought of this?" or "How can you possibly think that!" And he would have been making the same challenges to *her* work. In the old days.

But these weren't the old days. She didn't need him any more—she had her friends on the library staff. Nothing wrong with that, probably. After all, she wasn't *thinking* now, she was putting old thoughts into practice. She needed *them*, not *him*. But he still needed *her*. Did she ever think of that? I might as well have gone to Terminus—damn Hari for refusing to let me go. I stayed for Deet's sake, and yet I don't have her after all, not when I need her. How *dare* Hari decide what was right for Leyel Forska!

Only Hari hadn't decided, had he? He would have let Leyel go—without Deet. And Leyel hadn't stayed with Deet so she could help him with his research. He had stayed with her because . . . because . . .

He couldn't remember why. Love, of course. But he couldn't think why that had been so important to him. It wasn't important to *her*. Her idea of love these days was to urge him to come to the library. "You can do your research there. We could be together more during the days."

The message was clear. The only way Leyel could remain part of Deet's life was if he became part of her new "family" at the library. Well, she could forget that idea. If she chose to get swallowed up in that place, fine. If she chose to leave him for a bunch of— *indexers* and *cataloguers*—fine. Fine.

No. It wasn't fine. He wanted to *talk* to her. Right now, at this moment, he wanted to tell her what he was thinking, wanted her to question him and argue with him until she made him come up with an answer, or lots of answers. He needed her to see what he wasn't seeing. He needed her a lot more than *they* needed her.

He was out amid the thick pedestrian traffic of Maslo Boulevard before he realized that this was the first time since Hari's funeral that he'd ventured beyond the immediate neighborhood of his apartment. It was the first time in months that he'd had anyplace to go. That's what I'm doing here, he thought. I just need a change of scenery, a sense of destination. That's the only reason I'm heading to the library. All that emotional nonsense back in the apartment, that was just my unconscious strategy for making myself get out among people again.

Leyel was almost cheerful when he got to the Imperial Library. He had been there many times over the years, but always for receptions or other public events—having his own high-capacity lector meant that he could get access to all the library's records by cable. Other people—students, professors from poorer schools, lay readers—they actually *had* to come here to read. But that meant that they knew their way around the building. Except for finding the major lecture halls and reception rooms, Leyel hadn't the faintest idea where anything was.

For the first time it dawned on him how very large the Imperial Library was. Deet had mentioned the numbers many times—a staff of more than five thousand, including machinists, carpenters, cooks, security, a virtual city in itself—but only now did Leyel realize that this meant that many people here had never met each other. Who could possibly know *five thousand* people by name? He couldn't just walk up and ask for Deet by name. What was the department Deet worked in? She had changed so often, moving through the bureaucracy.

Everyone he saw was a patron—people at lectors, people at catalogues, even people reading books and magazines printed on paper. Where were the librarians? The few staff members moving through the aisles turned out not to be librarians at all—they were volunteer docents, helping newcomers learn how to use the lectors and catalogues. They knew as little about library staff as he did.

He finally found a room full of real librarians, sitting at calculators preparing the daily access and circulation reports. When he tried to speak to one, she merely waved a hand at him. He thought she was telling him to go away until he realized that her hand remained in the air, a finger pointing to the front of the room. Leyel moved toward the elevated desk where a fat, sleepy-looking middle-aged woman was lazily paging through long columns of figures, which stood in the air before her in military formation.

"Sorry to interrupt you," he said softly.

She was resting her cheek on her hand. She didn't even look at him when he spoke. But she answered. "I pray for interruptions."

Only then did he notice that her eyes were framed with laugh lines, that her mouth even in repose turned upward into a faint smile.

"I'm looking for someone. My wife, in fact. Deet Forska."

Her smile widened. She sat up. "You're the beloved Leyel."

It was an absurd thing for a stranger to say, but it pleased him nonetheless to realize that Deet must have spoken of him. Of course everyone would have known that Deet's husband was *the* Leyel Forska. But this woman hadn't said it that way, had she? Not as *the* Leyel Forska, the celebrity. No, here he was known as "the beloved Leyel." Even if this woman meant to tease him, Deet must have let it be known that she had some affection for him. He couldn't help but smile. With relief. He hadn't known that he feared the loss of her love so much, but now he wanted to laugh aloud, to move, to dance with pleasure.

"I imagine I am," said Leyel.

"I'm Zay Wax. Deet must have mentioned me, we have lunch every day."

No, she hadn't. She hardly mentioned anybody at the library, come to think of it. These two had lunch every day, and Leyel had never heard of her. "Yes, of course," said Leyel. "I'm glad to meet you."

"And I'm relieved to see that your feet actually touch the ground."

"Now and then."

"She works up in Indexing these days." Zay cleared her display.

"Is that on Trantor?"

Zay laughed. She typed in a few instructions and her display now filled with a map of the library complex. It was a complex pile of rooms and corridors, almost impossible to grasp. "This shows only this wing of the main building. Indexing is these four floors."

Four layers near the middle of the display turned to a brighter color.

"And here's where you are right now."

A small room on the first floor turned white. Looking at the labyrinth between the two lighted sections, Leyel had to laugh aloud. "Can't you just give me a ticket to guide me?"

"Our tickets only lead you to places where patrons are allowed. But this isn't really hard, Lord Forska. After all, you're a genius, aren't you?"

"Not at the interior geography of buildings, whatever lies Deet might have told you."

"You just go out this door and straight down the corridor to the elevators—can't miss them. Go up to fifteen. When you get out, turn as if you were continuing down the same corridor, and after a while you go through an archway that says 'Indexing.' Then you lean back your head and bellow 'Deet' as loud as you can. Do that a few times and either she'll come or security will arrest you."

"That's what I was going to do if I *didn't* find somebody to guide me."

"I was hoping you'd ask me." Zay stood up and spoke loudly to the busy librarians. "The cat's going away. The mice can play."

"About time," one of them said. They all laughed. But they kept working.

"Follow me, Lord Forska."

"Leyel, please."

"Oh, you're such a flirt." When she stood, she was even shorter and fatter than she had looked sitting down. "Follow me."

They conversed cheerfully about nothing much on the way down the corridor. Inside the elevator, they hooked their feet under the rail as the gravitic repulsion kicked in. Leyel was so used to weightlessness after all these years of using elevators on Trantor that he never noticed. But Zay let her arms float in the air and sighed noisily. "I *love* riding the elevator," she said. For the first time Leyel realized that weightlessness must be a great relief to someone carrying as many extra kilograms as Zay Wax. When the elevator stopped, Zay made a great show of staggering out as if under a great burden. "My idea of heaven is to live forever in gravitic repulsion."

"You can get gravitic repulsion for your apartment, if you live on the top floor."

"Maybe *you* can," said Zay. "But *I* have to live on a librarian's salary."

Leyel was mortified. He had always been careful not to flaunt his wealth, but then, he had rarely talked at any length with people who couldn't afford gravitic repulsion. "Sorry," he said. "I don't think I could either, these days."

"Yes, I heard you squandered your fortune on a real bang-up funeral."

Startled that she would speak so openly of it, he tried to answer in the same joking tone. "I suppose you could look at it that way."

"I say it was worth it," she said. She looked slyly up at him. "I knew Hari, you know. Losing him cost humanity more than if Trantor's sun went nova."

"Maybe," said Leyel. The conversation was getting out of hand. Time to be cautious.

"Oh, don't worry. I'm not a snitch for the Pubs. Here's the Golden Archway into Indexing. The Land of Subtle Conceptual Connections."

Through the arch, it was as though they had passed into a completely different building. The style and trim were the same as before, with deeply lustrous fabrics on the walls and ceiling and floor made of the same smooth sound-absorbing plastic, glowing faintly with white light. But now all pretense at symmetry was gone. The ceiling was at different heights, almost at random; on the left and right there might be doors or archways, stairs or ramps, an alcove or a huge hall filled with columns, shelves of books and works of art surrounding tables where indexers worked with a half-dozen scriptors and lectors at once.

"The form fits the function," said Zay.

"I'm afraid I'm rubbernecking like a first-time visitor to Trantor."

"It's a strange place. But the architect was the daughter of an indexer, so she knew that standard, orderly, symmetrical interior maps are the enemy of freely connective thought. The finest touch—and the most expensive too, I'm afraid—is the fact that from day to day the layout is rearranged."

"Rearranged! The rooms move?"

"A series of random routines in the master calculator. There are rules, but the program isn't afraid to waste space, either. Some days only one room is changed, moved off to some completely different place in the Indexing area. Other days, everything is changed. The only constant is the archway leading in. I really wasn't joking when I said you should come here and bellow."

"But—the indexers must spend the whole morning just finding their stations."

"Not at all. Any indexer can work from any station."

"Ah. So they just call up the job they were working on the day before."

"No. They merely pick up on the job that is already in progress on the station they happen to choose that day."

"Chaos!" said Leyel.

"Exactly. How do you think a good hyperindex is made? If one person alone indexes a book, then the only connections that book will make are the ones that person knows about. Instead, each indexer is forced to skim through what his predecessor did the day before. Inevitably he'll add some new connections that the other indexer didn't think of. The environment, the work pattern, everything is designed to break down habits of thought, to make everything surprising, everything *new*."

"To keep everybody off balance."

"Exactly. Your mind works quickly when you're running along the edge of the precipice."

"By that reckoning, acrobats should all be geniuses."

"Nonsense. The whole labor of acrobats is to learn their routines so perfectly they *never* lose balance. An acrobat who improvises is soon dead. But indexers, when they lose their balance, they fall into wonderful discoveries. That's why the indexes of the Imperial Library are the only ones worth having. They startle and challenge as you read. All the others are just—clerical lists."

"Deet never mentioned this."

"Indexers rarely discuss what they're doing. You can't really explain it anyway."

"How long has Deet been an indexer?"

"Not long, really. She's still a novice. But I hear she's very, very good."

"Where *is* she?"

Zay grinned. Then she tipped her head back and bellowed. "Deet!"

The sound seemed to be swallowed up at once in the labyrinth. There was no answer.

"Not nearby, I guess," said Zay. "We'll have to probe a little deeper."

"Couldn't we just *ask* somebody where she is?"

"Who would know?"

It took two more floors and three more shouts before they heard a faint answering cry. "Over here!"

They followed the sound. Deet kept calling out, so they could find her.

"I got the flower room today, Zay! Violets!"

The indexers they passed along the way all looked up—some smiled, some frowned.

"Doesn't it interfere with things?" asked Leyel. "All this shouting?"

"Indexers *need* interruption. It breaks up the chain of thought. When they look back down, they have to rethink what they were doing."

Deet, not so far away now, called again. "The smell is so intoxicating. Imagine—the same room twice in a month!"

"Are indexers often hospitalized?" Leyel asked quietly.

"For what?"

"Stress."

"There's no stress on this job," said Zay. "Just play. We come up here as a *reward* for working in other parts of the library."

"I see. This is the time when librarians actually get to *read* the books in the library."

"We all chose this career because we love books for their own sake. Even the old inefficient corruptible paper ones. Indexing is like—writing in the margins."

The notion was startling. "Writing in someone *else's* book?"

"It used to be done all the time, Leyel. How can you possibly engage in dialogue with the author without writing your answers and arguments in the margins? Here she is." Zay preceded him under a low arch and down a few steps.

"I heard a man's voice with you, Zay," said Deet.

"Mine," said Leyel. He turned a corner and saw her there. After such a long journey to reach her, he thought for a dizzying moment that he didn't recognize her. That the library had randomized the librarians as well as the rooms, and he had happened upon a woman who merely resembled his long-familiar wife; he would have to reacquaint himself with her from the beginning.

"I thought so," said Deet. She got up from her station and embraced him. Even this startled him, though she usually embraced him upon meeting. It's only the setting that's different, he told himself. I'm only surprised because usually she greets me like this at home, in familiar surroundings. And usually it's Deet arriving, not me.

Or was there, after all, a greater warmth in her greeting here? As if she loved him more in this place than at home? Or, perhaps, as if the new Deet were simply a warmer, more comfortable person?

I thought that she was comfortable with me.

Leyel felt uneasy, shy with her. "If I'd known my coming would cause so much trouble," he began. Why did he need so badly to apologize?

"What trouble?" asked Zay.

"Shouting. Interrupting."

"Listen to him, Deet. He thinks the world has stopped because of a couple of shouts."

In the distance they could hear a man bellowing someone's name.

"Happens all the time," said Zay. "I'd better get back. Some lordling from Mahagonny is probably fuming because I haven't granted his request for access to the Imperial account books."

"Nice to meet you," said Leyel.

"Good luck finding your way back," said Deet.

"Easy this time," said Zay. She paused only once on her way through the door, not to speak, but to slide a metallic wafer along an almost unnoticeable slot in the doorframe, above eye level. She turned back and winked at Deet. Then she was gone.

Leyel didn't ask what she had done—if it were his business, something would have been said. But he suspected that Zay had either turned on or turned off a recording system. Unsure of whether they had privacy here from the library staff, Leyel merely stood for a moment, looking around. Deet's room really was filled with violets, real ones, growing out of cracks and apertures in the floor and walls. The smell was clear but not overpowering. "What is this room *for?*"

"For *me.* Today, anyway. I'm so glad you came."

"You never told me about this place."

"I didn't know about it until I was assigned to this

section. Nobody talks about Indexing. We never tell outsiders. The architect died three thousand years ago. Only our own machinists understand how it works. It's like—"

"Fairyland."

"Exactly."

"A place where all the rules of the universe are suspended."

"Not all. We still stick with good old gravity. Inertia. That sort of thing."

"This place is right for you, Deet. This room."

"Most people go years without getting the flower room. It isn't always violets, you know. Sometimes climbing roses. Sometimes periwinkle. They say there's really a dozen flower rooms, but never more than one at a time is accessible. It's been violets for me both times, though."

Leyel couldn't help himself. He laughed. It was funny. It was delightful. What did this have to do with a library? And yet what a marvelous thing to have hidden away in the heart of this somber place. He sat down on a chair. Violets grew out of the top of the chairback, so that flowers brushed his shoulders.

"You finally got tired of staying in the apartment all day?" asked Deet.

Of course she would wonder why he finally came out, after all her invitations had been so long ignored. Yet he wasn't sure if he could speak frankly. "I needed to talk with you." He glanced back at the slot Zay had used in the doorframe. "Alone," he said.

Was that a look of dread that crossed her face?

"We're alone," Deet said quietly. "Zay saw to that. Truly alone, as we can't be even in the apartment."

It took Leyel a moment to realize what she was asserting. He dared not even speak the word. So he mouthed his question: Pubs?

"They never bother with the library in their normal spying. Even if they set up something special for you, there's now an interference field blocking out our conversation. Chances are, though, that they won't bother to monitor you again until you leave here."

She seemed edgy. Impatient. As if she didn't like having this conversation. As if she wanted him to get on with it, or maybe just get it over with.

"If you don't mind," he said. "I haven't interrupted you here before, I thought that just this once—"

"Of course," she said. But she was still tense. As if she feared what he might say.

So he explained to her all his thoughts about language. All that he had gleaned from Kispitorian's and Magolissian's work. She seemed to relax almost as soon as it became clear he was talking about his research. What did she dread, he wondered. Was she afraid I came to talk about our relationship? She hardly needed to fear *that*. He had no intention of making things more difficult by whining about things that could not be helped.

When he was through explaining the ideas that had come to him, she nodded carefully—as she had done a thousand times before, after he explained an idea or argument. "I don't know," she finally said. As so many times before, she was reluctant to commit herself to an immediate response.

And, as he had often done, he insisted. "But what do you *think*?"

She pursed her lips. "Just offhand—I've never tried a serious linguistic application of community theory, beyond jargon formation, so this is just my first thought—but try this. Maybe small isolated populations *guard* their language—jealously, because it's part of who they are. Maybe language is the most powerful ritual of all, so that people who have the same language are one in a way that people who can't understand each other's speech never are. We'd never know, would we, since everybody for ten thousand years has spoken Standard."

"So it isn't the size of the population, then, so much as—"

"How much they *care* about their language. How much it defines them as a community. A large population starts to think that everybody talks like them. They want to *distinguish* themselves, form a separate identity. Then they start developing jargons and slangs to separate themselves from others. Isn't that what happens to common speech? Children try to find ways of talking that their parents don't use. Professionals talk in private vocabularies so laymen won't know the passwords. All rituals for community definition."

Leyel nodded gravely, but he had one obvious doubt.

Obvious enough that Deet knew it, too. "Yes, yes, I know, Leyel. I immediately interpreted your question in terms of my own discipline. Like physicists who think that everything can be explained by physics."

Leyel laughed. "I thought of that, but what you said makes sense. And it would explain why the natural tendency of communities is to diversify language. We want a common tongue, a language of open discourse. But we also want private languages. Except a *completely* private language would be useless—whom would we talk to? So wherever a community forms, it creates at least a few linguistic barriers to outsiders, a few shibboleths that only insiders will know."

"And the more allegiance a person has to a community, the more fluent he'll become in that language, and the more he'll speak it."

"Yes, it makes sense," said Leyel. "So easy. You see how much I need you?"

He knew that his words were a mild rebuke—why weren't you home when I needed you—but he couldn't resist saying it. Sitting here with Deet, even in this strange and redolent place, felt right and comfortable. How could she have withdrawn from him? To him, her presence was what made a place home. To her, this place was home whether he was there or not.

He tried to put it in words—in abstract words, so it wouldn't sting. "I think the greatest tragedy is when one person has more allegiance to his community than any of the other members."

Deet only half smiled and raised her eyebrows. She didn't know what he was getting at.

"He speaks the community language all the time," said Leyel. "Only nobody else ever speaks it to him, or not enough anyway. And the more he speaks it, the more he alienates the others and drives them away, until he's alone. Can you imagine anything more sad? Somebody who's filled up with a language, hungry to speak, to hear it spoken, and yet there's no one left who understands a word of it."

She nodded, her eyes searching him. Does she understand what I'm saying? He waited for her to speak. He had said all he dared to say.

"But imagine this," she finally said. "What if he left that little place where no one understood him, and went over a hill to a new place, and all of a sudden he heard a hundred voices, a thousand, speaking the words he had treasured all those lonely years. And then he realized that he had never really known the language at all. The words had hundreds of meanings and nuances he had never guessed. Because each speaker changed the language a little just by speaking it. And when he spoke at last, his own voice sounded like music in his ears, and the others listened with delight, with rapture, his music was like the water of life pouring from a fountain, and he knew that he had never been home before."

Leyel couldn't remember hearing Deet sound so— rhapsodic, that was it, she herself was singing. She is the person she was talking about. In this place, her voice is different, that's what she meant. At home with me, she's been alone. Here in the library she's found others who speak her secret language. It isn't that she didn't want our marriage to succeed. She hoped for it, but I never understood her. These people did. Do. She's home here, that's what she's telling me.

"I understand," he said.

"Do you?" She looked searchingly into his face.

"I think so. It's all right."

She gave him a quizzical look.

"I mean, it's fine. It's good. This place. It's fine."

She looked relieved, but not completely. "You shouldn't be so *sad* about it, Leyel. This is a happy place. And you could do everything here that you ever did at home."

Except love you as the other part of me, and have you love me as the other part of you. "Yes, I'm sure."

"No, I mean it. What you're working on—I can see that you're getting close to something. Why not work on it *here*, where we can talk about it?"

Leyel shrugged.

"You *are* getting close, aren't you?"

"How do I know? I'm thrashing around like a drowning man in the ocean at night. Maybe I'm close to shore, and maybe I'm just swimming farther out to sea."

"Well, what do you have? Didn't we get closer just now?"

"No. This language thing—if it's just an aspect of community theory, it can't be the answer to human origin."

"Why not?"

"Because many primates have communities. A lot of other animals. Herding animals, for instance. Even schools of *fish*. Bees. Ants. Every multicelled organism is a community, for that matter. So if linguistic diversion grows out of community, then it's inherent in prehuman animals and therefore isn't part of the definition of humanity."

"Oh. I guess not."

"Right."

She looked disappointed. As if she had really hoped they would find the answer to the origin question right there, that very day.

Leyel stood up. "Oh well. Thanks for your help."

"I don't think I helped."

"Oh, you did. You showed me I was going up a dead-end road. You saved me a lot of wasted— thought. That's progress, in science, to know which answers aren't true."

His words had a double meaning, of course. She had also shown him that their marriage was a dead-end road. Maybe she understood him. Maybe not. It didn't matter—he had understood *her*. That little story about a lonely person finally discovering a place where she could be at home—how could he miss the point of that?

"Leyel," she said. "Why not put your question to the indexers?"

"Do you think the library researchers could find answers where *I* haven't?"

"Not the research department. *Indexing*."

"What do you mean?"

"Write down your questions. All the avenues you've pursued. Linguistic diversity. Primate language. And the other questions, the old ones. Archae-ological, historical approaches. Biological. Kinship patterns. Customs. Everything you can think of. Just put it together as questions. And then we'll have them index it."

"Index my *questions*?"

"It's what we do—we read things and think of other things that might be related somehow, and we connect them. We don't say what the connection means, but we know that it means something, that the connection is real. We won't give you answers, Leyel, but if you follow the index, it might help you to think of connections. Do you see what I mean?"

"I never thought of that. Do you think a couple of indexers might have the time to work on it?"

"Not a couple of us. *All* of us."

"Oh, that's absurd, Deet. I wouldn't even ask it."

"*I* would. We aren't supervised up here, Leyel. We don't meet quotas. Our job is to read and think. Usually we have a few hundred projects going, but for a day we could easily work on the same document."

"It would be a waste. I can't publish anything, Deet."

"It doesn't have to be published. Don't you understand? Nobody but us knows what we do here. We can take it as an unpublished document and work on it just the same. It won't ever have to go online for the library as a whole."

Leyel shook his head. "And then if they lead me to the answer—what, will we publish it with two hundred bylines?"

"It'll be *your* paper, Leyel. We're just indexers, not authors. You'll still have to make the connections. Let us try. Let us be *part* of this."

Suddenly Leyel understood why she was so insistent on this. Getting him involved with the library was her way of pretending she was still part of his life. She could believe she hadn't left him, if he became part of her new community.

Didn't she know how unbearable that would be? To see her here, so happy without him? To come here as just one friend among many, when once they had been—or he had thought they were—one indivisible soul? How could he possibly do such a thing?

And yet she wanted it, he could see it in the way she was looking at him, so girlish, so pleading that it made him think of when they were first in love, on another world—she would look at him like that whenever he insisted that he had to leave. Whenever she thought she might be losing him.

Doesn't she know who has lost whom?

Never mind. What did it matter if she didn't understand? If it would make her happy to have him pretend to be part of her new home, part of these librarians—if she wanted him to submit his life's work to the ministrations of these absurd indexers, then why not? What would it cost him? Maybe the process of writing down all his questions in some coherent order would help him. And maybe she was right—maybe a Trantorian index would help him solve the origin question.

Maybe if he came here, he could still be a small part of her life. It wouldn't be like marriage. But since that was impossible, then at least he could have enough of her here that he could remain himself, remain the person that he had become because of loving her for all these years.

"Fine," he said. "I'll write it up and bring it in."

"I really think we can help."

"Yes," he said, pretending to more certainty than he felt. "Maybe." He started for the door.

"Do you have to leave already?"

He nodded.

"Are you sure you can find your way out?"

"Unless the rooms have moved."

"No, only at night."

"Then I'll find my way out just fine." He took a few steps toward her, then stopped.

"What?" she asked.

"Nothing."

"Oh." She sounded disappointed. "I thought you were going to kiss me good-bye." Then she puckered up like a three-year-old child.

He laughed. He kissed her—like a three-year-old—and then he left.

For two days he brooded. Saw her off in the morning, then tried to read, to watch the vids, anything. Nothing held his attention. He took walks. He even went topside once, to see the sky overhead—it was night, thick with stars. None of it engaged him. Nothing *held*. One of the vid programs had a moment, just briefly, a scene on a semiarid world, where a strange plant grew that dried out at maturity, broke off at the root, and then let the wind blow it around, scattering seeds. For a moment he felt a dizzying empathy with the plant as it tumbled by—am I as dry as that, hurtling through dead land? But no, he knew even that wasn't true, because the tumbleweed had life enough left in it to scatter seeds. Level had no seed left. That was scattered years ago.

On the third morning he looked at himself in the mirror and laughed grimly. "Is this how people feel before they kill themselves?" he asked. Of course not—he knew that he was being melodramatic. He felt no desire to die.

But then it occurred to him that if this feeling of uselessness kept on, if he never found anything to engage himself, then he might as well be dead, mightn't he, because his being alive wouldn't accomplish much more than keeping his clothes warm.

He sat down at the scriptor and began writing down questions. Then, under each question, he would explain how he had already pursued that particular avenue and why it didn't yield the answer to the origin question. More questions would come up then—and he was right, the mere process of summarizing his own fruitless research made answers seem tantalizingly close. It was a good exercise. And even if he never found an answer, this list of questions might be of help to someone with a clearer intellect—or better information—decades or centuries or millennia from now.

Deet came home and went to bed with Leyel still typing away. She knew the look he had when he was fully engaged in writing—she did nothing to disturb him. He noticed her enough to realize that she was carefully leaving him alone. Then he settled back into writing.

The next morning she awoke to find him lying in bed beside her, still dressed. A personal message capsule lay on the floor in the doorway from the bedroom. He had finished his questions. She bent over, picked it up, took it with her to the library.

"His questions aren't academic after all, Deet."

"I told you they weren't."

"Hari was right. For all that he seemed to be a dilettante, with his money and his rejection of the universities, he's a man of substance."

"Will the Second Foundation benefit, then, if he comes up with an answer to his question?"

"I don't know, Deet. Hari was the fortune-teller. Presumably mankind is already human, so it isn't as if we have to start the process over."

"Do you think not?"

"What, should we find some uninhabited planet and put some newborns on it and let them grow up feral, and then come back in a thousand years and try to turn them human?"

"I have a better idea. Let's take ten thousand worlds filled with people who live their lives like animals, always hungry, always quick with their teeth and their claws, and let's strip away the veneer of civilization to expose to them what they really are. And then, when they see themselves clearly, let's come back and teach them how to be *really* human this time, instead of only having bits and flashes of humanity."

"All right. Let's do that."

"I knew you'd see it my way."

"Just make sure your husband finds out *how* the trick is done. Then we have all the time in the world to set it up and pull it off."

When the index was done, Deet brought Leyel with her to the library when she went to work in the morning. She did not take him to Indexing, but rather installed him in a private research room lined with vids—only instead of giving the illusion of windows looking out onto an outside scene, the screens filled all the walls from floor to ceiling, so it seemed that he was on a pinnacle high above the scene, without walls or even a railing to keep him from falling off. It gave him flashes of vertigo when he looked around—only the door broke the illusion. For a moment he thought of asking for a different room. But then he remembered Indexing, and realized that maybe he'd do better work if he too felt a bit off balance all the time.

At first the indexing seemed obvious. He brought the first page of his questions to the lector display and began to read. The lector would track his pupils, so that whenever he paused to gaze at a word, other references would begin to pop up in the space beside the page he was reading. Then he'd glance at one of the references. When it was uninteresting or obvious, he'd skip to the next reference, and the first one would slide back on the display, out of the way, but still there if he changed his mind and wanted it.

If a reference engaged him, then when he reached the last line of the part of it on display, it would expand to full-page size and slide over to stand in front of the main text. Then, if this new material had been indexed, it would trigger new references— and so on, leading him farther and farther away from the original document until he finally decided to go back and pick up where he left off.

So far, this was what any index could be expected to do. It was only as he moved farther into reading his own questions that he began to realize the quirkiness of this index. Usually, index references were tied to important words, so that if you just wanted to stop and think without bringing up a bunch of references you didn't want, all you had to do was keep your gaze focused in an area of placeholder words, empty phrases like "If this were all that could be . . ." Anyone who made it a habit to read indexed works soon learned this trick and used it till it became reflex.

But when Leyel stopped on such empty phrases, references came up anyway. And instead of having a clear relationship to the text, sometimes the references were perverse or comic or argumentative. For instance, he paused in the middle of reading his argument that archaeological searches for "primitiveness" were useless in the search for origins because all "primitive" cultures represented a decline from a star-going culture. He had written the phrase "All this primitivism is useful only because it predicts what we might become if we're careless and don't preserve our fragile links with civilization." By habit his eyes focused on the empty words "what we might become if." Nobody could index a phrase like that.

Yet they had. Several references appeared. And so instead of staying within his reverie, he was distracted, drawn to what the indexers had tied to such an absurd phrase.

One of the references was a nursery rhyme that he had forgotten he knew:

> Wrinkly Grandma Posey
> Rockets all are rosy.
> Lift off, drift off,
> All fall down.

Why in the world had the indexer put *that* in? The first thought that came to Leyel's mind was himself and some of the servants' children, holding hands and walking in a circle, round and round till they came to the last words, whereupon they threw themselves to the ground and laughed insanely. The sort of game that only little children could possibly think was fun.

Since his eyes lingered on the poem, it moved to the main document display and new references appeared. One was a scholarly article on the evolution of the poem, speculating that it might have arisen during the early days of starflight on the planet of origin, when rockets may have been used to escape from a planet's gravity well. Was that why this poem had been indexed to his article? Because it was tied to the planet of origin?

No, that was too obvious. Another article about the poem was more helpful. It rejected the early-days-of-rockets idea, because the earliest versions of the poem never used the word "rocket." The oldest extant version went like this:

> *Wrinkle down a rosy,*
> *Pock-a fock-a posy,*
> *Lash us, dash us,*
> *All fall down.*

Obviously, said the commentator, these were mostly nonsense words—the later versions had arisen because children had insisted on trying to make sense of them.

And it occurred to Leyel that perhaps this was why the indexer had linked this poem to his phrase—because the poem had once been nonsense, but we insisted on making sense out of it.

Was this a comment on Leyel's whole search for origins? Did the indexer think it was useless?

No—the poem had been tied to the empty phrase "what we might become if." Maybe the indexer was saying that human beings are like this poem—our lives make no sense, but we insist on making sense out of them. Didn't Deet say something like that once, when she was talking about the role of storytelling in community formation? The universe resists causality, she said. But human intelligence demands it. So we tell stories to impose causal relationships among the unconnected events of the world around us.

That includes ourselves, doesn't it? Our own lives are nonsense, but we impose a story on them, we sort our memories into cause-and-effect chains, forcing them to make sense even though they don't. Then we take the sum of our stories and call it our "self." This poem shows us the process—from randomness to meaning—and then we think our meanings are "true."

But somehow all the children had come to agree on the new version of the poem. By the year 2000

G.E., only the final and current version existed in all the worlds, and it had remained constant ever since. How was it that all the children on every world came to agree on the same version? How did the change spread? Did ten thousand kids on ten thousand worlds happen to make up the same changes?

It had to be word of mouth. Some kid somewhere made a few changes, and his version spread. A few years, and all the children in his neighborhood use the new version, and then all the kids in his city, on his planet. It could happen very quickly, in fact, because each generation of children lasts only a few years—seven-year-olds might take the new version as a joke, but repeat it often enough that five-year-olds think it's the true version of the poem, and within a few years there's nobody left among the children who remembers the old way.

A thousand years is long enough for the new version of the poem to spread. Or for five or a dozen new versions to collide and get absorbed into each other and then spread back, changed, to worlds that had revised the poem once or twice already.

And as Leyel sat there, thinking these thoughts, he conjured up an image in his mind of a network of children, bound to each other by the threads of this poem, extending from planet to planet throughout the Empire, and then back through time, from one generation of children to the previous one, a three-dimensional fabric that bound all children together from the beginning.

And yet as each child grew up, he cut himself free from the fabric of that poem. No longer would he hear the words "Wrinkly Grandma Posey" and immediately join hands with the child next to him. He wasn't part of the song any more.

But his own children were. And then his grandchildren. All joining hands with each other, changing from circle to circle, in a never-ending human chain reaching back to some long-forgotten ritual on one of the worlds of mankind—maybe, maybe on the planet of origin itself.

The vision was so clear, so overpowering, that when he finally noticed the lector display it was as sudden and startling as waking up. He had to sit there, breathing shallowly, until he calmed himself, until his heart stopped beating so fast.

He had found some part of his answer, though he didn't understand it yet. That fabric connecting all the children, that was part of what made us human, though he didn't know why. This strange and perverse indexing of a meaningless phrase had brought him a new way of looking at the problem. Not that the universal culture of children was a new idea. Just that he had never thought of it as having anything to do with the origin question.

Was this what the indexer meant by including this poem? Had the indexer also seen this vision?

Maybe, but probably not. It might have been nothing more than the idea of becoming something that made the indexer think of transformation—becoming old, like wrinkly Grandma Posey? Or it might have been a general thought about the spread of humanity through the stars, away from the planet of origin, that made the indexer remember how the poem seemed to tell of rockets that rise up from a planet, drift for a while, then come down to settle on a planet. Who knows what the poem meant to the indexer? Who knows why it occurred to her to link it with his document on that particular phrase?

Then Leyel realized that in his imagination, he was thinking of Deet making that particular connection. There was no reason to think it was her work, except that in his mind she was all the indexers. She had joined them, become one of them, and so when indexing work was being done, she was part of it. That's what it meant to be part of a community— all its works became, to a degree, your works. All that the indexers did, Deet was a part of it, and therefore Deet had done it.

Again the image of a fabric came to mind, only this time it was a topologically impossible fabric, twisted into itself so that no matter what part of the edge of it you held, you held the entire edge, and the middle, too. It was all one thing, and each part held the whole within it.

But if that was true, then when Deet came to join the library, so did Leyel, because she contained Leyel within her. So in coming here, she had not left him at all. Instead, she had woven him into a new fabric, so that instead of losing something he was gaining. He was part of all this, because *she* was, and so if he lost her it would only be because he rejected her.

Leyel covered his eyes with his hands. How did his meandering thoughts about the origin question lead him to thinking about his marriage? Here he thought he was on the verge of profound understanding, and then he fell back into self-absorption.

He cleared away all the references to "Wrinkly Grandma Posey" or "Wrinkle Down a Rosy" or whatever it was, then returned to reading his original document, trying to confine his thoughts to the subject at hand.

Yet it was a losing battle. He could not escape from the seductive distraction of the index. He'd be reading about tool use and technology, and how it could not be the dividing line between human and animal because there were animals that made tools and taught their use to others.

Then, suddenly, the index would have him reading an ancient terror tale about a man who wanted to be the greatest genius of all time, and he believed that the only thing preventing him from achieving greatness was the hours he lost in sleep. So he invented a machine to sleep for him, and it worked very well until he realized that the machine was having all his dreams. Then he demanded that his machine tell him what it was dreaming.

The machine poured forth the most astonishing, brilliant thoughts ever imagined by any man—far wiser than anything this man had ever written during his waking hours. The man took a hammer and smashed the machine, so that he could have his dreams back. But even when he started sleeping again, he was never able to come close to the clarity of thought that the machine had had.

Of course he could never publish what the machine had written—it would be unthinkable to put forth the product of a machine as if it were the work of a man. After the man died—in despair—people found the printed text of what the machine had written, and thought the man had written it and hidden it away. They published it, and he was widely acclaimed as the greatest genius who had ever lived.

This was universally regarded as an obscenely horrifying tale because it had a machine stealing part of a man's mind and using it to destroy him, a common theme. But why did the indexer refer to it in the midst of a discussion of tool-making?

Wondering about that led Leyel to think that this story itself was a kind of tool. Just like the machine the man in the story had made. The storyteller gave his dreams to the story, and then when people heard it or read it, his dreams—his nightmares—came out to live in their memories. Clear and sharp and terrible and true, those dreams they received. And yet if he tried to *tell* them the same truths, directly, not in the form of a story, people would think his ideas were silly and small.

And then Leyel remembered what Deet had said about how people absorb stories from their communities and take them into themselves and use these stories to form their own spiritual autobiography. They remember doing what the heroes of the stories did, and so they continue to act out each hero's character in their own lives, or, failing that, they measure themselves against the standard the story set for them. Stories become the human conscience, the human mirror.

Again, as so many other times, he ended these ruminations with his hands pressed over his eyes, trying to shut out—or lock in?—images of fabrics and mirrors, worlds and atoms, until finally, finally, he opened his eyes and saw Deet and Zay sitting in front of him.

No, leaning over him. He was on a low bed, and they knelt beside him.

"Am I ill?" he asked.

"I hope not," said Deet. "We found you on the floor. You're exhausted, Leyel. I've been telling you—you have to eat, you have to get a normal amount of sleep. You're not young enough to keep up this work schedule."

"I've barely started."

Zay laughed lightly. "Listen to him, Deet. I told you he was so caught up in this that he didn't even know what day it was."

"You've been doing this for three weeks, Leyel. For the last week you haven't even come home. I bring you food, and you won't eat. People talk to you, and you forget that you're in a conversation, you just drift off into some sort of—trance. Leyel, I wish I'd never brought you here, I wish I'd never suggested indexing—"

"No!" Leyel cried. He struggled to sit up.

At first Deet tried to push him back down, insisting he should rest. It was Zay who helped him sit. "Let the man talk," she said. "Just because you're his wife doesn't mean you can stop him from talking."

"The index is wonderful," said Leyel. "Like a tunnel opened up into my own mind. I keep seeing light just *that* far out of reach, and then I wake up and it's just me alone on a pinnacle except for the pages up on the lector. I keep losing it—"

"No, Leyel, we keep losing *you*. The index is poisoning you, it's taking over your mind—"

"Don't be absurd, Deet. You're the one who suggested this, and you're right. The index keeps surprising me, making me think in new ways. There are some answers already."

"Answers?" asked Zay.

"I don't know how well I can explain it. What makes us human. It has to do with communities and stories and tools and—it has to do with you and me, Deet."

"I should hope we're human," she said. Teasing him, but also urging him on.

"We lived together all those years, and we formed a community—with our children, till they left, and then just us. But we were like animals."

"Only sometimes," she said.

"I mean like herding animals, or primate tribes, or any community that's bound together only by the rituals and patterns of the present moment. We had our customs, our habits. Our private language of words and gestures, our dances, all the things that flocks of geese and hives of bees can do."

"Very primitive."

"Yes, that's right, don't you see? That's a community that dies with each generation. When we die,

Deet, it will all be gone with us. Other people will marry, but none of them will know our dances and songs and language and—"

"Our children will."

"No, that's my point. They knew us, they even think they *know* us, but they were never part of the community of our marriage. Nobody is. Nobody *can* be. That's why, when I thought you were leaving me for this—"

"When did you think that I—"

"Hush, Deet," said Zay. "Let the man babble."

"When I thought you were leaving me, I felt like I was dead, like I was losing everything, because if you weren't part of our marriage, then there was nothing left. You see?"

"I don't see what that has to do with human origins, Leyel. I only know that I would never leave you, and I can't believe that you could think—"

"Don't distract him, Deet."

"It's the children. All the children. They play Wrinkly Grandma Posey, and then they grow up and don't play anymore, so the actual community of these particular five or six children doesn't exist any more—but other kids are still doing the dance. Chanting the poem. For ten thousand years!"

"This makes us human? Nursery rhymes?"

"They're all part of the same community! Across all the empty space between the stars, there are still connections, they're still somehow the *same kids.* Ten thousand years, ten thousand worlds, quintillions of children, and they all knew the poem, they all did the dance. Story and ritual—it doesn't die with the tribe, it doesn't stop at the border. Children who never met face-to-face, who lived so far apart that the light from one star still hasn't reached the other, they belonged to the same community. We're human because we conquered time and space. We conquered the barrier of perpetual ignorance between one person and another. We found a way to slip my memories into your head, and yours into mine."

"But these are the ideas you already rejected, Leyel. Language and community and—"

"No! No, not just language, not just tribes of chimpanzees chattering at each other. *Stories,* epic tales that define a community, mythic tales that teach us how the world works, we use them to create each other. We became a different species, we became *human,* because we found a way to extend gestation beyond the womb, a way to give each child ten thousand parents that he'll never meet face-to-face."

Then, at last, Leyel fell silent, trapped by the inadequacy of his words. They couldn't tell what he had seen in his mind. If they didn't already understand, they never would.

"Yes," said Zay. "I think indexing your paper was a very good idea."

Leyel sighed and lay back down on the bed. "I shouldn't have tried."

"On the contrary, you've succeeded," said Zay.

Deet shook her head. Leyel knew why—Deet was trying to signal Zay that she shouldn't attempt to soothe Leyel with false praise.

"Don't hush me, Deet. I know what I'm saying. I may not know Leyel as well as you do, but I know truth when I hear it. In a way, I think Hari knew it instinctively. That's why he insisted on all his silly holodisplays, forcing the poor citizens of Terminus to put up with his pontificating every few years. It was his way of continuing to create them, of remaining alive within them. Making them feel like their lives had purpose behind them. Mythic and epic story, both at once. They'll all carry a bit of Hari Seldon within them just the way that children carry their parents with them to the grave."

At first Leyel could only hear the idea that Hari would have approved of his ideas of human origin. Then he began to realize that there was much more to what Zay had said than simple affirmation.

"You knew Hari Seldon?"

"A little," said Zay.

"Either tell him or don't," said Deet. "You can't take him this far in, and not bring him the rest of the way."

"I knew Hari the way you know Deet," said Zay.

"No," said Leyel. "He would have mentioned you."

"Would he? He never mentioned his students."

"He had thousands of students."

"I know, Leyel. I saw them come and fill his lecture halls and listen to the half-baked fragments of psychohistory that he taught them. But then he'd come away, here to the library, into a room where the Pubs never go, where he could speak words that the Pubs would never hear, and there he'd teach his real students. Here is the only place where the science of psychohistory lives on, where Deet's ideas about the formation of community actually have application, where your own vision of the origin of humanity will shape our calculations for the next thousand years."

Leyel was dumbfounded. "In the Imperial Library? Hari had his own college here in the library?"

"Where else? He had to leave us at the end, when it was time to go public with his predictions of the Empire's fall. Then the Pubs started watching him in earnest, and in order to keep them from finding us, he couldn't ever come back here again. It was the most terrible thing that ever happened to us. As if he died, for us, years before his body died. He was part of us, Leyel, the way that you and Deet are part of each other. She knows. She joined us before he left."

It stung. To have had such a great secret, and not to have been included. "Why Deet, and not me?"

"Don't you know, Leyel? Our little community's survival was the most important thing. As long as you were Leyel Forska, master of one of the greatest fortunes in history, you couldn't possibly be part of this—it would have provoked too much comment, too much attention. Deet could come, because Commissioner Chen wouldn't care that much what she did—he never takes spouses seriously, just one of the ways he proves himself to be a fool."

"But Hari always meant for you to be one of us," said Deet. "His worst fear was that you'd go off half-cocked and force your way into the First Foundation, when all along he wanted you in this one. The Second Foundation."

Leyel remembered his last interview with Hari. He tried to remember—did Hari ever lie to him? He told him that Deet couldn't go to Terminus—but now that took on a completely different meaning. The old fox! He never lied at all, but he never told the truth, either.

Zay went on. "It was tricky, striking the right balance, encouraging you to provoke Chen just enough that he'd strip away your fortune and then forget you, but not so much that he'd have you imprisoned or killed."

"You were making that happen?"

"No, no, Leyel. It was going to happen anyway, because you're who you are and Chen is who he is. But there was a range of possibility, somewhere between having you and Deet tortured to death on the one hand, and on the other hand having you and

Rom conspire to assassinate Chen and take control of the Empire. Either of those extremes would have made it impossible for you to be part of the Second Foundation. Hari was convinced—and so is Deet, and so am I—that you belong with us. Not dead. Not in politics. Here."

It was outrageous, that they should make such choices for him, without telling him. How could Deet have kept it secret all this time? And yet they were so obviously correct. If Hari had told him about this Second Foundation, Leyel would have been eager, proud to join it. Yet Leyel couldn't have been told, couldn't have joined them until Chen no longer perceived him as a threat.

"What makes you think Chen will ever forget me?"

"Oh, he's forgotten you, all right. In fact, I'd guess that by tonight he'll have forgotten everything he ever knew."

"What do you mean?"

"How do you think we've dared to speak so openly today, after keeping silence for so long? After all, we aren't in Indexing now."

Leyel felt a thrill of fear run through him. "They can hear us?"

"If they were listening. At the moment, though, the Pubs are very busy helping Rom Divart solidify his control of the Commission of Public Safety. And if Chen hasn't been taken to the radiation chamber, he soon will be."

Leyel couldn't help himself. The news was too glorious—he sprang up from his bed, almost danced at the news. "Rom's doing it! After all these years—overthrowing the old spider!"

"It's more important than mere justice or revenge," said Zay. "We're absolutely certain that a significant number of governors and prefects and military commanders will refuse to recognize the overlordship of the Commission of Public Safety. It will take Rom Divart the rest of his life just to put down the most dangerous of the rebels. In order to concentrate his forces on the great rebels and pretenders close to Trantor, he'll grant an unprecedented degree of independence to many, many worlds on the periphery. To all intents and purposes, those outer worlds will no longer be part of the Empire. Imperial authority will not touch them, and their taxes will no longer flow inward to Trantor. The Empire is no longer Galactic. The death of Commissioner Chen—today—will mark the beginning of the fall of the Galactic Empire, though no one but us will notice what it means for decades, even centuries to come."

"So soon after Hari's death. Already his predictions are coming true."

"Oh, it isn't just coincidence," said Zay. "One of our agents was able to influence Chen just enough to ensure that he sent Rom Divart in person to strip you of your fortune. That was what pushed Rom over the edge and made him carry out this coup. Chen would have fallen—or died—sometime in the next year and a half no matter what we did. But I'll admit we took a certain pleasure in using Hari's death as a trigger to bring him down a little early, and under circumstances that allowed us to bring you into the library."

"We also used it as a test," said Deet. "We're trying to find ways of influencing individuals without their knowing it. It's still very crude and haphazard, but in this case we were able to influence Chen with great success. We had to do it—your life was at stake, and so was the chance of your joining us."

"I feel like a puppet," said Leyel.

"Chen was the puppet," said Zay. "You were the prize."

"That's all nonsense," said Deet. "Hari loved you, *I* love you. You're a great man. The Second Foundation had to have you. And everything you've said and stood for all your life made it clear that you were hungry to be part of our work. Aren't you?"

"Yes," said Leyel. Then he laughed. "The index!"

"What's so funny?" asked Zay, looking a little miffed. "We worked very hard on it."

"And it was wonderful, transforming, hypnotic. To take all these people and put them together as if they were a single mind, far wiser in its intuition than anyone could ever be alone. The most intensely unified, the most powerful human community that's ever existed. If it's our capacity for storytelling that makes us human, then perhaps our capacity for indexing will make us something better than human."

Deet patted Zay's hand. "Pay no attention to him, Zay. This is clearly the mad enthusiasm of a proselyte."

Zay raised an eyebrow. "*I'm* still waiting for him to explain why the index made him *laugh*."

Leyel obliged her. "Because all the time, I kept thinking—how could librarians have done this? Mere librarians! And now I discover that these librarians are all of Hari Seldon's prize students. My questions were indexed by psychohistorians!"

"Not exclusively. Most of us *are* librarians. Or machinists, or custodians, or whatever—the psychologists and psychohistorians are rather a thin current in the stream of the library. At first they were seen as outsiders. Researchers. *Users* of the library, not members of it. That's what Deet's work has been for these last few years—trying to bind us all together into one community. She came here as a researcher too, remember? Yet now she has made everyone's allegiance to the library more important than any other loyalty. It's working beautifully too, Leyel, you'll see. Deet is a marvel."

"We're *all* creating it together," said Deet. "It helps that the couple of hundred people I'm trying to bring in are so knowledgeable and understanding of the human mind. They understand exactly what I'm doing and then try to help me make it work. And it *isn't* fully successful yet. As years go by, we have to see the psychology group teaching and accepting the children of librarians and machinists and medical officers, in full equality with their own, so that the psychologists don't become a ruling caste. And then intermarriage between the groups. Maybe in a hundred years we'll have a truly cohesive community. This is a democratic city-state we're building, not an academic department or a social club."

Leyel was off on his own tangent. It was almost unbearable for him to realize that there were hundreds of people who knew Hari's work, while Leyel didn't. "You have to teach me!" Leyel said. "Everything that Hari taught you, all the things that have been kept from me—"

"Oh, eventually, Leyel," said Zay. "At present, though, we're much more interested in what you have to teach *us*. Already, I'm sure, a transcription of the things you said when you first woke up is being spread through the library."

"It was recorded?" asked Leyel.

"We didn't know if you were going to go catatonic on us at any moment, Leyel. You have no idea how you've been worrying us. Of course we recorded it— they might have been your last words."

"They won't be. I don't feel tired at all."

"Then you're not as bright as we thought. Your body is dangerously weak. You've been abusing yourself terribly. You're not a young man, and we insist that you stay away from your lector for a couple of days."

"What, are you now my doctor?"

"Leyel," Deet said, touching him on his shoulder the way she always did when he needed calming. "You *have* been examined by doctors. And you've got to realize—Zay is First Speaker."

"Does that mean she's commander?"

"This isn't the Empire," said Zay, "and I'm not Chen. All that it means to be First Speaker is that I speak first when we meet together. And then, at the end, I bring together all that has been said and express the consensus of the group."

"That's right," said Deet. "*Everybody* thinks you ought to rest."

"*Everybody* knows about me?" asked Leyel.

"Of course," said Zay. "With Hari dead you're the most original thinker we have. Our work needs you. Naturally we care about you. Besides, Deet loves you so much, and we love *Deet* so much, we feel like we're all a little bit in love with you ourselves."

She laughed, and so did Leyel, and so did Deet. Leyel noticed, though, that when he asked whether they all *knew* of him, she had answered that they cared about him and loved him. Only when Zay said this did he realize that she had answered the question he really meant to ask.

"And while you're recuperating," Zay continued, "Indexing will have a go at your new theory—"

"Not a theory, just a proposal, just a *thought*—"

"—and a few psychohistorians will see whether it can be quantified, perhaps by some variation on the formulas we've been using with Deet's laws of community development. Maybe we can turn origin studies into a real science yet."

"Maybe," Leyel said.

"Feel all right about this?" asked Zay.

"I'm not sure. Mostly. I'm very excited, but I'm also a little angry at how I've been left out, but mostly I'm—I'm so relieved."

"Good. You're in a hopeless muddle. You'll do your best work if we can keep you off balance forever." With that, Zay led him back to the bed, helped him lie down, and then left the room.

Alone with Deet, Leyel had nothing to say. He just held her hand and looked up into her face, his heart too full to say anything with words. All the news about Hari's byzantine plans and a Second Foundation full of psychohistorians and Rom Divart taking over the government—that receded into the background. What mattered was this: Deet's hand in his, her eyes looking into his, and her heart, her self, her soul so closely bound to his that he couldn't tell and didn't care where he left off and she began.

How could he ever have imagined that she was leaving him? They had created each other through all these years of marriage. Deet was the most splendid accomplishment of his life, and he was the most valued creation of hers. We are each other's parent, each other's child. We might accomplish great works that will live on in this other community, the library, the Second Foundation. But the greatest work of all is the one that will die with us, the one that no one else will ever know of, because they remain perpetually outside. We can't even explain it to them. They don't have the language to understand us. We can only speak it to each other.

AFTERWORD

"A THOUSAND DEATHS"

MY EARLY FICTION won me a reputation for cruelty. The most memorable line was from a review in *Locus:* "Reading Card is like playing pattycake with Baby Huey." This sort of comment, however well-phrased, worried me more than a little. Clearly my fiction was giving the impression of being bloodier than most writers' stories, and yet that was never my intent. I'm an innately nonviolent person. I have almost never struck another person in anger; my custom in school when the subject of fighting came up was to talk my way out when I couldn't simply run. I never tortured animals. I don't enjoy pain. So why was I writing fiction that made grown men gag?

This story, "A Thousand Deaths," was one of a

pair (the other is "Kingsmeat") that did most to earn me that reputation. It is the one story I've written that was so sickening that my wife couldn't finish reading it—she never has, as far as I know. And yet I couldn't see at the time—and still can't—how it could be written any other way.

The story is about noncompliance. It was triggered in part by a line in Robert Bolt's *A Man for All Seasons*, which dwells in my memory in this form: "I do none harm, I think none harm, and if this be not enough to keep a man alive, then in faith I long not to live." There are times when a government, to stay in power, requires that certain people be broken, publicly. Their noncompliance with the will of the government is a constant refreshment to the enemies of the state. One thinks of Nelson Mandela, who, to be set free, would have had only to sign a statement renouncing violence as a means of obtaining the rights of his people. One thinks of the wonderful line from the movie *Gandhi* (which had not been made when I wrote this story, though the line expresses the theme of this story almost perfectly): "They can even kill me. What will they have then? My dead body. Not my obedience." It is the power of passive resistance, even in the face of a government that has the power to inflict the ultimate penalty, that eventually breaks the power of that government.

With "A Thousand Deaths" I simply did what satiric science fiction always does—I set up a society that exaggerates the point in question. In this case, it was the power of the state to inflict punishment in order to control the behavior of others, and my *what-if* was, "What if a government could, not just threaten to kill you, but actually kill you over and over until it finally got the confession it needed?" The mechanism was easy enough—I had already developed the drug somec and had stolen the idea of brain-taping from many other writers years before, for my *Worthing Chronicle* series. What mattered to me, though, was to focus on the point where coercion ultimately breaks down, and that is on the rock of truth. The government kills the story's hero, trying to break him to the point where he will confess his wrong, and confess the rightness of the government. The trouble is that the government will only measure his confession against a standard too high for him to meet. It isn't enough that his confession be passionate. It must also be *believed.* And that is the one thing that the hero cannot deliver—a believable confession. He can't believe it himself; neither can anyone else. That is what coercion cannot do. It can win compliance from fearful people. But it cannot win belief. The heart is an unstormable citadel.

How, tell me please, could I possibly have told this story without making you, the reader, believe absolutely in the hero's deaths? You have to experience some shadow of the suffering in order to understand the impossibility of his confession. If you find the story unbearable, remember that there have been far more deaths than this, and more terrible ones as well, in the same struggle in the real world.

A footnote: In the late seventies, I set this story in a United States ruled by a Soviet government. In this I was not seriously predicting something I believed likely to happen. But I was trying to place the story of a totalitarian state within the United States if only to bring home the idea to American readers, who, outside of the experience of American blacks in many a Southern town, are ignorant of the suffering and terror of totalitarianism. Once the decision to set the story here was made, I had two choices: to show an America ruled by a homegrown demagogue, or to show an America ruled by a foreign conqueror.

I rejected the former, in part because at that time it had lately become a cliché of American litterateurs to pretend that the only danger to the U.S. was from conservative extremists. I preferred to show America ruled by the most cruel and efficient totalitarian system ever to exist on the face of the Earth: the Stalinist version of the Communist Party.

The events of 1989 in eastern Europe do not change this; it was the very unwillingness of Gorbachev to play Stalin that led to the unshackling of the captive nations. Had he been willing to resort to the machine gun and the tank, as his predecessors did, there would be no more Solidarity, no second Prague Spring, no holes in the Berlin Wall, no bullet-riddled body of Ceausescu, no Hungarian border open to Austria. Or would there? Gorbachev was the man who brought Russia over that moral cusp—but I think it would have had to come eventually, with him or someone else. "A Thousand Deaths" is a true story, and I used the Soviets in it because they are the most recent world power to prove that it is true.

"CLAP HANDS AND SING"

Once, back in the mid-1970s, I had a conversation with a young woman I had once thought myself to be in love with. "I had such a crush on you before you went on your mission," she said. "And the poems you wrote me while you were gone . . . I thought something would come of it when you got home. But when you returned from Brazil, I waited and waited and you never even called."

"I thought of calling," I said. "Often."

"But you never did. And on the rebound from you I fell in love with someone else."

Here's the funny thing: I never guessed how *she*

felt. One reason I never called her was because I thought she might think I was weird to try to convert a friendship to something more. Thus do adolescents manage to work at cross-purposes often enough to make romantic tragedies possible.

In the years since, I have found a much deeper love and stronger commitment than anything I ever imagined in those days. But when I was exploring the idea of time travel, and thought of an ironic story in which two people, unknown to each other, both journey back in time to have a perfect night together, my mind naturally turned to that moment of impotent frustration when I realized that this young lady and I, had I but acted a bit differently, might have ended up together. Since it's much easier to use real events than to make up phony ones, I stole from my own life to find, I hoped, that sense of bittersweet memory that is the stuff of movie romances.

"DOGWALKER"

Cyberpunk was all the rage, and I was driving home from ArmadilloCon, the science fiction convention held in Austin, the see of the bishop of cyberpunk, Bruce Sterling. I had long had an ambivalent feeling toward cyberpunk. Bruce Sterling's ideas about science fiction fascinated me greatly, if only because he was the one person I could hear talking about science fiction in terms that weren't either warmed-over James Blish and Damon Knight or stolen from the mouldering corpse of Modernism that still stinks to high heaven in the English departments of American universities. In short, Sterling actually had Ideas instead of Echoes.

At the same time, I could not help but be a bit disgusted at what was being done in the name of cyberpunk. William Gibson, though quite talented, seemed to be writing the same story over and over again. Furthermore, it was the same self-serving story that was being churned out in every creative writing course in America and published in every little literary magazine at least once an issue: the suffering artist who is alienated from his society and is struggling to find out a reason to live. My answer is easy enough: An artist who is alienated from his society *has* no reason to live—as an artist, anyway. You can only live as an artist when you're firmly connected to the community to whom you offer your art.

But the worst thing about cyberpunk was the shallowness of those who imitated it. Splash some drugs onto brain-and-microchip interface, mix it up with some vague sixties-style counterculture, and then use really self-conscious, affected language, and you've got cyberpunk. Never mind that the actual stories being told were generally clichés that were every bit as stupid and derivative as the worst of the stuff Bruce Sterling had initially rebelled against. Even if the underlying stories had been highly original, stylistic imitation and affectation are crimes enough to make a literary movement worthy of the death sentence.

So, being the perverse and obnoxious child that I am, I challenged myself: Is the derivativeness of cyberpunk the source or a symptom of its emptiness? Is it possible to write a good story that uses all the clichés of cyberpunk? The brain-microchip interface, the faked-up slang, the drugs, the counterculture . . . Could I, a good Mormon boy who watched the sixties through the wrong end of the binoculars, write a convincing story in that mode—and also tell a tale that would satisfy *me* as good fiction?

One thing was certain—I couldn't imitate anybody else's *story*. It was the language, the *style* that I was imitating. So I had to violate my own custom and start, not with the story, but with the voice. With a monologue. The first two paragraphs of *Dogwalker* were the first two I wrote, pretty much as they stand now. The plot came only after I had the voice and the character of the narrator pretty well established.

I got the thing done soon after returning home, and sent it off to Gardner Dozois at *Asimov's*. I expected the story to get bounced. I had a mental picture of Gardner staggering out into the hall at Davis Publications, gagging and choking, holding out the manuscript as if it were a bag of burning dog dung. "Look at this. *Card* is trying to write cyberpunk now." Instead, Gardner sent me a contract. It rather spoiled my plans—I expected to use the story as my entry at Sycamore Hill that summer, but since it had sold I couldn't do that. The result was that I ended up writing my novella "Pageant Wagon" during that workshop, so it wasn't a total loss.

In the meantime, however, Gardner never published "Dogwalker." He held it two-and-a-half years before I finally sent a note pointing out that our contract had expired and if they didn't have immediate plans to publish it, I wanted it back to sell it elsewhere. At that point they seemed to have suddenly remembered that they had it, and it was scheduled and published barely in time to be included in this book.

In a way, though, Gardner did me a favor—perhaps on purpose. By holding the story so long, he had seen to it that "Dogwalker" appeared in print *after* the spate of cyberpunk imitations was over. The story was not so clearly pegged as derivative. And though it was clearly not like a "typical Card story" on its surface, it could more easily be received as my work than as pale-imitation Gibson. Thus was I spared the fate of appearing as pathetic as, say, Barbra Streisand singing disco with the BeeGees.

"BUT WE TRY NOT TO ACT LIKE IT"

For a short time, Kristine's and my favorite restaurant in Salt Lake City was the Savoy, a purportedly English restaurant that nevertheless had wonderful food. We brought friends, we went alone—we did everything we could to make that restaurant succeed. Furthermore it was always crowded. And six months later, it was out of business.

It happens over and over. TV shows I like are doomed to cancellation. Authors I fall in love with stop writing the kind of book I loved. (Come on, Mortimer and Rendell! Rumpole and Wexford are the reason you were born! As for you, Gregory McDonald, write Fletch or die!) Trends in science fiction and fantasy that I applaud quickly vanish; the ones that make me faintly sick seem to linger like herpes. For one reason or another, my tastes are just not reflected in the real world.

That's what gave rise to this story. Unfortunately, I never let the story rise above its origin. I have learned since then that I shouldn't write a story from a single idea, but rather should wait for a second, unrelated idea, so that out of their confluence can come something truly alive. The result is that this story bears the curse of most of science fiction—it is idea-driven rather than character-driven, which means that it is ultimately forgettable. That doesn't mean it's valueless—I hope it's kind of fun to read it once. But you'll certainly not be rewarded for reading it again. You already received everything it had to offer on the first reading.

"I PUT MY BLUE GENES ON"

Jim Baen wrote an editorial in *Galaxy* magazine in which he called on science fiction writers to stop writing the same old "futures" and take a look at what science was doing *now*. Where, for example, were the stories extrapolating on current research in recombinant DNA?

I was still working at *The Ensign* magazine then, and Jay and Lane and I took this as a personal challenge. Naturally, in the tradition of young sci-fi writers, I mechanically took the idea of gene-splicing (I'd been reading *Scientific American* like a good boy, so I could fake it up pretty well), carried it to an extreme, and served it up in a stereotypical plot about two nations in a life-and-death struggle—only one of the nations doesn't realize that the other one was wiped out long ago and that its struggle is now against the very world they have destroyed. As a let's-stop-messing-up-the-world polemic, I think the story still holds up pretty well. As an artful story, it's definitely a work of my youth. Recombining DNA has been treated far better since then, both in my own stories (*Wyrms*, *Speaker for the Dead*) and in the works of writers who've done the subject more justice. (I think particularly of the magnificent work Octavia Butler has done with *Dawn*, *Adulthood Rites*, and *Imago*.) If you want proof that I was but an adolescent playing at fiction-writing, you have only to look at the title, a bad pun on a fun-but-dumb popular song that was, I believe, written as the theme music for a jeans ad.

I notice now, however, that some later interests of

mine were already cropping up in "I Put My Blue Genes On." For one thing, I actually put Brazilians in space. I was not the first to do it, but it was the beginning of my deliberate effort to try to get American sci-fi writers to realize that the future probably does *not* belong to America. Science fiction of the pre–World War I era always seemed to put Englishmen and Frenchmen into space; now, in this post-imperialist world, we think of that as a rather quaint idea. I firmly believe that in fifty years the idea of Americans leading the world anywhere will be just as anachronistic, and only those of us who put Brazilians, Thais, Chinese, and Mexicans into space will look at all prescient.

Of course, maybe I'm wrong about the specific prediction I'm making. But there's another reason to open up science fiction to other cultures, and that is that science fiction is the one lasting American contribution to prose literature. In every other area, we're derivative to the—well, not to the core, because in those areas we *have* no core. Nobody in other countries aspires to write Westerns, and nobody in Russia or Germany or Japan looks to Updike or Bellow to teach them how to write "serious" fiction. They already have literary traditions older and better than our so-called best. But in science fiction, they *all* look to us. They want to write science fiction, too, because those who read it in every nation see it as the fiction of possibility, the fiction of strangeness. It's the one genre now that allows the writer to do satire that isn't recognized as satire, to do metaphysical fiction that isn't seen as philosophical or religious proselytizing. In short, it is the freest, most open literature in the world today, and it is the one literature that foreign writers are learning first and foremost from Americans.

Why, then, do science fiction writers persist in imagining only American futures? Our audience is much broader than these shores. And there are countries where our words are taken far more seriously than they are here. If we actually aspire to change the world with our fiction—and I can't think of any other reason for ever setting pen to paper—then we ought to be talking to the world. And one sure way to let the world know we are talking to them is to put them—citizens of other countries, children of other cultures—into our futures. To do otherwise is to slap them in the face and say, "I have seen the future, and you aren't there." Well, I *have* seen the future, and they *are* there—in great numbers, with great power. I want my voice to have been one of the voices they listened to on their way up to be king of the hill. And, in "I Put My Blue Genes On," I took my first step along that road.

"IN THE DOGHOUSE" (with Jay A. Parry)

What if the aliens don't come to us in alien form? What if they come in a form we already recognize, that we already think we understand? Jay Parry and I toyed with the idea of telling this story differently— with the aliens coming in the form of an oppressed minority. American Indians or blacks, we thought. But the problems at the time seemed insurmountable—particularly the political problems. It's a very tricky business, for a white writer to try to express the black point of view without being politically incorrect. It seemed to me then that there were things that black writers could say about and on behalf of blacks that white writers couldn't, not without the message being taken wrong. In the years

since then, I've learned that a writer of any race or
sex or religion or nation can write about any other
race or sex or religion or nation; he only needs to:

1. Do enough research that he doesn't make an
   ass of himself.
2. Tell the truth as he sees it without pander-
   ing or condescending to any group.
3. Have a thick enough skin to accept the fact
   that he'll be impaled with a thousand darts
   no matter how well he does at 1 and 2.

Being timid, Jay and I worked out the plot using
animals that have been as firmly pegged in our human prejudices as any human group. Faithful, beloved dogs. Man's best friend. All the same
possibilities were there—the White Man's Burden,
the condescending affection (some of my best friends
are dogs), and, above all, the rigid determination to
keep them in their place.

"THE ORIGINIST"

In my review column in *The Magazine of Fantasy
and Science Fiction*, I wrote a diatribe deploring the
1980s trend of trying to turn sci-fi authors' private
worlds into generic brand name universes where
other writers can romp. It began with *Star Trek*, and
it was not part of anybody's grand design. There were
these *Star Trek* fans, you see, who got impatient
with Paramount's neglect of their heroes and began
to write their *own* stories about the crew of the
starship Enterprise. (In a way this was singularly appropriate: The original series was written and per-
formed like somebody's garage production anyway,

so why not continue the tradition?) Legend has it that Paramount at first intended to sue, until it dawned on them that there might be *money* in publishing never-filmed stories about Kirk, Spock, and the other crew members of *Wagon Train among the Cheap Interplanetary Sets*. They were right, to the tune of many readers and many dollars. A new industry was born: Science fiction written in somebody else's poorly imagined but passionately studied universe.

I suppose it was inevitable that publishers who weren't getting any of those *Star Trek* bucks would try to turn other successful imagined futures into equally lucrative backdrops where one writer's work would be as good as any others'. There ensued in the late 1980s a spate of novels set "in the world of———," in which journeyman writers who often didn't have a clue about the inner truth that led the Old Pro to create his or her world tried to set their own stories in it. The result was stories that nobody was proud of and nobody cared about.

What was unspoken (I hope) was the true premise of all these worlds-as-brand-names books: The readers won't be able to tell the difference. Here's what they found out: Unlike the *Star Trek* audience, the readers of most science fiction *can* tell the difference and they care very much. Written science fiction has an author-driven audience. The *real* science fiction audience doesn't want to read John Varley's Dune novel or Lisa Goldstein's Lensman novel or Howard Waldrop's Dragonworld novel. (Well, actually, I would *love* to read Howard Waldrop's Dragonworld novel, but not for any reason I'm proud of.)

So I laid down the law in my column: Writers should not waste their time or talent trying to tell stories in someone else's universe. Furthermore, established writers should not cooperate in the wasting of younger writers' talent by allowing their worlds to be franchised.

As soon as that column hit print, Martin Harry Greenberg mentioned to me that he was preparing a festschrift anthology commemorating Isaac Asimov's fiftieth year in publishing, a book called *Foundation's Friends.* And for this one anthology, Dr. Asimov was allowing the participants to set stories within his own closely-held fictional universes, using his own established characters. We could actually write robot stories using the three laws and positronic brains and Susan Calvin. We could actually write Foundation stories using Hari Seldon and Trantor and Terminus and the Mule.

Suddenly I was sixteen years old again and I remembered the one story I wanted so badly to read, the one that Asimov had never written—the story of how the Second Foundation actually got started in the library at Trantor.

Did I forget that I had just gotten through banning the franchising of universes for all time? No. I simply have a perverse streak in me that says that whenever somebody lays down a law, that law is meant to be broken—even when I was the lawgiver. So I wrote "The Originist" as both a tribute to and, perhaps, a sidelight on Asimov's masterwork.

This doesn't mean that I think the law I stated isn't true. In fact, I stand by it as firmly as ever. It's just that, like all laws, this one *can* be circumvented if you work hard enough. The reason why franchised worlds generally don't work is because the junior writers don't understand the original world well enough, don't know what it is about the original writer's work that made his stories work, and don't feel enough personal responsibility to do their best work under these circumstances. Well, in my arrogance, I thought I *did* know the Foundation universe well enough—not in the trivial details, but in the overall sweep of the story, in what it *means* (Yes, I've read *Decline and Fall*, too, but that isn't the foundation of Foundation, either.) Also, I thought I understood something of how the stories worked— the delight of discovering that no matter how many curtains you peel back, you never find the *real* curtain or the *real* man behind it in Asimov's Oz. There are always plans underlying plans, causes hidden behind plausible causes.

And, finally, I had a compelling story of my own to tell. I had already made a stab at it, with a fragment of a novel that was to be called *Genesis*—a book I may still write someday. In it I was trying to show the borderline between human and animal, the exact comma in the punctuational model of evolution that marked the transition between non-human and human. For me, that borderline is the human universal of storytelling; that is what joins a community together across time; that is what preserved a human identity after death and defines it in life. Without stories, we aren't human; with them, we are. But *Genesis* became impossible to write, in part because to do it properly I had to visit Kashmir and Ethiopia, two places where it is not terribly safe to travel these days.

But I *could* develop many of the same themes, though at a greater distance, in my story of "The Originist." Moreover, Asimov himself had broached a related question in *Foundation*, when he presented a character who was searching through libraries in order to find the planet of origin of the human species. I was able to take a purely Asimovian point— the futility of secondary research—and interlayer it with my own point—the fundamental role of story- telling in shaping human individuals and communities. I went further in my effort to make "The Originist" a true Foundation story. I also used a form that Asimov has perfected, but I had never tried before: the story in which almost nothing happens except dialogue. Asimov can make this work because of the piercing clarity of his writing and the sublime intelligence of his ideas—it is never boring listening to his characters discuss ideas, because you are never lost and the ideas are always worth hearing. The challenge was to come as close as I could to matching that clarity; I had to trust that others would find my ideas as interesting as I had always found Asimov's.

So it was that, even though I knew "The Originist" would never be received as standing on its own, I poured a novel's worth of love and labor into it. In the long run, I proved my own law—I wrote this story at the expense of a purely Orson Scott Card novel that will probably never be written. Yet I think it was worth doing—once—partly to prove it could be done well (if in fact I did it well), and partly because I'm proud of the story itself: because of the achievement of it, because of what the story says, and because it is a tribute to the writer that I firmly believe is the finest writer of American prose in our time, bar none.

Would you like to linger in the worlds of Orson Scott Card?

This is your invitation to join

Starways Congress
or
The Hatrack River Town Meeting

As a citizen of the future or of the magical past, you will receive quarterly newsletters, giving you a chance to get answers to questions about Card's books—and to engage in open, freewheeling conversations with him and with other readers about ideas and experiences connected with his stories.

You'll also get news about his upcoming publications and previews of his works in progress, along with notice of his occasional speeches, book signings, and visits at conventions.

Write for more information to:

Hatrack River
P.O. Box 18184
Greensboro NC 27419-8184